The System Has Failed:

Out for Self Series, Book 2

The System Has Failed:

Out for Self Series, Book 2

by

Ms. Michel Moore

www.urbanbooks.net

Urban Books, LLC
300 Farmingdale Road, NY-Route 109
Farmingdale, NY 11735

The System Has Failed: Out for Self Series, Book 2
Copyright © 2018 Ms. Michel Moore

ISBN 13: 978-1-945855-53-5
ISBN 10: 1-945855-53-3

First Trade Paperback Printing November 2018
Printed in the United States of America

10 9 8 7 6 5 4 3 2 1

Distributed by Kensington Publishing Corp.
Submit Orders to:
Customer Service
400 Hahn Road
Westminster, MD 21157-4627
Phone: 1-800-733-3000
Fax: 1-800-659-2436

The System Has Failed:

Out for Self Series, Book 2

by

Ms. Michel Moore

Chapter One

Big Ace sat back, shaking his head in disbelief. Focusing on one son, then the other, he reached for his glass. With one short swallow, followed by a huge gulp, Big Ace let the dark top-shelf liquor warm his throat. He knew his boys were half crazed. The entire city of Detroit knew it as well. The sometimes-wannabe-proud father knew his offspring were both born acting a fool. Since they'd come out of their mother's womb, it'd been that way. Although he'd tried his best to mold them into mirror images of himself, he'd failed. Some would say maybe not miserably, but close enough. Big Ace was different. He was a polished gangster. He'd been that way for some time. With the way his boys acted he wanted to question their DNA, but they looked too much like him to do so. The judge and half the jury would run him clear out of town if he ever did try to deny them. Back in the day, in his youth, Big Ace had his own demons of being wild. He and his homeboy Kamel ran the streets. They were reckless and were known to clown on more than several occasions. Yet they were never idiots as big as his seeds were. But he continued to hope for miracles when it came to their behavior, both business and personal.

Big Ace and his sons were content. The stuffed trio was seated in the rear of the crowded Detroit-area restaurant.

Finishing up their dinner, each felt that they'd gotten their money's worth. The hardworking waitress cleared the table of several huge plates of broken shells from jumbo crab legs. Moments later she returned, bringing the three of them dessert. While devouring that as well, they plotted. Deep into the conversation, they began to exchange ideas. While some of their schemes would involve much more time to achieve hood results, others didn't.

What was needed and agreed upon was a temporary solution to the boys' problem at hand, which was an almost-complete halt to business at a few of their east-side weed spot locations due to some still-nameless dudes with some hellava strong bud. Normally Big Ace wouldn't even entertain the notion of helping them nurse their own hustle, but after receiving calls from both his sons raising the Bat-Signal for his assistance or least advice, the loyal father stepped in.

"Okay, y'all two. I done finished my food, so go ahead. It ain't no way I wanted to hear y'all whining on a fucking empty stomach!"

"Dad," Elon complained as he lied, "come on. It ain't even like that. We already know what we gonna do about the slowdown. We just wanted to run it past you first because we might have had to borrow some of them thangs to make shit unfold faster."

"That's right," Donte automatically concurred.

Big Ace leaned back and disapprovingly grinned at his sons' weak attempt to fool him. "Look here, if you cats knew what to do, then why in the hell we here? And as for borrowing my Peacemakers, that shit's definitely out the equation. You two make more than enough bread to purchase ya own damn artillery! So if somebody is stepping out of line and on your territory, then do what y'all gotta do! That's my best advice!"

Both brothers, knowing that if they really told their father the real deal he'd most definitely clown them, wisely decided to figure shit out on their own. "Matter of fact, Dad, we about to head to the crib and meet up with our crew," Elon said, continuing to lie as he looked down at his constantly ringing cell phone and put it on mute.

"Look, Elon, you and your brother go on and handle y'all little situation while I sit here and eat my dessert. Besides, you ain't the only one whose phone is ringing," Big Ace informed his son. "And please pull up those sagging jeans and act like a grown-ass man!"

Elon, who followed his father's orders and pulled his pants up on his waist, and Donte excused themselves and headed out of the restaurant and toward the parking lot. As they drove off in their separate trucks, Stuff and Marie were driving in through the other parking lot's entrance.

"What it do, baby doll?" Big Ace raised the last bit of his double-layer chocolate cake to his lips. "What you need from your big daddy?"

"You ain't gonna believe this wild-ass bullshit I'm about to tell you!" Simone whispered into the phone's receiver as the warm water in the tub soothed her body. "First of all, when I got back to my house this afternoon you wouldn't believe how this little motherfucker had my crib looking. And if that shit weren't bad enough, his behind wanna go for bad now and sling goddamn trees."

"Okay, and?" Big Ace swallowed, tossing his fork down onto the table and overlooking what she'd just said about Terrell selling weed. "Big deal, he selling to a couple of his schoolmates!"

Simone relit the half-smoked blunt and choked two good times before delivering the shocking "gotcha gotcha" punch line to their conversation. "Well, the weed ain't the big deal! It seems like Kamal's son is running around here fucking stank-ass project bitches like you and his no-good daddy used to do back in the day!"

"Damn, Simone! Good for Terrell!" Big Ace laughed out loud and signaled for the waitress to bring his bill. "Ain't nothing wrong with a little bit of low-class ghetto booty every so often. And don't forget me and you both was raised in the projects too."

Immediately offended that Big Ace had thrown up her humble beginnings smack dab in her face after she was trying to put him on to game, she blurted out what she'd originally called to say. "Oh, since you being so Obama this evening, I guess you don't care either that my son is sticking his dick all up in Monique's daughter's pussy!"

"Monique?"

"Yeah, nigga, you heard me! Monique!"

"Monique who?" Big Ace, tired of the cat-and-mouse game Simone was intent on playing, stood up to leave after paying the bill. "I know lots of chicks named Monique!"

"Oh, well how many of them set your dumb, good-tricking ass up at the Red Roof the same damn night Kamal and Joey died, then mysteriously somehow ended up dead as a motherfucker her damn self? Now tell me, do any of that shit ring a bell with ya self-righteous ass?"

"Where you at right now?" Big Ace's tone got very serious. "I need you to meet me at my house ASAP!"

"Boy, bye," Simone snickered, knowing she'd knocked him off his square bringing up Clip-N-Dip Moe and that awful night he'd gotten his balls damn near stomped out of his asshole. "I'm relaxing taking a hot bubble bath, and then maybe my future daughter-in-law and me might watch a movie."

"I'm not fucking around with you, Simone." He demanded, "I'm leaving out now so be there in thirty minutes, period!"

Let his ass wait for me for once and see how he feels. Simone leaned back smugly as her phone rang loudly once again. *I know this ain't him calling right back, is it?*

Chapter Two

"What took you so long to call me back?" Marie questioned Stuff as she and he headed hand in hand into the cool, air-conditioned Red Lobster. "I thought you forgot about me like you've been doing all week."

Overcome with guilt from spending so much time with Shauntae during the past week and ignoring Marie's never-ending calls and texts, Stuff avoided eye contact, looking downward at the carpet. As the hostess politely led them to their seats, an oversized, burly man dressed in a tracksuit with an expensive LYNX chain with a diamond-encrusted cross dangling at the end bumped into Stuff, throwing him off-balance.

"Oh, my bad. Please excuse me, sir. I wasn't paying attention. I apologize."

"Not a problem." The man hurriedly rushed off while wishing in the back of his mind that his two sons looked and acted half as respectfully as Stuff.

After being seated, the couple glanced at the menu, deciding what appetizers to get, as a jealous Marie kept the questions coming. An order of mozzarella cheese sticks, shrimp cocktail, and three sodas later, Stuff grudgingly agreed to take Marie to Detroit's annual Barristers' Ball, where his father would be one of the prestigious keynote speakers of the evening. He'd already promised Shauntae he'd spend at least the earlier part of that day with her, since it coincidently was her birthday, and then he would possibly take her to the prestigious event. Stuff knew at this point that things between him and her were definitely up in the air.

Damn, why didn't I stop Terrell when I saw that look in his eyes? That shit was so fucked up! Damn! Damn! he repeated over and over in his head. During every moment he spent at the table, watching Marie's lips make idle chitchat about this and that, Stuff couldn't seem to stop thinking of Shauntae and the way she took Terrell's ass whooping so calmly. *Maybe I'll go back later on and see if she's okay,* he thought as he planned on cutting the evening short.

"You know what we gotta do, don't you?" Donte, who tried his best to avoid violence if possible, informed his brother of the obvious.

"Hell fuck yeah. Ain't no question," Elon yelled into his cell phone. "Find out just exactly who these fake crab niggas is and smash they bitch asses."

"No doubt." Donte stayed focused as he steered his truck down to the freeway and toward home. "I'll see you at the crib."

"That's a bet." Elon hung up with his brother just in time to catch another incoming call from the suspiciously elusive Shauntae, whom he hadn't been able to get up with in days. "Yeah, speak on it!"

"Hey, baby." Shauntae tried sounding sexy despite her still-growing fat lip and the ice wrapped in a washcloth pressed to her eye. "How you been?"

"Bitch, please." Elon leaned back in the driver's seat after turning up some old Tupac. "Don't 'hey, baby' me! Where the fuck ya good dick-sucking ass been hiding?"

"Nowhere, E. I just been doing me!"

"Whatever. Get the fuck on with that stupid Oprah bullshit, bitch! What's really good?"

"Can you come over?"

"For what?"

"Just come by, okay?"

"Look, Shauntae. Me and my brother gotta politick on some important shit, so I'll get up with you later. Peace!"

"Like what, maybe some niggas around the way with better weed than y'all got?" she said, catching him before he hung up the phone in her ear. "Now politick on that!"

"Hold up, bitch. What you just say?"

"Oh, so now you got time to talk to me, huh?" Shauntae was truly feeling herself as she stared into the mirror, wondering how long it'd take for the swelling to go down.

"Stop playing." Elon reached up, turning down the radio's volume. "I knew that was them same-ass cornball fools at the liquor store you was posted up with a few weeks back! Where you know them from?"

"Bring ya fine ass on over here, baby, and after I give you some of this good pussy, I'll tell you all about them."

"Yeah, all right then. I'm on my way."

"And oh, yeah, swing by the store and bring me some painkillers. The strongest ones they got." Shauntae cracked a slight yet painful smile as she revengefully got ready to put her "payback is a true motherfucker" plan into effect.

Her agenda was crystal clear, and just like her deceased moms, setting niggas up was about to become second nature. Scheming on Terrell for not wanting to get with her but her baby sister instead, Stuff for not taking up for her earlier, and lastly Yankee for clowning her about the old janitor she used to bang, her mind clicked like a ticking time bomb. Sympathetically, Shauntae figured God had already punished Wahoo's dumb half-retarded ass enough by taking his elderly, drugged-out grandmother out of the game for good, so she mercifully gave his simple butt a pass.

Chapter Three

It'd only been a few weeks, but Prayer was going half out of her mind with worry. Terrell was her baby, her son, her only child despite what his birth certificate had written on it. She had raised him and spent more time with him than Simone ever could, so in her eyes, he was hers by default.

Even when Drake was in and out of town, she still had Li'l T to tend to, and that made her life worth living. Sure, she had her career, but certainly, anyone who knew her knew her son was the center of her universe and the sun rose and set by his wants and needs.

"Why hasn't he called me in two days?" Prayer paced the floor of the bedroom. "I know you told me to give him space, but just how much?"

Drake had just gotten out of the shower after a long day of dealing with other niggas' bullshit, and he was definitely not in the mood for his wife's overprotective rants about Terrell and his growing up and away from her grip. Reaching for the half-drunk glass of Hennessy he'd poured before undressing, Drake gulped it down in hopes of drowning her voice out.

"Prayer, ya ass can't control everything that boy does! You making him more handicapped than that chair he's in ever can! You need to fall back for once!"

"That's my son. And am I so wrong for wanting to protect him from bullshit and heartache? Does that make me a freaking monster?"

"Naw, Prayer, but I do think that what's done in the dark will come to the light someday someway!" Drake insisted. "Trying to keep him away from Simone, not to mention his grandfather who's in that nursing home you conveniently nudged him into, ain't gonna be a good look when the boy finds out! You know that temper of his ain't shit to be played with!"

"Real talk, Simone herself didn't want to deal with that Willy Dale character when he came around claiming to be Kamal's long-lost father, so why in the hell would I?" Prayer snarled, not knowing that after all these years Big Ace was still going to visit Willy Dale, giving him photos as well as updates on Terrell. "Besides, a paternity test was never done to establish Kamal as the daddy, so that old fool, half drunk out his mind, is lucky that all I did was put a restraining order out on him for showing up on our doorstep!"

"Look, I'm done debating who's right and who's wrong. Bottom line, if it makes ya feel any better, why don't you call Simone and check on him?" he said, giving in while not admitting that he himself had checked up on Terrell during the earlier part of the week.

"What?" Prayer paused with a look of utter disgust for her husband and his suggestion. "I wouldn't give her the satisfaction of a phone call!"

"Oh, well, then you just have to let Terrell be then, don't you?" He shook his head as his body still dripped water.

"Drake, sweetie." She wrapped her arms around her husband's neck. "Maybe you could call Simone for me."

After a few minutes of persuasion, and the annoying thought of hearing Prayer's nagging all night long, he grabbed the cordless and dialed Simone's number.

A few rings later, Simone answered, sounding relaxed. "Hello."

"Hey, Simone." Drake felt a strange tingling in his manhood as he thought about the outfit Simone had on the last time he'd seen her. "It's me, Drake."

"I know ya voice, silly," she cooed, always in the mood to flirt with him. "What's good with you?"

"Well, I'm sitting here with my wife, and we were both wondering how Terrell was getting along."

Angry that he was bringing up Prayer in his second unexpected call this week, Simone started to flip the script and rub shit in. "Damn, Drake." She teasingly splashed the water in the tub so he could hear the wet sounds. "If I weren't lying back, covered in bubbles and rubbing soap over my legs, I'd get up and call him to the phone."

"Oh, yeah," Drake said, playing off what Simone was saying as his overweight wife looked on with anticipation with news of Li'l T. "Is that right?"

"And I know you wouldn't want a chick to catch a cold all up in my perfectly trimmed kitty cat, now would you?" Simone grinned.

"Ummmm." Drake shivered at the thought. "Why don't you have him call home when you get a chance?"

"That's not a problem." Simone laughed at his nervous reaction. "And by the way, he's already at home!"

No sooner than Drake hung up, he glanced up, telling Prayer, who was now stuffing her mouth with barbeque potato chips, to sit down and expect Terrell's call shortly. As she happily waited, still crunching away, hastily the alpha male of the household slyly headed back to the steamy confines of the slick, marble-wall shower to beat his meat, lustfully imagining what it'd feel like to have his wife's former best friend and Li'l T's mother on her knees in front of him with her lips wrapped around his pipe.

Joi and Terrell spent a few hours in deep discussion about his childhood and why his mother was the way she was. Then Joi felt it was best for her to go home and check in on her big sister, who she knew was in some serious pain, which her overzealous mouth had gotten her into. Even though she hadn't totally forgiven Terrell for his inexcusable actions, Joi knew he was troubled, and her trusting ways made her want to solve the problems of the world, including her boyfriend.

Standing near the rear kitchen door, waiting for Terrell to get his van keys and drive her home, Joi was once again met by Simone, who was fully dressed with her purse dangling off her arm. With a lump in her throat, the young girl knew she had to say something, but at this point, she was at a total loss for words. Scrambling around in her own small handbag, fumbling with a pack of Big Red gum, Joi finally spoke up, breaking the ice. "So, Miss Harris, do you happen to have any old pictures of my mother and you?"

"Ummm naw, I don't think so, sweetie." Simone took a deep breath while lying through her teeth and trying to control her emotions at having her son's tactless girl-friend question her about her no-good mother. "I used to, but I think someone stole them out my photo album." *As if I'd really let that dirtball Monique hang out with me and my crew!* Simone thought as she faked a smile.

"Oh." A disappointed Joi sighed as Terrell rolled into the room with his navy blue Detroit Tiger cap twisted to the side and his cell phone on his lap.

"Are you ready to go or what?" He leaned his wheelchair backward, doing one of the many tricks he'd learned over the years he'd been stuck in it. These tricks often caused many others, including his family, to cringe while their hearts skipped a beat, hoping he wouldn't lose control, flip out, and bust his head wide open.

"Where are you about to go?" Simone asked with her hands on her hips as if she were really concerned and not just plain nosy and a straight-out hater. "And I done told you to stop doing that dumb shit!"

"Dang, Ma! I'm about to shoot her to her crib," Li'l T fired back as he let the chair assume its correct and safe position. "Is that all right with you or do I need you to sign my permission slip?"

Truly not wanting her son anywhere near Joi, not to mention her sister, Simone volunteered to drop the young girl off since she was leaving anyway. "Why don't you just go relax and let me take her home? Besides, it'll give me and Joi a much better chance to get acquainted and you a chance to call Drake's pesky ass. Shit, he done called me twice checking up on you!"

Knowing it would be like pulling teeth to disobey his mother's overbearing actions, Terrell grudgingly gave in against his better judgment. After suspiciously watching his half-baked mother and his girlfriend disappear into the garage then pull out of the driveway, he rolled back into his room and called Yankee to check up on the ticket that was out in the street, then followed it up with a call to Drake.

Shauntae checked the mirror, hoping some of the swelling had gone down, before she flung the door open to let Elon come inside. "Hey, love."

"Damn! Who mollywopped ya ass up like that?"

"Ain't nobody do shit like that to me," she protested as she walked away from the door, switching. "Thangs just got a little out of control at one point, but a bitch like me is down for you and only you! I took one for the team!"

"Oh, yeah?" Intrigued by her blasé attitude to the obvious stomp down she encountered, Elon cautiously sat down on the couch with his best friend, his nine, on his lap and waited for what Shauntae had to say that was so relevant to his and Donte's current problems.

It took all of twenty minutes for her to give him the complete rundown of the events that had taken place over the last couple of weeks since she'd been hanging out with Stuff and Terrell. Not leaving out the fact that they not only had a gang of weed in their possession but they were rich as a motherfucker living on the other side of the Gates and out far into the suburbs, Shauntae gloated, thinking she had led Elon to the motherland.

Even though that plush lifestyle they were living and Shauntae constantly yearned for meant absolutely nothing to Elon, who was raised with just as many advantages as Terrell and Stuff, he still had to knock them out of the picture so his and Donte's business could continue to flourish at a rapid pace. "Dig this here," he said, plotting as his dick got hard at the thought of money, murder, and mayhem. "Find out their plans for the next week or so step by step, hour by hour if you can. Then when they asses least expect the bullshit, they'll regret the day they wanted to play with the big boys!"

"I know, baby." Shauntae, horny as hell, tried to snuggle up on Elon, massaging his thick dick. "They ain't got shit on you!"

Elon took one look down at her bruised-up mug and started to lose his erection. "Damn, bitch!" He pushed her back across the couch. "A nigga want some of that pussy, but you gotsta turn over and let me hit it from the back so I don't have to see ya busted smile!"

"Oh, it's like that?" Shauntae, who was turned on by his disrespectful bad-boy demeanor, raised her skirt, revealing that she had no panties on, and turned over, propping her ass up into the air so Elon would have no trouble getting to her dripping wet kitty cat.

After slipping a rubber on, Elon went to town, pounding all his frustrations from the Detroit streets out on her body. Shauntae was in seventh heaven as her face, already in pain, continuously hit the arm of the couch.

Getting out of eye and ear range of her son, Simone turned the music up loudly, halting any more thoughts that Joi might've had of making petty conversation. No sooner than Simone drove through the black steel gates, she sped up, almost pushing the gas pedal to the floor in an attempt to get the goody-goody mother-in-law act over. Unfortunately for Joi, the act was over sooner than she thought as Terrell's mother slammed down on the automobile's brake, bringing the car to a sudden stop on a dimly lit corner near the liquor store down the street and three blocks over from her house.

"Listen," Simone said, "is this good enough? Because I'm running late, and I don't have time to creep down them pothole-filled streets on the block you said you live on."

Hesitant to make waves or disagree with Simone, Joi politely nodded, gathered her things, and got out of the car. Before she could say goodbye and shut the door good, she heard the automatic door locks go down, and she watched the taillights of the car peel off as she stood on the litter-lined curb. *Dang gee. Everything Terrell said about his mother really is true. No wonder he acts the way he does.*

She headed off down the block, cutting across a couple of vacant lots. Making a left then a quick right, she was a few yards from home when she noticed Elon's truck pulled up in her unpaved driveway. "Oh, my God! Not him! He's so rude!" Standing in front of the abandoned house next door, Joi got herself together. She could only imagine what her sister looked like, and she wondered why in the world she would let Elon, or anyone else for that matter, see her in that state.

"All right then." Elon suddenly emerged from the house with his always-present gun down at his side.

"Hi," Joi softly spoke, walking up toward the porch.

"Hey, baby." Elon openly flirted with her, knowing he'd pay almost anything Shauntae's sister wanted to be able to hit them guts like he'd been yearning to do for months. "I heard you got a little boyfriend and shit!" he taunted. "Just in case something ever happens to that crippled lame, just remember a nigga like me always in the game of needing some young, pretty, tight-pussy-having chick on my arm!"

"Excuse me?" Joi paused. "Don't talk to me like that. Plus aren't you dating my sister?"

"Dating?" Elon laughed as he stuffed his gun in the front of his jeans and grabbed Joi up by her waist all in one smooth motion. "I don't date hoes. I regulate they punk asses!"

Struggling to get away from his grip, Joi finally broke loose, running up the stairs and into the house. As Elon jumped into his truck and hit his headlights, he drove past two different vehicles that were inconspicuously parked on separated parts of the block but both within view of Shauntae and Joi's house.

Well, damn. I guess Joi isn't as innocent as she pretends to be. And all along I've been thinking I had the wild sister. Stuff sat silently, thinking, as he held on his lap a dozen red roses he'd picked up for Shauntae after dropping Marie off at home. *And now that I think about it, that's the same truck from the store that day!* He read the license plate in his rearview mirror. I GO HARD. *It is! Ahhh, man! I've gotta call Terrell later!*

Parked discreetly behind a huge, old cargo van, Simone's car vibrated from the old-school rap music blasting from the truck barreling past with no regard for the dirt and pebbles its oversized tires kicked up on the sides of her doors. Slumping over toward the passenger seat of her Vette and out of sight of the mystery driver, she thought, *ump, ump ump! She work quick! Ain't this some foul bullshit! Homegirl was busy acting all "stand by my man" in love at my house, and she over here posted in the next motherfucker's grill, getting her mack game on in full swing just like that! She ain't no better than her dead-ass mama or that stank-mouth sister of hers!* Simone read the truck's license plate. I GO HARD.

Simone was now glad that at Big Ace's insistence she'd doubled back, braving the chance of bending her shiny rims on the dark road to see exactly where Monique's kids laid their heads at just in case any of them chose to relive the day their mother and her crew were murdered and give the cops any additional information that could ultimately lead to his arrest after all these years. Catching Joi cheating with ol' boy, who unbeknownst to her was one of Big Ace's sons, was an extra bonus, icing on the cake to Simone. With her car lights still turned off, she crept out of the hood as quietly as she'd crept in.

Chapter Four

"I can't believe that fool just had the nerve to call me and check up on me and what the fuck I'm doing out here in these streets," Yankee fumed as Wahoo, still grief-stricken, listened. "His crippled ass got me twisted!"

"Yeah, well, can you blame him?" Wahoo asked as he held his grandmother's obituary. "Him and Stuff do have a lot of their own money still invested."

"So fucking what! That still don't make me Terrell's goddamn slave and shit. He ain't no boss!"

"Whatever," Wahoo disinterestedly replied.

"Plus that sucker Stuff just bogarted all up on Shauntae," Yankee hissed as he pounded his fist inside his other hand. "I got some real plans in store for his punk ass! Then the script really gonna flip and I'm gonna be a boss around these parts!"

Wahoo, still clutching the obituary and picture, looked up. "Dude, what you talking about now?"

"I'm talking about hitting the ultimate lick of a lifetime and getting some of that serious bread for once." Yankee was glad he'd finally sparked Wahoo's interest because most definitely he needed a partner if what he was planning would work. "I've been thinking about this caper ever since we met dude, but I was just holding back."

"Met who, Terrell?" Wahoo asked with guilt in his tone as he quickly thought about all the nice things his boy had done to support him and his brothers and sisters since his grandmother's death, including buying the dress she was buried in along with paying for the very paper he was holding in his hands.

"Naw, that nigga Stuff! His rich ass could have all the hoes he wants and he down here in the D slumming with our bitches! I swear to God on my word, son!"

"So what you saying?"

Yankee grinned, rubbing his sweaty palms together. "I'm saying let's follow that dude to the crib late one night and rob him and that high-profile family of his. After that lick, we should be set for life. I can get my own package and really step my game up, and you can shoot a move on the social worker and take the kids down South or someplace out of the way that don't nobody know y'all and start over fresh."

"Maybe you right." Wahoo thought about what it would feel like living in a new place where he and his family weren't the neighborhood joke, and he quickly informed Yankee that he was all in for whatever.

As Joi entered the house, she saw Shauntae come out of the bathroom with a cold rag pressed to her face. "Hey."

"Hey yourself." Shauntae smiled as she removed the rag to reveal her face to her little sister.

"Oh, my God! It looks awful." Joi turned away.

"I'm all right."

"Terrell is so sorry. He don't know what came over him. He swears he's gonna get some help!"

"Don't worry, it's all good." Shauntae kept smiling, knowing that one day soon Terrell along with Stuff and Yankee would all get what they had coming.

The phone rang. Looking at the caller ID, Shauntae immediately changed her smile to a frown, catching a serious attitude as she saw Stuff's name and number flashing. But knowing what she and Elon discussed about playing the role until it was time, she put on her best voice and answered. "Hello."

"Hey, it's me."

"Oh, hey. What up doe?"

"You."

"Oh, yeah?"

"Yeah. Are you still mad at me? How you feeling?"

"I'm good. I just took some aspirin and Joi just got home."

Not wanting to let her know he'd been parked down the street and had seen her sister and the nigga in the truck have words before Joi came in, he kept quiet. Having no idea that Shauntae had just finished giving up the pussy to the same dude, naively Stuff asked her if she could come out to his car because he was about to pull up.

"Naw, babe. I'm lying down."

"Well, can you send out Joi? I've got something for you."

"Yeah, okay."

Eager to please Shauntae, Joi went outside and to the car where Stuff was waiting. As he handed her the flowers through the window along with a crisp hundred-dollar bill, Joi noticed a strange look of disgust in his eyes. He drove his BMW away and down the street. She couldn't figure it out, but she wanted to get back in the house as soon as possible before Elon's roguish ass popped back up.

Upon Joi's return, Shauntae was overjoyed, snatching the flowers from her sister's hands. The money was of no true consequence to her, but the long-stemmed flowers were a horse of a different color. No man had ever given her flowers, and she felt her heart slightly warm.

I hope the swelling goes down before my birthday and that Barristers' Ball dance thing Stuff promised to take me to, Shauntae prayed as if she just didn't give Elon the green light to mash Stuff and his friends. *I really wanna go.*

Driving back to the house with the information he'd just gotten from Shauntae, Elon knew that his and his brother's little slowdown in sales and productivity would soon come to an abrupt halt. He had not only the names of the rich mama-boy busters who were trying to step on their toes but one of their addresses, too. Stopping by the store first to get a beer and a shot of Hennessy, he looked back just in time to see a brand-new Vette, which was sitting on the hottest rims he'd ever seen, fly by and head toward the freeway. *I need to get one of them joints when business picks back up,* he thought as he went into the entrance.

A solid week flew by after that twisted day, and all seemed calm on the callous, black-hearted, unfeeling streets of Detroit. All residents, having their own jobs to do, were hard at work making that shit go down. Copper thieves were stealing wire out of the lampposts, leaving the darkness of night to rule. Drug addicts were posted at the gas stations, begging for spare change. Hoes were tucked behind dumpsters, sucking dick for a dollar. Small kids were roaming the street in dirty diapers while their unfit mothers slept off hangovers from the night before. Niggas and true gator-wearing pimp players were out slanging that work, knowing the slow-responding police were busy kicked back somewhere with doughnuts stuffed in their mouths. It was business as usual in the D.

All seemed well for an elated Prayer who was satisfied that in less than forty-eight hours she'd be reunited with Terrell, who was bringing his new girlfriend over for dinner. Her name was Joi, and that was all she knew about the girl.

Busily she worked on the menu as Drake tossed an outfit in a bag for yet another unexplained, unexpected two-to-three-day trip. When Drake pulled out of the driveway, she never once said goodbye or even kissed him on the cheek. One could easily guess that it was that type of self-absorbed behavior that kept her once-loyal man up in the comforting arms of the next female.

Drake had spoken to Li'l T several times during the week, advising him to stop what he was doing and finish his education, but since Terrell was hell-bent on following in his, Joey's, and Kamal's footsteps, putting in that street work, Drake had to let the youngster learn on his own exactly what the world was offering to an uneducated, young black male with a fucked-up criminal record: not jack shit!

Simone was chilling at home, at this point feeling the complete opposite. She'd embraced that her son wanted to live the thug life, and she proudly encouraged it. It was all she herself had known for the past two decades, and to her way of thinking anything that got her son farther away from Prayer, even if it was a jail cell, she was fine with.

After divulging the information she'd found out about Monique's kids, Big Ace, whom Simone was loyal to, advised her to stick near the crib and try to monitor Joi's moves and thoughts to see if she or her sister had any memory of the day he'd murdered her mother. With Big Ace's assurance that if one of them did say anything, he'd quickly handle it, Simone watched her only child shower the young girl with gifts the same way Kamal and Joey used to do to her back in her prime. She pondered making the call, lying, just because she was jealous.

Simone was so caught up in Joi getting the fast street money that Terrell could've spent on her, she had no worldly idea that all three of them had been watched and followed from afar for several days by Mitts and LoLo.

On the other side of the Gates, while Joi, whose diary her sister violated nightly giving updated information to Elon, was picking out the perfect outfit to wear to meet Terrell's step-mother Prayer, Shauntae was feeling guilty as she rearranged the new dozen roses that Stuff had sent her for the fourth time this week. With the swelling almost completely down, she could see just how beautiful the diamond tennis bracelet, also courtesy of Stuff, looked on her wrist. Even though she had yet to give up the pussy, he was serving her like a true queen, which no Negro in the hood ever had. He was too good to be true.

With the clock ticking, Shauntae felt remorse because she knew that at any given moment Elon and his crew might strike, bringing harm to Stuff, which meant an end to his kindness and possibly his life. *Fuck Terrell's and Yankee's trifling asses,* was all she could think, but Stuff in her eyes had made amends. Wanting nothing more than to call Elon and recant the information about Stuff and his involvement in the bullshit, she just couldn't bring herself to do it. Besides, Elon was a lunatic and might bug out and kick her ass behind the bullshit, and bottom line, she'd suffered enough ass kickings to last a hundred damn lifetimes.

Even though Stuff hadn't mentioned the Barristers' Ball in days, secretly hoping Shauntae's face would still be too bruised to go out in public since he'd promised Marie Averez he'd take her instead, the underprivileged female had marked the calendar weeks ago and since it was on her birthday she was definitely counting on going. For Shauntae it was a one-in-a-million chance to actually go somewhere where people who she always admired and wanted to be like were hobnobbing in the same place.

Donte and Elon were content knowing that soon their problems would be completely over. Starting today, their plan of taking care of the competition would be placed in full swing, and their lives would go back to normal. Elon had several of their tight-knit crew set to split the wigs of all the little niggas Yankee and Terrell had on the corners, gas stations, and city parks. This Saturday night in the city would be like no other.

Terrell had just dropped off the last pound of weed that Juan had blessed them with to Yankee, who was posted up at the greasy Chicken Shack on the corner of his block. Spending time with Prayer and his girl was at the top of his list, and he wasn't gonna let anyone or anything, including grief from Simone, stand in his way. The young, wheelchair-bound man didn't care what his mother or Drake claimed to have seen happen between Joi and some dude. He trusted her.

He, Drake, and Prayer all had tickets to attend the local Barristers' Ball to see Stuff's dad get an award, but Drake was called away on business, leaving Prayer on her own. This was a perfect time to have Joi meet Prayer.

When Yankee got the package from Li'l T, he was more than heated at the stipulations Terrell had the nerve to put on how he was to pay it back. Not giving five hot-fire shits that they had to pay Juan a ticket, Yankee wanted to do what he'd been doing for weeks, which was jacking off money at Northland Mall, eating like a fucking kingpin, and tricking with different bad-ass bitches who would've never given him the time of day if he hadn't been paying them. In his paranoid mind and twisted way of thinking, he felt like not only were Terrell and Stuff already blessed with money, but they also were getting one over on him, shortchanging his share of the revenue on the weed sales.

With the scorching hot day dragging by, Yankee, who wore a baseball cap backward, and Wahoo, still deep in mourning, sat on the front stoop of Yankee's house, going over the loosely concocted robbery game plan that was only hours from going down. Bragging to every crackhead, whore, and drunk in the alley, bragging to the mailman and even to the Arab at the party store, Shauntae, cocky and proud, had let it be known all across one side of the ghetto hood to the next that she was gonna go to the highly publicized, uppity-ass lawyers' bullshit party with Stuff. Knowing that information, when Stuff and Shauntae left the event, Wahoo and Yankee would make their move and follow him back to his house.

Sitting on the edge of his bed, Stuff carefully looked over the bills he'd accumulated over the past week, trying to show Shauntae he was sorry for allowing things to get so out of hand between her and Terrell. Sure, he thought she was rough around the edges, but she was different from any other female he'd ever encountered, and that intrigued him beyond belief. Everyone always said good girls loved bad boys. Well, in this case, it was the complete opposite.

After he and Marie Averez returned from their date at the ball, Stuff was gonna make sure to spend all his available time the rest of summer before he went off to college with Shauntae and only Shauntae, even if it did make Juan cut off them and their supply of weed. After all, this was nothing more than a temporary thing to do to make some extra bread before he received his trust fund, not an occupation.

Chapter Five

It was Saturday morning, and the sun was shining bright. Shauntae had spoken to Stuff several times during the week, thanking him for all the flowers and especially her birthday gift bracelet. Never once confirming that she was still going with him to the ball, Shauntae took it for a given. After tricking with an old white man to get some extra loot, she used the money to buy a brand-new expensive dress, shoes, and of course to top it off, some cheap-ass accessories.

"I'm about to be out." Shauntae snatched her cell phone off the charger and headed toward the door. "I got an eleven o'clock appointment at the salon and a bitch don't wanna be late."

"Okay," Joi yelled out the kitchen doorway. "I'll still be here when you get back. Terrell isn't picking me up until four or five."

"Fuck that nigga Terrell and his crippled ass that can't walk and probably can't fuck! I told you to stop saying that fag's name to me!" she screamed, looking at the mirror near the door and making sure all the swelling was gone, which it was. The dark bruise marks were still visible, but she'd already planned on putting extra makeup on those spots. When Stuff, the same dude she'd set up to get fucked up, picked her up for her fairy-tale evening, she'd be perfect. "Now I'm out!"

"I heard you the first time! So just go!" Joi understood her sister still being angry, and she felt she had every right to be, but that still didn't stop her from not wanting to hear that dumb shit about her boyfriend Terrell.

Despite having an appointment, Shauntae waited her turn to even get shampooed. Now she was almost finished getting the last track sewn in and ironed, and it was not soon enough for the other tired customers and stylists who had to hear her brag about her plans of being the baddest bitch at a ball most of them had never heard of, let alone been invited to.

After flagging down a cab, Shauntae settled in the rear seat for the four-mile trip back to her house. As the car hit every unavoidable pothole, the overjoyed female felt her cell phone vibrating in her bootleg Coach purse. She hoped it wasn't Elon again for the fifteenth time. After blowing up Stuff's phone three times earlier in the morning herself and getting his voicemail, she was glad it was him finally returning her call.

"Hello."

"Hey, happy birthday. It's me, Stuff."

"I know your voice by now." A smile graced her face.

"Oh." Stuff felt he was making some headway in cracking through Shauntae's concrete exterior. "What you doing?"

"I just got my hair done!" she excitedly yelled as the cab driver glanced back to see why she was so loud. "I paid damn near a hundred and fifty for this sew in!"

"Oh, yeah? What you got up?"

"Don't act silly, nigga," Shauntae laughed. "What time you picking me up? Or are we going in a limo?"

"Limo?" Stuff questioned. "What you talking about a limo for? I don't get it."

"Dang, boy, I was just asking. You know I ain't never been to a party like the one tonight, so I don't be knowing how y'all be flossing on the other side of the law."

It was then and only then that Stuff realized she was talking about the Barristers' Ball he was attending later on. He had mentioned it to her weeks ago in passing, but he assumed she'd forgotten all about it since neither he nor she had brought the subject back up. Even if he hadn't confirmed he was taking a refined and equally educated Marie, considering all the disrespectful, crude, and obnoxious behavior Shauntae displayed at Simone's, there was no way in sweet hell he'd take her around his father and his father's peers. The young man who lived by the book had to come up with something to fix this situation without hurting her feelings, but there was only one way he could see to do it: lie.

"Well," he stammered, "that's what I was calling to tell you. My mom is pulling one of her major headache, 'I'm about to have a heart attack' routines and wants me to stay home with her."

"What?" Shauntae screamed out, causing the cab driver to swerve.

"Yeah. Since my parents divorced, she does it all the time when I'm going to spend some time with my dad."

"So fucking what? Can't one of your sisters stay with her good faking ass? That some straight-up bullshit she pulling!"

"Naw." Stuff continued to let the lie grow bigger, knowing he couldn't take her out in public. "Their husbands are all lawyers like my pops, so they have to be there too. I'm the only one."

Feeling like a child who'd lost her dog, Shauntae hung up the phone after Stuff promised to call her if he could find someone else to chill with his mother.

Joi was a nervous wreck as she and Terrell made their way up the long driveway of the house that he grew up in and called home. After reassuring her that Prayer was easygoing and laid-back, nothing at all like what she witnessed firsthand when she met Simone, Li'l T turned the van's engine off and got out, and then sat in his wheelchair, which Joi had quickly brought around to the side. Before they could reach the ramp located on the left side of the front porch, they were met on the stairs by a jubilant Prayer.

"Hey, baby." She tightly hugged him, not wanting to let go. "I missed you so much!"

"I missed you too."

"Hello, sweetie. You must be Joi."

"Hello, Mrs. Martin." Joi smiled, feeling welcomed. "It's so nice to finally meet you."

"You also. Y'all two come on in."

Prayer was the perfect hostess to her surrogate son's girlfriend the rest of the evening until they got ready to leave. Even when she found out that coincidentally she was the youngest daughter of Monique Richard, who she, Chari, and especially Simone despised and beefed out with every time they came into contact, she still was hospitable, knowing that you can't choose whom you're related to.

As the happy couple was making their way back to the van, Prayer's cordless phone rang, causing her to get angry. "This ain't nobody but Stuff's mother again acting a straight-up fool. She's been clowning all day."

"Dang, why now?" Terrell asked as Joi's ears perked up at the mention of her sister's newfound love interest.

"You know that Barristers' Ball is going on and that boy is with his daddy. And you know how she gets when he ain't all up under her."

"Oh, yeah?" Li'l T knew low-key that Prayer was just like Stuff's mother: over-possessive.

"Yeah. He took Marie Averez." Prayer nonchalantly dropped the bomb not knowing Joi's sister thought she was the one supposed to be on his arm tonight. "You know that girl always had a crush on him since y'all was kids."

The ride home was a solemn one as Joi tried to figure out the best way possible to break the news to her big sister that Stuff wasn't about shit and was playing her.

"What's wrong with you?" Terrell asked as he rubbed her on the leg. "Auntie Prayer loved you."

"I love her too." Joi smiled as she leaned over and kissed him on the cheek. "I just got something on my mind, that's all."

Before he could say another word, his cell phone starting ringing. "Yeah, what up doe?"

"Dawg, ya ain't gonna believe this dumb shit!"

"What is it, Yankee? What the hell is wrong?"

"Mannnn, some of the young cats from around da way just called me saying some crazy guys with bats jumped out on them swinging and shit." Yankee had panic in his voice mixed with rage. "They said two of our runners' shit is split wide the fuck open and they on their way to the goddamn hospital bleeding like a son of a bitch!"

"You bullshitting." Li'l T felt his heart start to race and his adrenalin rise as he drove faster toward Joi's house. "What the fuck!"

"Naw, nigga, but . . ." Yankee saw his other line was ringing, and it was Wahoo. "Hold on, T, this Wahoo."

While Terrell was on hold, his anger increased, scaring Joi once again as she saw the same bizarre expression he had on his face when he bugged out on Shauntae. She hesitated to ask what was wrong, but since he was driving fanatically, she felt the need to at least try to calm him down before he got into an accident and got them both killed.

"Baby, what's happening?" She massaged his shoulder as he drove twenty or thirty miles per hour over the speed limit.

"Nothing," he exhaled before Yankee got back on the line. "Hello!"

"Yeah, dude, I'm back!" Yankee, who was secretly scheming on Terrell himself, was talking loudly enough now for Joi to hear him. "My cousin just told me them other workers we got posted down the street from him just ran up on his front porch after being chased off Jefferson. And dig this here, them fools had bats too!"

"Where you at? 'Cause I'm on my way as soon as I drop Joi off at the crib. Then somebody gonna pay for trying to mess up our fucking hustle!" Terrell bent the corner of his girl's street. After they decided to meet up at Wendy's across from the old, abandoned KFC, he hung up and brought his van to a quick halt at Joi's front door. "All right, baby, I gotta dip."

"Are you gonna be okay?" she asked, worried.

"Babe, I got this. Now I gotta be out. Something ain't right!"

As Terrell skidded off, Joi entered her house to find Shauntae sitting on the couch with a blunt up to her lips and a bottle of Rémy Martin on the coffee table smack dab in front of her. The ten o'clock news was on the television, and the sound was loud enough for a deaf man to hear it.

"Hey, Tay." Joi could tell her sister was not in a good mood and still depressed since she had missed going to the Barristers' Ball with Stuff. Joi hated to add fuel to the fire on her sister's birthday, but she knew she had to deliver the devastating blow that Stuff had lied to her and really did go to the ball, and worse than that, with some other chick named Marie.

"Oh, hey," Shauntae grumbled, barely looking away from the screen. "Wanna see something I recorded off the news?"

"Ummmm, I guess so." Joi was glad to avoid telling her about Stuff when she saw the unthinkable. It was a report from downtown Detroit featuring a collection of Motown's who's who of local celebrities, honorees, and fashionable upper crust who were attending the Barristers' Ball. Just when the report was over, Shauntae pointed the remote and pressed the hold button. Joi's mouth dropped open in disbelief as she saw Stuff (Kenneth Ian Spencer III) and Marie Averez hand in hand, walking the red carpet. They posed for media pictures. Unbeknownst to them, the watchful, predatory eye of Wahoo was parked across the street, waiting for Stuff to leave.

"Ain't that a bitch." Shauntae relit the blunt, gagging as she reached for the bottle that she was taking straight to the head like it wasn't shit but water. "He played me for some Spanish broad! It's all good, 'cause that nigga and ya boyfriend gonna all get theirs soon!"

"What you talking about?" Joi quizzed her sister, who was drunk and high as a kite. "What does Terrell have to do with it? What did you do now, Shauntae? I hope that's not why he was so mad! What did you do?"

Slurring her words as she started to dance around the room with the new dress she'd brought up to her body, Shauntae laughed. "They think they're better than us! Elon knows where both they bitch asses live at, and we about to see what's really good when some mama's boys try to go hard. Fuck 'em! Fuck 'em all!"

Joi immediately wasted no time trying to get in touch with Terrell, but she had no luck, getting nothing but his voicemail. *Damn, he's not picking up.*

When Shauntae realized that her baby sister was trying to throw salt in her revenge game plan, she vindictively snatched Joi's cell phone from her hand, causing the two of them to struggle. Having the strength of a bull and accustomed to taking ass kickings from different dudes on the regular, an intoxicated Shauntae easily won the battle, knocking Joi off-balance. Fuming with envy, Shauntae shoved her against the wall, knocking the wind out of Joi. With contempt and malice in her heart, Shauntae then took the sibling fight to an all-time low. When Joi tried to get back up on her feet, without a second thought the older of the two grabbed one of Joi's many academic award plaques off the wall, striking her sister across the face and knocking her out cold.

"You always think you're so smart." She towered over Joi, dizzy and out of breath. "I ain't liked you since the day Mama brought your ass home from the hospital!"

Ten minutes after that wild confrontation, Elon, hyped that his plan was going down, pulled up in the girls' front yard and ran up on the porch. He pushed open the unlocked door. To his surprise, he found Shauntae delirious, smelling like she'd bathed in liquor, and Joi unconscious alongside the china cabinet.

"Damn, bitch! What went on here? What's wrong with your sister?" Elon tried getting a straight response from Shauntae. "Me and my people out there putting in that work and you clowning!"

"Leave me alone!" She raised her voice, forgetting who she was talking to, and she swung. She connected a right hook directly with Elon's jaw. "Before I fuck you up too!"

"That's it, ho! I done had it!" He rubbed the side of his face and then lunged at her. "You done hung out with them soft-ass niggas too long! Now daddy gonna really show you and your sister who's boss in the D!"

Chapter Six

Just as Yankee bit into his cheeseburger, an infuriated Terrell turned into the parking lot with murder on his mind. Disloyal and having his own separate agenda that Wahoo was working on, Yankee couldn't waste any time getting a handle on who or what the cause was of these sudden bat-wielding niggas who had declared war on them.

"What up doe?"

"What up doe with you, my dude?" Terrell nodded as he leaned out the open window. "What's the deal? Ya heard anything more?"

"Naw. Them young boys say they lost they stash, but who knows if that shit true or not."

"Yeah, true that. But yet and still they shit is busted, right?"

"Hell yeah." Yankee tossed the sandwich on the ground, losing his appetite. "I stopped by Wahoo's cousin's crib, and it was blood all over the porch!"

Plotting what moves to make next after about a good thirty minutes or so reliving what the young cats said happened step by step, they still were at a loss as to who their enemy was.

"Well, we need to gather all the fellas together and get strapped. At least that way if them hating busters come back, we'll be ready!"

"Yeah, that'll work." Yankee looked nervously at the time on his cell phone, knowing he was on the clock for his plan to go off without a hitch.

"Anyway, where is Wahoo?" Terrell scanned the parking lot as his ever-present gun now occupied the passenger seat. "I know he said he out this bullshit, but right about now we need his ass. He gotta have our backs!"

"Oh, ummm . . ." Yankee had to think quickly. "I think he's over on the deep west side, checking on some job."

"Oh, okay. Well, get in touch with him and tell him we all need to meet up tonight. I'm about to go to the crib and see how much bread we working with now to re-up, 'cause my boy Juan is gonna fall through later to pick it up. I don't wanna keep him waiting. I'll holler."

Here this nigga go again thinking he's a goddamn boss! After me and Wahoo hit this lick in a few, it's gonna be a pleasure telling his crippled ass to kick rocks! Yankee grinned at Terrell.

Terrell wasn't experienced in really what to do next or what course of action to take. Everything Simone had said about him was true, and now that some dudes whose toes he and his friends had stepped on were obviously on their heads, the shit was fucked up. He wasn't a gangster with that real hardcore gangster mentality in him. Prayer and Drake hadn't raised him to be a killer despite his psychotic inherited bloodline. Even though he kept his gun with him at all times, it was for protection, not what he was now involved in.

Lost in deep concentration thinking about what in the hell he'd gotten himself into trying to prove that he was a man, a loud sound came from nowhere, snatching him from his thoughts. Turning down the radio, he heard the sounds getting louder and heard the thud of gunshots rip through the rear sliding door of the van. As he looked in his mirror, Terrell noticed a dark maroon old-school Regal turn off a side street and accelerate, coming up behind him. Reaching over for his pistol Li'l T put one up top and prayed for the car, whose headlights were off, to hopefully realize they were shooting at the wrong motherfucker and get the hell on.

Speeding down Jefferson Avenue then dipping in and out of the raggedy streets of Detroit, a few short blocks later they were still on his trail. The passenger of the car leaned out the window, getting boogie and shattering the van's rear window with a shot that almost separated Terrell's head from the rest of his body.

These niggas act like they trying to kill me for real! His mind-set quickly changed, and Kamal appeared to take over. *I ain't going out like no punk. If they wanna do something, then fuck it!* Suddenly Terrell picked up his leg and pressed his foot down on the brake and cut the steering wheel, making the custom van do a dough-nut, resulting in him facing the old-school Regal head-on. Seeing his father's face, Li'l T moved his foot onto the gas pedal and hit the custom buttons on the steering column, lowering his own window. The closer he got, the more Kamal's spirit consumed him, and he just didn't give a fuck about living or dying.

Several loud, thunderous sounds popped off. Kamal's bastard son got off four rounds directly into the late-model car, causing the driver to swerve into an abandoned car. Li'l T got away unharmed. But that wasn't enough as he swerved around once more, letting off three more "fo' sho" shots into the driver's side. Cautiously rushing to get back to the safety of the other side of the Gates and get a couple of his mother's many guns she thought she had secretly stashed in the back of her closet, Li'l T was stopped by the security guard at the shack.

"What up doe, Mr. Johnson?" Terrell kept looking over his shoulder, keeping his gun on his lap just in case his attackers returned.

"Hello, Terrell. Somebody in a black truck left this package for you about an hour ago."

"A black truck?" he asked, puzzled. "I don't know anybody in a black truck."

"Yeah, well, the young man said he was a new friend of yours, and I believe he said something like, 'Welcome to the neighborhood.'"

"What the hell?" Hesitantly he took the long package, which had a huge black bow on it, and set it on the passenger seat. He drove through the steel gates with perspiration pouring down his face.

As he sat in the driveway, the crazy bullshit started to make a little sense of who might've been on their heads so tough. Slowly opening the mysterious box, Terrell was shocked to see one long-stemmed black rose with a card attached that read:

> *For ya mama to carry when I'm done with you!*
> *I GO HARD*

That's the same dude I keep seeing! It hit him as he got out of the van and into his wheelchair. He rolled into the house. *I need to get in touch with the fellas.* Terrell first called Yankee, followed by Wahoo, getting no answer from either. Before he could put his cell back on his hip, a ringing sound signaled he had a text message with a picture attached from an unknown number. As his strong hands shook from all the drama that'd just jumped off, Li'l T grabbed some of his painkillers off his dresser and waited for the picture to download.

"Damn, I wish these pills would hurry the fuck up and kick in." He went back into the living room.

Terrell's nerves were starting to stimulate movements he couldn't quite control in both the left and right legs. After setting his cell phone down on the marble table, he

gripped both his thighs in an attempt to stop the trembling. The handicapped teenager momentarily forgot
about the picture slowly downloading. He assumed it
was only one of those junk texts that he received on the
regular from his former classmates.

After calming down from being shot at and getting the
strange threat attached to the black rose, he leaned up to
try calling Yankee once more. He felt his blood pressure
rise as his eyes bucked to almost twice their regular size.
"Ahhhh, hell naw," Li'l T yelled as he shook with fury. The
picture on his cell was now completely revealed, and he
continued to process in his brain what he was seeing.
"What kinda bullshit is this!"

It was Joi, lying back on what seemed like a burgundy
and gray couch, with her eyes closed. Whoever sent him
the text had a handful of Joi's long hair wrapped around
his hands and his dick stuffed down her open mouth.

I'm gonna kill somebody's ass! If that sight weren't
enough to send Terrell off into an easy, predictable
rage, not giving a fuck about the consequences, the next
picture attached showed the foul-ass nigga with his hand
shoved up into Joi's pussy. The same caption under each
picture read: I GO HARD. *This ho-ass nigga done messed
with my girl! Fuck that! He gonna die!*

Without so much as a second thought about what to
do next, Kamal's son was in full lunatic effect. Raising
back his arm, he slammed his cell phone against the wall
of his house. Then he grabbed his gun back off the table,
securing it into the rear of his jeans waistband. Opening
the front door, Li'l T then rolled his wheelchair to the
edge of the porch and slid out onto the cool concrete
pavement. Tossing his chair down all five of the stairs,
empowered with anger, he quickly used his arms for legs
and followed it.

After practically throwing the steel chair to the driveway, he finally got inside his vehicle and drove off en route to Joi's house, not knowing what he'd find when he got there. The only thing the deranged teenager knew was that Joi loved him and would never ever do shit like that to disrespect him. And whoever the brazen nigga was riding around Detroit in the black truck claiming "I GO HARD" and causing havoc in Terrell Harris's once-calm life was about to get fucked the fuck up! Period! No ifs, ands, or buts, he would be dealt with!

Chapter Seven

"Dawg, where is you at? I don't see you." Yankee crept around the corner to Woodward Boulevard near the far entranceway of the Fox Theater where the Barristers' Ball was being held.

"I'm about to flash the headlights twice," Wahoo stated as he stayed stooped down in the seat. "Look to ya left!"

"Oh, okay. I see you." Yankee, making sure no one around was watching him, made his way to the car and jumped inside. "Have you seen him and Shauntae come out yet?"

"Naw, not yet. And dig this, he ain't even bring that bucket head Shauntae with him."

"Say word, son!"

"Yeah, dude was hugged up with some bad-ass model-type Mexican skank!"

"Whatever! Whoever he brought, he still getting got! And that ho-ass coward nigga Terrell keeps calling my phone like he done lost his mind." Yankee took off his baseball cap, wiping the sweat off his forehead. "I don't know who got on those little dudes' heads like that with bats, but ain't nothing gonna stand in the way of us and this lick tonight."

"Yeah, he been hitting me up too!" Wahoo kept a keen, watchful eye on the front door of the theater so when Stuff did leave they'd be right behind him and close on his tail. "I do kinda feel bad but . . ."

"But what? Fuck that. I know you ain't going soft and shit!" Yankee said. "Stuff's ho ass got enough of that cheese to share with us. Plus as much as we sit around taking orders from that crippled bitch Terrell, he owes us too, and later on, I'm going for that!"

Twenty long minutes later of the robbery-minded duo staring and avoiding the suspicious patrols of Detroit's finest, Stuff and Marie emerged as the crowd poured out of the bright, neon-lit venue, setting their plan into action. Dodging in and out of traffic, Yankee and Wahoo maintained a safe, inconspicuous distance behind the clean BMW as it glided down the freeway ramp heading out of the city limits. When they thought they couldn't drive any farther without running out of gas, Stuff and the female finally came up.

"Where the hell we at?" Wahoo tried to see if he recognized the area as he continued to stay several yards back. "Him and Terrell is out here in the for-real boonies!"

"That's what I'm talking about! You know it ain't shit out here but a bunch of white motherfuckers with that major bread!" Yankee smiled in anticipation of going back to the D with his pockets on bump. "Hold up, slow down a little bit. They about to make a turn."

Following them down a back road, Wahoo turned off his headlights so Stuff wouldn't become aware that he was being tailed. After passing four or five huge mini mansions, Stuff hit his brakes slightly as he made a quick left into a driveway of a brightly lit home with a cobble-stone wall around it. Making sure the car was parked all the way to the side of the road, the two soon-to-be intruders got out, creeping toward the entrance. Before they could safely get near the wall, they saw Stuff get back in his car and drive around the horseshoe-shaped driveway and back in their direction.

"Oh, shit! Duck!" Yankee and Wahoo crouched near some bushes as Stuff, now alone, drove by.

"Hurry up," Wahoo whispered as they rushed to the car before Stuff got out of their sights.

Less than half a mile later, once again the pair pulled over to the side of the road as their intended target entered another driveway that undoubtedly was his. Seeing him disappear through the front door, Yankee and Wahoo let at least ten or fifteen minutes pass before they both removed black ski masks from their pockets and went around back. They eased open a lower unlocked window.

Not knowing what to expect as they crawled inside, Yankee slipped his gun out of his waistband. Tiptoeing around each corner of the expensively furnished home, Yankee led the way as he and Wahoo followed the voices of two women and Stuff, who was preoccupied telling them about his evening. Before the innocent women and Stuff knew what was happening, they were staring down the barrels of unmerciful pistols held by two masked gunmen.

"Yo! Don't say a motherfucking word and ain't nobody gonna get hurt!" Yankee tried disguising his Brooklyn accent as he pressed the muzzle of his 9 mm to Mrs. Spencer's temple.

"What do you want?" Prayer begged as she instantly regretted coming over to keep her neighbor and Terrell's best friend's mother company. "Who are you?"

"Listen, you uppity, fat bitch! Didn't I say keep your mouth quiet?" Yankee turned his gun on Prayer, causing her to flinch and draw up. He snatched her hand, twisting her wedding ring off her finger. "Now don't make me hurt your ass!"

Stuff consoled his mother as well as Prayer as he attentively watched the mannerisms of the two cruel assailants. They systematically removed his mother's rings along with a necklace his father had given her. It had a flawless diamond pendant that was worth more than Yankee and Wahoo would probably make in three lifetimes. *It can't be,* Stuff thought. *These dudes gotta be kidding me if they think I don't know who they are.*

Moving around the huge house from room to room, gathering anything that he thought was of value, Yankee left Wahoo to stand guard over their victims to ensure none of them made a move to get help. Stuff saw the weight of the gun causing Wahoo's hand to shake. He took the opportunity to try to talk some sense into Wahoo.

"Wahoo," he whispered as the women looked on in horror and shock that Stuff appeared to know at least one of their captors. "I know it's you. Why you doing this? Do you wanna go to jail over a couple of dollars?" Wahoo tried his best not to pay attention, but Stuff's words were getting to him. "I know your grandmother just died, and I know you're confused, but why take a chance of your family losing you too? Wahoo, listen to me."

"Shut up, nigga!" Wahoo said threateningly, trying to keep his voice down. He knew Yankee was already itching to turn a simple robbery into a murder. "I'm doing this to help my family. We ain't got it like you!"

"So what, dude?" Stuff kept at him, attempting to work on his emotions. "Just think about what your little brothers and sisters are gonna do when you locked up in jail or dead!"

"What you mean dead? I'm the one with the gun." Wahoo waved it around recklessly as the women huddled together and ducked, trying to avoid the possibility of getting shot if the pistol accidentally went off. "Now I'm the boss and ya taking the loss around here!"

"Listen, son," Prayer calmly interjected, "it's obvious that the other young man is the one calling all the shots.

You can have everything we have and leave, but I assure you if you harm us, my husband and son will leave no stone unturned until they find you. Now, why would you want to live like a hunted animal the rest of your life because you let someone else talk you into something that you know is wrong?"

"Yeah, and if Terrell and his uncle don't kill you, my dad is definitely going to make sure that you and Yankee spend the rest of y'all life in prison."

"Terrell? Terrell?" Wahoo was confused. "What he got to do with this?"

"That's my son." Prayer spoke up, hoping Li'l T's name would carry some type of weight with the young man and he'd opt to let them go free. "Do you know him too?"

"What the hell?" Wahoo was having second thoughts about the robbery because he had heard rumors about the legendary Drake Martin and his underworld big-name connections from back in the day, not to mention that Terrell had always kept it one hundred with him. Now he had his people backed up in a corner with guns to their heads and was robbing them blind. *Damn, I done fucked up.*

"Look, Yankee ain't trying to hear shit y'all saying. So y'all need to shut y'all mouths before he comes back."

"Dude, think for yourself. You're smarter than that to let the next man mess you around." Stuff could tell he was finally making headway. Wahoo lowered his gun temporarily while peeling back the mask that was covering his face. "It still ain't too late."

"Maybe you're right." Desperation fueled his tone. "It's just that I wanted to get my family out of Detroit before the State snatches them up! I'm all they got!"

"I promise I'll help you. But first, you gotta help yourself and let us go," Prayer urged.

"Yes, let us go," Stuff's mother pleaded before she collapsed into her son's arms.

Just as they believed they'd gotten through to Wahoo, Yankee fumbled down the staircase with a few pillowcases stuffed full of stolen items. Shaking his head when seeing his partner in crime had revealed his true identity, Yankee knew immediately that no living witnesses could be left to testify in case he was ever caught.

"Damn dumb-ass nigga! Y'all ain't leaving me no choice! Now I gotta waste three bullets on these rich motherfuckers!" Yankee dropped his stolen goods to the thick, plush carpet, and then he slid back the gun's grip, putting one up top. "But oh well, so be it!"

Chapter Eight

Turning left out of the Gates and back onto the main road, Terrell wasted no time dodging in and out of the summer night's heavy traffic, blowing his horn in hopes of persuading the slower drivers to get the hell out of his way. Swerving right when he got to Joi's street, Terrell just avoided striking a bum who was resting on the dumpster near the alleyway, as he barreled his van recklessly down the bumpy road, which had no working streetlights.

With one more block to go, he quickly glanced over his shoulder to see if anyone else was following him. *Then fuck what else happens!*

In the midst of his adrenaline escalating to an all-time high, Terrell sharply cut the steering wheel, making the custom van jump the already-crumbling concrete curb. He brought it to an abrupt halt on Joi's front grass. With no concerned neighbors on the densely populated block to care one way or the other what was taking place with the next motherfucker, Li'l T swung the van door open.

Without bothering to get his wheelchair, feeling like he was untouchable, Terrell lowered himself onto the grass. With palms down, he proceeded to use his upper-body strength to get him to the stairs, which were badly in need of repair, and truth be told, needed to be demolished. Secure in the fact that his 9 mm was fully loaded and stuffed in the rear of his jeans, pressing against his spinal cord, he made his ascension toward the front door. He could see it was slightly cracked opened.

"I hope whoever did that shit to Joi is still here so I can blast his ho ass!" Li'l T yelled out, giving the perpetrator a heads-up that he meant business.

Since he'd smashed his cell phone prior to leaving the house, Terrell couldn't call Joi and see if at least she'd answer and tell him who was inside her crib. Yet, he didn't give a fuck at this point. Li'l T reached his huge, muscular arm upward, opening the door with one hand as he tightly gripped his gun's handle with the other. Like his black-hearted, mentally unbalanced father Kamal, who roamed the streets of Detroit like he owned each and every one of them raggedy sons of bitches, Terrell had no fear in his veins as he prepared himself to face the unknown like he was a true warrior and an official old-school G.

This is it! I'm about to go for mines! I'm tired of these pussy-ass niggas thinking this cripple shit is a fucking joke! I'm a grown-ass man just like they are! "Joi!" he shouted out as soon as he crossed over the threshold, pausing just long enough to pull out his pistol and place it onto his lap. "Joi! Are you here? Where you at?"

Cautiously entering the house, small bits of debris that were on the carpet pressed into the palms of his hands with each movement he made. Unfamiliar with the interior layout since he'd never actually been inside the place Joi called home, his eyes darted from wall to wall, door to floor, and floor to window, scrutinizing every sight his widened pupils took in. Considering the lower-level view the handicapped teenager was forced to observe things from, Terrell easily saw Shauntae first. She was lying near the coffee table. Knowing that he and she were still not on speaking terms, leery in demeanor he approached her slowly. He did not know exactly what, if any, part of all the shenanigans of the evening she was playing.

"Hey, Shauntae," Terrell whispered, reaching down for his gun. "Where's Joi?" His finger sweated on the trigger. The closer Li'l T eased to Shauntae, the more he smelled the strong, distinct odor of liquor reeking from her pores. "Hey!" He nudged her as he got in arm's reach. Despite the force pushed on her leg, the troubled female did not move or flinch. Terrell naively assumed Shauntae was no more than merely passed out cold from all the drinking her little sister alleged she did on the regular, until he tried to go around her in his search of Joi and his hand mashed down on a thick, viscous substance. *What the fuck!* Li'l T raised his hand, and from the light that was shining from the bootleg *Scarface* DVD that Elon had left playing on the television, he could see that his fingers and half his hand were covered in blood. *Ahhhhh shit!* He wiped his dripping palm on the floor the best he could as he frowned. Then he noticed a huge, gaping hole, which had to be a gunshot wound, on the left side of Shauntae's head.

Li'l T had no idea whatsoever that history was indeed hereditary and had eerily repeated itself. Years ago, Big Ace had silenced Monique once and for all for being a "setup queen." Her eldest daughter, who had taken after her dead mama, had suffered that same fate less than an hour earlier at the hands of Big Ace's son Elon. He shot one through her two packs of 1B ultra-straight freshly sewn-in weave and directly into the bitch's cranium.

Oh, my God! I can't believe this shit! This is so fucked up! Terrell was now more panicked and anxious than ever to find Joi. Searching the room with his eyes and ears, Li'l T's heart raced as he scooted his body against a wall so he could try to survey what he was dealing with. "Joi!" he yelled out repeatedly, hoping his girl was all right. "Joi! Joi! Joi!"

The roaring sounds of a car drove down the street, its muffler dragging on the ground. Terrell once again tried to hear over the annoying sounds of Tony Montana's and Manny's not-good-English-speaking-ass voices blaring from the television set. Just as he had focused in on where the electrical cord was plugged in, he suddenly caught a glimpse of Joi's sandal sticking out from behind the couch.

Shit! Ah, fuck! Naw! Dragging his legs, which were trembling from all the strenuous movements he was putting them through, quickly Terrell got to his girl-friend's side, swooping her half-naked body up in his arms. *Damn! Damn!* As her arm flung to the side and hit the carpet, Li'l T felt enraged watching his real first love attempt to speak. With her lips dry and cracked, a swollen eye, and small amounts of glistening red blood trickling down her temple, Terrell was relieved Joi hadn't suffered the same seemingly cruel fatal fate as Shauntae had: death.

"I'm sorry," Joi managed to say before she passed out.

With the strength of three bulls, Terrell grabbed Joi, tossing her over his strong, broad shoulders. He slid across the floor toward the door and onto the porch. "It ain't no way in hell I'm gonna leave you here to deal with all this bullshit. Ain't nothing here for you!" he vowed as he struggled going down the stairs with his weight as well as Joi's dead weight in tow. Lucky for him, with his passionate fury of revenge combined with the high-dosage painkillers he'd taken earlier, Terrell's legs were able to endure the trauma he was putting them through.

Chapter Nine

Across town, about three or four miles outside the city limits, Big Ace and Simone had just been seated at his regular booth located in the rear of one of the best and more expensive Italian restaurants. Having been turned on to this low-key, discreet spot a few years back by a major connect, Big Ace felt like somewhat of a big deal every time he and one of his many women broke bread there. But this was his regular evening. It was Saturday night, and like every Saturday night for years, he and Simone kinda had a standing engagement to kick the willy bo bo's, chill out, and vent if need be. Back in the day, after Kamal's death, things were shaky between them, but after a while, Big Ace got over the dumb shit of feeling animosity and blaming Simone for his boy's death. He knew Kamal for what he really was, a cold-blooded murderer, so he knew if dude came over to her house pissed, he only had one thing that ultimately stayed on his mind if he felt he was being slighted or disrespected in any shape, form, or manner.

Plus, when the truth surfaced that Kamal was the one who crippled an innocent Li'l T for life, it was more than easy to see why Joey shot Kamal and why Simone seemed not to care one bit that her supposed baby daddy and heinous-ass monster was dead and gone, nine outta ten probably straight to hell.

"So damn, baby, what's good with you?" Simone looked over the menu as if she didn't already know what she was ordering.

"I'm good," Big Ace replied as he chomped down on the huge cigar that was in the corner of his mouth. "I'm just tired as shit. In between business, that Clip-N-Dip Moe bullshit that done resurfaced, not to mention my wild-ass sons who call themselves in some sort of small-scale territory war over near your crib, thangs is gravy."

"Damn, Big Ace! Please don't talk to me about being tired. Not tonight!" Simone rolled her eyes, sighing as she folded her arms. "Li'l T and his friends done just about took over the house. And real talk, at least your boys were raised in the streets, so you ain't gotta worry about them. They already cut for the street life. Terrell ain't never gonna be ready for that type of bullshit even if he really is Kamal's son. Prayer got that boy out in them suburbs all the way fucked up and soft as a son of a bitch! Even Drake can't do shit with Prayer's overbearing ass. That tramp act like she birthed his sorry behind, not me!"

"Slow the hell down and take a deep breath!" Big Ace took a small swig of the strong drink the waitress had just brought over to him. "Just be happy the boy got a second chance at a good, normal life, because you know damn well you wasn't ready to step up and do that mama thang back then! Shittttt, matter of fact, keeping it a hundred, ya ass still ain't ready! Some of y'all Detroit hoes just ain't mother material. That's why I got my sons with me now!"

"Nigga, fuck you," Simone laughed as she also reached for her drink in an attempt to take the edge off. "And for the record, fat boy, I ain't no ho!"

"Damn, excuse me, Ms. Thang. Bitch!"

About twenty minutes into their main course, Big Ace's cell phone continued to constantly ring. Normally he was accustomed to cutting it off while he ate dinner, but since he was with Simone and she was an old-school rida, he knew she didn't mind if he took business calls during the middle of dinner, especially if it meant him making more money.

"Yeah, speak on it." Big Ace chewed his meatball as he spoke. "What's going on, Elon?"

Three seconds into Big Ace's conversation with his son, Simone's ESP "Get It Girl" radar kicked in, and her antenna went straight upward. She could tell that something was drastically wrong. A veteran to the game of being a dope dealer's girl, Simone had seen Big Ace's expression on more than a few niggas' faces throughout the years of her loyal, devoted service dedicated to hustling dudes to sponsor her lavish lifestyle. *Damn! Here the hell we fucking go!* she thought as she signaled the young white ponytail-swinging waitress for a doggie bag to wrap up her lobster and spaghetti meal she'd scarcely had a chance to enjoy. *Oh well, somebody ass done got done in the D!*

"What?" Big Ace yelled as he jumped up from the table, causing both drinks, along with their plates and the food piled on them, to fall to the floor. "Relax, relax! I'm on my way!"

Selfishly looking at her perfectly seasoned food now ruined on the carpet, Simone cursed the waitress for not being fast enough to bring her a carry-out container. *What a freaking waste!* But knowing she had to play the concerned role like she really gave a fuck about shit other than herself, one of her Academy Award–worthy performances she always kept on standby kicked into full gear. "Oh, my God! Baby, baby, what is it? What's wrong?" she whined, grabbing her purse, knowing they were about to make a quick exit. "What happened? Is everything okay? Who was that on the phone?" Glancing back once more at her plate upside down on the floor, Simone threw shade once more on the poor waitress who was left to clean up the mess, and worse than that, miss out on a nice tip that Big Ace was famous for leaving.

"Come on, we gotta roll." Big Ace peeled off a couple of hundred-dollar bills and tossed them at the hostess as they headed out the door. "My son's been shot!"

Damn! I guess I really called that one! Simone followed Big Ace, who'd just taken the keys from the valet, choosing to run across the parking lot and get his own car. *I wonder, do he have time to drop me off at my whip, or am I gonna have to take a fucking cab?* she plotted as if he'd just said he had a headache, not that his child had been shot and was possibly dead. *If I do have to take a cab, I swear to God he giving me some money for the bullshit! Plus some dough so a bitch can eat!*

By the direction Big Ace was recklessly driving in, it was easy for Simone to figure out they were en route to Receiving Hospital. As she wondered if her makeup was still looking fresh, the always out-for-self female deviously changed her mind, scheming that maybe her showing up at the hospital on Big Ace's arm was a good thing and might ward off any other stray-ass sluts he was fucking with who might've shown up just to show his good pay master ass they cared.

Besides, excluding about nine or ten years ago in passing, Big Ace never ever let chicks, including his long-time friend and fuck buddy Simone, around his boys. He loved them to death, being both mother and father, and didn't want to confuse them. Having a gang of bitches swinging on your nut sack wasn't the true way a man was supposed to carry himself. Donte, who was now another gunshot victim statistic in Detroit, got that lesson, but of course, Elon chose to emulate his pops and be a player.

Not caring about blocking traffic, Big Ace pulled up at the emergency entrance where he saw a huge group of young men he knew to be his sons' faithful crew and road dawgs, along with several scantily dressed females crying like there was no tomorrow. Flinging the car door open, Big Ace jumped out with urgency and ran through the double doors. Simone, who was left in the car, eased her door open and stepped out in the midst of the quickly growing crowd of young people. She made her grand entrance into the hospital like she was on the verge of walking the red carpet at the Soul Train Music Awards.

Upon entering the emergency room, Simone shuddered, noticing that it was almost sheer pandemonium as several families other than those obviously there for Donte were acting straight fools. *Damn! Another night in the D.* The condescending Simone looked down on some of the other females who were there as she stuck by Big Ace's side.

"What in the hell happened to your brother?" Big Ace asked Elon, who was enraged. He banged his clenched fist against the wall, causing the plaster to crack. "What the doctors doing? Have you went back there?"

"He was on a mission with Mitts and shit must've got outta control," Elon argued. "All I know at this point was the car they was driving ran into a pole or some shit like that after Donte got hit by a bullet. They said they need to take him into surgery immediately."

As Big Ace, consumed with worry, marched up to the information desk, Simone stood there feeling slighted that he was so rude that he didn't even take the time out to introduce her to his son. *Ain't that a bitch! Who that nigga think he is?* Feeling like she was just one in a sea of many, Simone pulled out her cell phone. She placed a call to one of her girlfriends, talking loud and putting on a front like anyone there truly cared that she was going shopping at Saks tomorrow or that she'd just had her brand-new Vette detailed. *These hoes wish they lived like me!* she silently snarled. *And damn what in the hell is that one wearing? I wish I would come outside looking a hot mess like her broke ass!*

When Big Ace returned from the desk to update Elon, who had just been spoken to by the security guards and told to calm down, Simone assuming the role of wifey, posted up on his arm and massaging Big Ace's shoulders in hopes of relaxing him. Just as the waiting room appeared to get some sort of order restored to it, Mitts emerged from the back with a square bandage taped to the side of his head and small cuts that onlookers imagined had to have occurred on impact when the Regal crashed.

"Mitts, Mitts, my nigga!" Elon rapidly ran up to his street soldier who was injured during the commission of putting in that work. "What exactly happened, dude? What went down? Did they say anything about Donte back there?"

"Yo." Mitts leaned on the wall, still dizzy from the slight concussion the doctors said he suffered when his head struck the dashboard. "That shit went down so fucking fast. One minute we was driving, chilling on the side street near the liquor store and throwing back a few beers, then the next thing I know, Donte spotted ol' boy in the van, and it was on!"

"Oh, yeah?" Elon was confirming for sure who his target was gonna be for gunning his brother down, even if it was a case of self-defense. Straight up his crew was all on Terrell's, Yankee's, and Stuff's heads, all in that order. But he and his boys started so much bullshit and stayed up in the middle of so much foolishness, it was hard to pinpoint without a firsthand witness who did what and to whom. "You talking about that custom boy, right? The one with the rims and shit?"

Hearing what the young guy was saying about a custom van caused Simone's ears to get on high alert. As she rested her weight all on one hip, she waited anxiously for the small-time thug to finish his account. *Wait a minute. What did he just say?*

"Yeah, dude." Mitts licked his dry lips as he spoke softly since his head was pounding. "We was on his crippled ass good for at least a few blocks until that nigga did some old gangsta suicide mission–type shit and somehow flipped the script. Next thing I know, we spun the fuck out, and he was the one doing the blasting!"

"Well, I'm about to get it popping! That nigga about to pay," Elon vowed.

"Hold up," Simone yelled in the boy's face as Elon paced the floor. "What you mean crippled nigga in a van?"

"Man, who the fuck is you?" Mitts fired back, never before in his life having seen the woman who was all of a sudden demanding answers. "You need to step off!"

Big Ace was also confused as he pulled Elon to the side of a vending machine, grilling him about what exactly he and his brother were into, leaving a livid Simone arguing with Mitts. "What is y'all beefing about?"

"Dad, that's the young cats who've been stepping on our territory." Elon took his truck keys out of his pocket because he was about to ride out on Terrell.

"Well, why didn't you come talk to me first before y'all started all this bullshit?"

"'Cause you told me and Donte to handle our own business, and that's what we've been doing, and that's what I'm about to do now!"

Simone, who was done trying to bully information out of Mitts, bolted over to Big Ace and Elon, trying to still find out for certain if they were talking about Li'l T. "Babe, who is they talking about? I know it ain't Terrell." She hung on to Big Ace's arm.

"Yeah, that's that crippled-ass nigga's government name, Terrell Harris," Elon answered for his father. "And that's what they can put on his ho-ass motherfucking tombstone for shooting my goddamn blood! And that's on my word." Elon spun around and headed for the door.

He jumped inside his truck, which was parked illegally up on the curb, blocking the walkway.

"Ain't you gonna go and stop his stupid ass? That's Li'l T your retarded son is talking about hurting!" Simone told Big Ace as she watched the black truck with the license plate that read I GO HARD disappear into the night. "Go after him!" Simone screamed out as she realized that was the same truck that was parked at Joi's and Elon was the same dude she was talking to. *That ho done set my kid up! I'm gonna kill that bitch!*

Before Big Ace, distraught about what had happened to his own child, could respond to Simone's unreasonable demands, one of the doctors came out the back, calling for the family of Donte James. "That's me." He quickly brushed passed a frantic Simone. "I'm his father!"

"Wait! Where you going?" Simone angrily argued, snatching the oversized man by his forearm. "Did you hear what I just said about my son? Are you deaf?"

"Your son?" Big Ace finally had enough of the "world revolves around me" routine Simone was playing, and he cut the game instantly short. "Listen, bitch! You said that shit right! Your son! Now real talk my boy is lying back there because some mess your boy might've done, and I'm about to go check on his status, ya feel me? And for the record, flat out, ain't you or no other skank who sucks my dick or gives me the pussy on a daily basis gonna stop or slow that shit down." Big Ace got louder as the doctor, clad in a white jacket and chart in hand, held the door impatiently, waiting for his patient's father to follow him. "Now, Simone, if you wanna take ya slap-happy self over there and try stopping Elon's hot-tempered ass from clowning on your seed, then so be it. Good luck with that! Do you! But with me, it's family over any bitches all day every day, baby doll! Now peace!"

After putting Simone in her place, Big Ace vanished with the doctor behind the gray metal doors, leaving her looking like a total and utter fool. Turning around humiliated, Simone stared into the faces of all the people she was trying so hard to make feel bad when she first entered. With mostly friends of Elon's and Donte's standing around waiting for any news of their fallen comrade, it was simple for Simone to distinguish that she was on her own and completely out of place. Clutching her purse tightly, the previously boisterous female made her way out of the hospital and thankfully flagged down a cab that had just dropped off a mother and two small children at the emergency room entrance.

"Take me to the Gates, and hurry! I'll give you a hundred dollars plus the fare if you step on it!" Simone instructed the driver of African descent. She tried calling Terrell on his cell phone to warn him of Elon's intended rage of revenge. "Run the red lights if you have to! Just hurry!" Pushing the REDIAL button time and time again in her sudden concern, the distressed parent constantly got her son's voicemail. *Damn! Pick up, Li'l T! Damn! Answer the fucking phone!* Simone prayed as the cab driver dipped in and out of traffic in hopes of receiving the bonus promised to him.

Chapter Ten

Stuff nervously stared down the barrel of Yankee's gun, listening to him rant and rave about the world dealing him and Wahoo both fucked-up hands in life. As the out-of-control thief was trying to convince a hesitant Wahoo that somehow stealing from his friend Stuff and his family would right that wrong, Stuff took a deep breath and got prepared for his one chance, maybe his last, to stand up and be a man. For once in his young life, Stuff was not trying to find some sort of logic or reasoning as to why something was happening. This wasn't the time to attempt to dissect Yankee's brain or figure shit out. With the expressions of jealousy, envy, and hatred plastered on Yankee's face, Stuff knew if he, his mother, and Prayer were going to survive the rest of the night and see daybreak, right here, right now was do or die.

"What you're doing is wrong, son," Prayer said to distract Yankee as Stuff watched his overly dramatic mother still passed out on the floor next to him. "There's always a better way than murdering three innocent people."

"I'm not your son, ho, and stop trying to make excuses for why you and all your stuck-up-ass friends think y'all better than the rest of the world!" Yankee demanded, shaking his gun around as Wahoo continued having second thoughts about what was taking place. "My mama sent me here from Brooklyn on the Greyhound to live with my aunt, who always treated me like a piece of shit. Wahoo's granny ain't been dead thirty days, and the State wanna tear the family apart! You know why? Because we ain't got that loot!" Yankee paced the floor, still pointing his pistol.

"And is that our fault?" Prayer grew irritated that he felt like she was to blame for the problems of humanity.

"Hell yeah! You just like Terrell's old girl, Simone, looking down on a motherfucker for not being born with a silver spoon in their mouth!"

"Nigga, please! Are you serious? That shit ain't nothing but a front!" Prayer instantly fired back with some revelations of her own and got back to her roots of being ghetto born. "Me and Simone was raised up in the Truth Homes, nigga! So how 'bout it! We ain't have shit to eat some nights but goddamn white rice and a stale piece of bread. And if our mothers were busy drinking or out somewhere running the streets, we were lucky to get that! Sometimes I had to wear the same thing to school for three days straight because I ain't have shit else, but fuck it. I wanted that free lunch in my empty stomach, so I went anyhow!" Prayer was yelling at the top of her lungs as she got her point across. "Times were hard for me too when I was your age, but I found a way out without breaking the law! I struggled night and day and paid my hood taxes in full, Negro! So don't come your roguish ass all up in here acting like you and your little thug friend is the only ones who done had it fucking bad in life. We all did! Don't ever get the shit twisted about how a chick is blessed to be living now, because make no mistake about the dumb shit. Bitch! I am from the D!"

Shocked that Prayer, who at first glance seemed so refined and meek, had just gone off, momentarily lowering their guard, Yankee nor Wahoo were prepared for what came next. Stuff, dressed in his expensive suit and Big Block Gators, using every move he'd learned from three years of being on his high school wrestling team, bravely charged Yankee, knocking the gun out of his hand and onto the floor near Wahoo's feet. With the force of the will to survive the battle on each teenager's side, they fought by the coffee table, where Stuff almost choked Yankee out. They then struggled beside the couch, with Yankee's knee pressed into Stuff's chest while he repeatedly socked him in his jaw, resulting in blood spilling from Stuff's mouth. The pair then rolled over near the antique grandfather clock, resulting in the irreplaceable timepiece crashing to the floor, barely missing Stuff's mother. The angry son then retaliated with several strong punches directly into Yankee's midsection, causing the young boy to gasp for air as he continued fighting. Both warriors were persistent in wanting to emerge victorious as they reached out over one another's body to grab for the pistol.

"You think you better than me, nigga?" Yankee hungered for air with each insane movement that was packed full of animosity. "You all in the hood running up behind Shauntae's nasty pussy like you own that bitch! You giving that tramp money and shit, making it hard for the next average neighborhood dude to get on! Why don't you just run up in that Mexican slut you was just all hugged up with and leave our females alone!"

"Fuck you, Yankee," Stuff said as he fought for survival. "You crazy! I told Terrell he couldn't trust you or your boy, but he wouldn't listen!"

"Naw, fuck you!" Yankee violently challenged.

With the gun still idly resting near Wahoo's feet, Prayer thought about her option to also make a move either going for the weapon or trying to escape out the side door, which was located off the driveway. Seeing that Yankee's pistol was only a few yards away but still much closer to Wahoo made the desperate female choose the second of the two options. She wanted to stay and try to convince

Wahoo that what he was doing was wrong and maybe help Stuff's mother who was still conveniently passed out, but at this point chaos was in effect, and any hope of a peaceful solution to this robbery, which was on the verge of turning to first-degree, premeditated, cold-blooded murder, was little to none. This might be Prayer's only chance, and she definitely had to take it.

As Wahoo stood motionless in a trance trying to figure out if he really wanted to possibly spend the next fifty years of his life in jail for burglary, kidnapping, and murder, Prayer cleverly eased her way from the commotion of the fight and tried breaking for the hallway. Just as she thankfully made it to the side door unharmed, she heard a single gunshot go off and Wahoo's voice calling out to his friend and partner in crime. Not once slowing up to see who had come out victorious between Yankee and Stuff, she twisted the knob and snatched the door open. She took off down the long driveway, stumbling past Stuff's parked BMW.

Placing the palm of her trembling hand on the still-warm hood of the automobile to catch her balance, Prayer screamed out in terror as she heard a second gunshot ring out from the house, followed by a third. Taking off once again, she dashed out to the main road, never looking back to see or care if Wahoo or Yankee were behind her in pursuit. *Yea, though I walk through the valley of the shadow of death, I will fear no evil: for thou art with me; thy rod and thy staff they comfort me.* Prayer repeatedly prayed with each desperate step she made to get help, *Oh, my God! Oh, my God! Please let Stuff and his mother be okay. God, please let Li'l T not be hurt! Oh, my God, please!*

Coming into an empty house after his short trip away, Drake opened the refrigerator door. He took out a carton of juice and poured himself a tall cup. Just as his lips felt the cold wetness of the liquid, he dropped the glass on the floor after hearing screams for help off in the distance. Swinging the door open to investigate the cries, Drake soon discovered those screams were coming from his distraught wife. *What the hell?* he thought as he headed out the door, meeting her halfway down the driveway near the huge oak tree in their front yard. "Prayer, Prayer, what's wrong?" Drake questioned as she fell into his arms, out of breath and looking over her shoulder. "Where are you coming from?"

"Ummmm, ummmmm. Oh, my God. I'm so glad to see you!" Prayer tried frantically to breathe as she clutched her chest, panting heavily. "Ummmm . . . Two boys . . . at Stuff's!" she managed to say. "With guns, they shot him! They shot him!"

"Say what?" Drake was confused as he escorted her toward the house. "Shot who? Calm down and tell me what you're talking about! Where is Stuff?"

Prayer rambled on while still keeping a watchful, suspicious eye on the main road as a car with its headlights off roared past, breaking the speed limit. "They know Terrell, and they have guns! I heard the shots! We gotta get help!" She jumped up and down like a child having a tantrum. "Hurry up, please, Drake, please!"

Grabbing his gun off his hip where he kept it, Drake, not fearing anyone, jumped in his car, backed it out, and gunned it toward Stuff's house. With a hysterical Prayer on the passenger side with big tears streaming down her face, he handed her his cell phone as he drove with his pistol on his lap.

"Here, you call the police and let them know to send some cars out here, and then try calling Terrell!"

When they cautiously turned sharply up at Stuff's house, Prayer immediately noticed that Stuff's BMW was now missing. "The car is gone," she blurted out after getting nothing but Terrell's voicemail time and time again. "It was parked right here! I remember! Now it's gone!"

"Listen, Prayer, you stay here and get behind the wheel," Drake demanded as he got out with his gun in his hand. "And keep calling Terrell. If he doesn't pick up, call Simone. Maybe she knows where he's at!"

"All right," she whined, keeping her teary eyes on the side of the house and the thick bushes that lined the driveway. "Please be careful, baby. They have guns!"

Drake bossed up, ready to enter the house and face whatever was waiting for him. "Yeah, well, so do I!"

No more than three or four minutes passed before Drake made his exit from the side door, signaling to Prayer that the coast was clear and she could safely come inside.

While still terrified of being held hostage at gunpoint by some unknown hooligans, hesitantly Prayer opened the car door, turning the still-running engine off. Peeking over her shoulder, still in fear, her eyes searched the perimeter as she heard the relieving sounds of police sirens in the near distance. Touching the cold metal door handle slowly, Prayer opened it and stepped back inside the house of recent horrors.

Closing her eyes tightly to temporarily drown out the sounds of the loud moans of pain that were coming out of the living room, Prayer eased around the corner and couldn't believe what she was seeing. As she had expected but hated to see, Stuff was on his back with his body shivering as if he was cold. Agonizing with pity and fighting not to vomit from the sight of Terrell's friend suffering, she held on tightly to the wall. Getting closer at Drake's urging, she immediately held her mouth as she saw a golf ball–sized spill of blood flowing out of Stuff's chest area. *Oh, my God! Hurry!* Prayer thought as she listened to the sirens pull up into the driveway.

Then, glancing over to the other side of the room, she saw Stuff's mother scrunched up under the huge baby grand piano, rocking back and forward probably in shock. Slumped over limp on the side of the now-destroyed grandfather clock was Wahoo. *I'm so confused,* filled her thoughts as she crept closer to her now unarmed and obviously injured captor.

"Please help my family," Wahoo begged for mercy as he tried to wet his dried, cracked lips. "I'm sorry. I tried to stop him. Please help them! Please!"

"What happened in here?" Prayer quizzed him as clots of dark blood started to flow from the gunshot wound that was on the side of his temple. "What happened?"

It didn't take a rocket scientist to put two and two together and figure out what had taken place. From what Prayer could get out of the young, dying thug, Yankee did indeed win the struggle and shot Stuff. When he wanted to shoot his mother as well, Wahoo courageously decided he'd had enough of the crime spree and tried to stop Yankee, which erupted in both of them firing off a round at the other. Once again, Yankee had come out on top, obviously. Then he stole Stuff's BMW and made his escape.

As the police entered the house, Drake got on his feet, identifying himself as well as his wife before he headed to his car. Soon he was en route to Detroit, straight to the Gates, in search of Terrell. Normally there would be a hundred questions to ask before the police would let you leave the scene of a crime, but Yankee was a hundred percent right when he said shit was different when you had that bread. The quick-responding authorities were familiar with all the well-to-do residents in their high-priced community and knew they were trustworthy and had enough money to fight any criminal case, even capital murder.

Pressing the REDIAL button time and time again, Prayer, unfortunately, got nothing but Terrell's voicemail. When the worried parent tried to leave yet another message, she received a recording informing her that Li'l T's mailbox was full. With the police leading Stuff's grief-stricken mother out into another room of the huge house, sorrowfully watching the EMS technicians pull white sheets over the faces of both Stuff and Wahoo, signifying their deaths at the hands of Yankee, Prayer increased her fear of Terrell's safety, knowing a killer was on the loose.

Please let Drake get to the Gates and find Terrell before anything else happens. Prayer was diligent in her thoughts as the detectives started to ask her questions concerning the first homicides they'd had in their fairly crime-free city since the early nineties.

Enduring the excruciating pain of the gunshot wound in his left shoulder, Yankee still sinisterly enjoyed finally feeling the comfort of driving Stuff's expensive high school graduation gift. As he entered the freeway, pushing the BMW, the young hustler now turned murderer quickly came to the realization that he had to get out of town. The three king-sized pillowcases stuffed with various items he'd stolen riding shotgun with him would definitely not generate a sufficient amount dough for him to live on. Calculating his next move, the envious teenager wasn't satisfied he'd caused enough turmoil and heartache for the evening.

I wanna pop bottles like the next nigga out here in these wicked streets! I wanna buy the club out! Shitttt, I'm gonna be giving dudes da true business back in NYC! If Yankee was gonna have to relocate back to Brooklyn, it was gonna be in style, with his brand-new BMW and his pockets fat. *Terrell better be ready to give me my share of what I got coming along with his, Stuff's, and Wahoo's backstabbing asses or else!*

In pain but feeling no remorse for the crimes he'd just committed, including shooting his childhood friend, Yankee turned up the sounds, pumping out some old-school rap as he headed to the Gates to confront his boy Terrell with a proposition that he wasn't willing to take no for an answer to.

Chapter Eleven

Terrell and a semi-coherent, battered, and bruised Joi drove past the guard shack as Mr. Johnson waved them through. She laid her head on his shoulder for comfort. The still-furious Terrell glanced down at his girl, kissing her on the forehead and trying to find a way to break it to her that her big sister Shauntae was back at her house, dead as a motherfucker, lying in a pool of her own blood.

"Don't worry. I got you," he promised the young girl as they pulled up in his driveway. "You can stay with me and my mother as long as you want to."

After making their way around the back entrance of the house, the couple went inside, where Li'l T led Joi into his bedroom. Tossing his dirty clothes and a few mix CDs onto the floor, Terrell made space for Joi to lie down and get some much-needed rest whenever she was ready. Knowing that she was ashamed of what had happened to her, Li'l T opted to not throw a gang of questions at her that he already knew the answers to. Instead, he gave her a towel and a washcloth and respectfully shut the door.

I can't believe my sister did this to me. Joi felt the lump on the side of her face, as the throbbing pain between her legs intensified thanks to Elon and the crude way he'd violated her. *Oh, my God!* Having sudden flashes of Elon's face while he raped her, and still being able to smell the awful mixed stench of weed, beer, and liquor he breathed into her mouth, an overwhelmed Joi bent over in disgust, vomiting on the floor at the foot of

Terrell's bed. *And why would Shauntae let him do that to me? Does she hate me that much?*

After rolling his wheelchair into the living room, Li'l T grabbed the house phone off the charger to call Yankee and Wahoo and give them an update on what had gone down. With both of them being from the hood, Terrell knew that one or the other had to know some information on the nigga driving the black truck or the dudes in the Regal who tried to kill him earlier. Holding the pieces of his smashed cell phone in his hands, he hoped he could at least remember their numbers after realizing the screen was shattered.

Elon came up on the Jefferson Avenue exit, doing almost double the speed limit. Flying around the corner at an extreme rate almost caused the huge black truck to flip over on its side and make several other automobiles also crash. Gripping the steering wheel, the deranged Elon regained control of the vehicle just in time to avoid a head-on collision with a carload of teenagers trying to get home before their curfews.

With the sounds of horns blowing in protest of the way he was driving, Elon acted as if he owned the road, veering the oversized truck up into the entranceway of the Gates. He was just here earlier in the evening, dropping off the box for Terrell. Not having the patience to wait for the guard to question him about this and that before he made the decision whether to allow him entry, as soon as Mr. Johnson approached him with his clipboard in hand, Elon slid his hand over, retrieving his pistol from where he had it stashed, turned the volume up on his radio, and shot the husband and father of five to death.

After shoving Mr. Johnson's lifeless body over into the thick line of green bushes that conveniently blocked the view of outsiders into the elite, small, privileged community of Detroit, Elon pushed the button himself, making the black steel gates slide open. Jumping back inside his truck, he then drove through them and got confused, not really knowing where the house was located. Mitts had been the one watching Terrell's crib, and because the walls of the hospital blocked all cell phone reception, Elon couldn't get a call through to confirm the address.

"Fuck it! I'll look for that pussy's van. It's gotta be parked somewhere around here. I'll find it. Ain't shit gonna stand in the way of what I got for that crippled son of a bitch!"

The cab driver earned his hundred-dollar tip as he and Simone neared her house in record, law-breaking time. While still trying helplessly to get in touch with Li'l T, Simone got a call from Prayer, which she automatically sent to voicemail. *What that bitch want now of all times?* she fumed as they hit a major pothole. Less than a half mile later, after placing three or four more unsuccessful calls to Terrell, her cell phone rang again. This time it was Drake.

"Hello," she eagerly answered.

"Hey, Simone! Where's Terrell at?" Drake wasted no time with the preliminaries. "Is he with you?"

"Naw, he ain't, but I keep calling him, and I can't get through. Oh, my God. Drake, he done messed around and got himself in some real fucked-up shit!" Simone yelled as the cab driver nosily eavesdropped on her conversation from the front seat. "I'm on my way to the crib now. Can you come?"

"Listen," Drake replied, "I'm already on my way down there. Some bullshit just jumped off out my way, and some of his so-called running buddies was behind it."

"What?" In shock, Simone couldn't believe what she was hearing. "Are you serious?"

"Yeah, and don't tell Terrell, but Stuff got shot. From the looks of things when I left his house, he ain't gonna make it."

"What?" Simone repeated as her cold heart seemed to skip a beat hearing that tragic news. "This entire night is going from bad to fucking worse!"

"Yeah, I know, but I'm on my way. I'll see you in a few minutes and fill you in on all the details when I get there. You need to call the police, Simone, because this fool ain't playing around!"

"All right then, I'll call you as soon as I get home and see if Li'l T's there."

Approaching the front of the guard shack, the cab driver slowed down, naturally assuming that someone would come out to give him the okay to pass through and gain access to the upscale community.

"Why in the hell is this gate wide open and unattended like this?" Simone suspiciously leaned up, staring through the thick plastic partition separating her and the driver. *I'm gonna call the management office on Mr. Johnson's old ass first thing in the morning.*

"What should I do, miss?" the driver inquired, glancing back as he stopped.

"Just keep going," she instructed him. She knew full well that without directions he would certainly get lost on the twisted, confusing, dead-end, unmarked blocks the Gates was famous for. "I'll tell you the rest of way from here."

With the cab following the exact path she and Terrell took to their house daily, Simone, anxious to get out and locate her son, had the driver drop her off on the curb. She wished him good luck on finding his way back to the main entrance. Taking notice that all appeared quiet around the general vicinity, meaning there were no signs of Big Ace's vindictive offspring Elon, Simone wasted no time rushing up on the front porch past her son's parked van. She stuck her key in the lock. From the first moment she stepped foot inside the doorway, the deeply concerned mother could immediately tell something was drastically wrong.

"Terrell! Terrell," Simone screamed out as soon as her foot touched the carpet. "Are you in here? Terrell!"

"Yeah, Ma," Li'l T answered, rolling from the rear of the house with yet another box of ammunition to put on the dining room table to accompany the stock pile of artillery he'd taken out of Simone's locked closet. "I'm right here!"

"Why in the fuck you ain't been answering your damn phone? I've been calling the dog shit outta your dumb ass!"

"My cell is broke."

"Whatever, boy," Simone blew off his excuse, running up to the table. "Where did you get all my shit from? And matter of fact, fuck that question. What in the hell you done did getting mixed up with Big Ace's kids? Oh, my God, we need to call the damn police before some more shit jumps!"

Still vigilant in loading all the illegal weapons as if his mother hadn't just mentioned the police, Terrell spoke up. "Big Ace? My father's friend?"

"Yeah, Negro, what other Big Ace you know?" Simone quickly grabbed one of the guns off the table, realizing that Elon was supposed to be on his way, although she didn't exactly know when. "They claiming you ran one of his sons and his friend off the road earlier, and then they saying you shot him!"

"In that old-school Regal?"

"What the fuck! How I know what kinda car it was? I'm just saying what I heard at the hospital before I caught a cab here."

"What was you doing at the hospital in the first place seeing about a motherfucker who was trying to kill me? And do you know who this other dude who hang with them is?"

"What dude?"

"He drives a black truck."

"Yeah, stupid." Simone ran over to peek out the living room curtains. "That's the same bald fucker I saw that tramp daughter of Monique's with! He got them I GO HARD plates on his shit! That's Big Ace's other son, the one ya little girlfriend was so damn cozy with!"

"What?" Terrell overlooked his mother insulting Joi, forgetting for the time being that she was even sleeping in his room. "Good, well, now I'm about to kill his ho ass, and that's my word!"

"What is you saying?" Simone was confused. "How did this shit even jump off? How you even know them? I don't understand."

"It don't matter if you understand." Terrell got angrier each time he thought about the pictures sent to his cell phone and the way his girl was violated. "That coward is already fucking dead, and I'm about to show him that I go hard too!"

"Well . . ." Simone didn't know what to do next but put one up top herself and get prepared for what was gonna happen after what in the fuck came next. "That crazy idiot Elon said he was gonna be on his way here, so you need to post up, because he acted like he meant business!"

"So the fuck do I," Li'l T vowed as he rolled his chair near the couch.

"I knew you should've stayed your ass out in them suburbs, 'cause now you done fucked shit all the way up between me and Big Ace! Now I gotta find me the next meal ticket! Thanks a lot!"

"That's all the fuck you damn care about?" Terrell questioned his mother. "His sons tried to kill me, and you worried about the old dude's bread? You real foul, Ma!"

Ring. Ring. Ring. The sound of Simone's cell phone chiming startled her and her enraged son both. She answered, putting it on speaker and not wanting to take her hand off the gun she was clutching, not to mention her finger off the trigger.

"Hello."

"Yeah, is he there?" Drake's voice filled the silent room.

"Yeah, he's here, but you need to hurry up." Simone had the sound of urgency in her tone. "How far are you?"

"About a good ten or fifteen minutes away," Drake estimated. "Did you call the police yet or what?"

"Not yet." Simone looked on the table at the guns that were a felony case waiting to happen. "I'm about to."

"Well, you didn't tell him about Stuff, did you? Prayer just called me with the updated news."

"Stuff?" Terrell interrupted their conversation, yelling across the room. "What's wrong with him? Where he at?"

"Hey, Terrell." Drake regretted that he'd said anything, now realizing he was on speakerphone. "Sit tight. I'll be there in a few."

"Naw, fuck that! Where's my nigga Stuff at?"

"Watch your damn tone, son." Drake got heated. "I know you going through some shit right about now, but don't ever bite the hand that feeds you. I'm on your side. Now I said to sit tight and I'll be there. Ya feel me?"

"Whatever." Li'l T rolled over to the other side of the room after hearing the sound of a vehicle pulling in the driveway.

Rushing to snatch the cordless phone off the couch to finally call the cops before it was too late, Simone was stopped by her son informing her that a cab was shining its light up on the house and the short, dark-skinned driver had gotten out and was headed to the porch.

Confused, with her gun in her hand down at her side, Simone flung the door open and started a verbal assault on the man. "Yes, what's wrong? What do you want?"

"Hello again, miss." The driver spoke in his deep, rich African tone. "I finally made it out of this puzzle and back to the main road."

"Okay and?" Simone sarcastically asked as Terrell attentively watched him from the other room. "Then why in the hell are you back? You got your money!"

"I know, miss, and I thank you." The driver remained polite in spite of Simone's foul mouth and bad disposition. "But when I looked in the rear of my cab, I saw that you had left your purse, and I wanted to return it to you."

Dropping her head down in shame for being so rude, Simone stuck out her hand to take her expensive designer handbag out of the honest cab driver's hand. "Damn, my bad. I'm sorry. Thanks for bringing it back."

"Not a problem, miss," the driver replied, never once returning Simone's crude tone in his response. "I could tell you were in a hurry. So I'll let you go, and good luck to you."

Walking off the porch and back to his cab, the driver shook his head in pity. The way the seemingly beautiful woman was obviously so tortured and cursed on the inside to behave and speak as she did made him wonder why any of his fellow countrymen came here to the United States and married a black woman instead of their own kind.

"Oh, hell yeah!" Elated that his search was over, Elon smiled as he cut the truck's headlights off and watched from afar. Thanks to the bright side light of the yellow Checker Cab that was shining on the house a few yards down, Elon was able to make out Terrell's custom van.

He wasn't sure if he'd driven past this street before, and at this point, he was so confused and twisted around, who knew for certain? "That crippled up nigga can run, but he can't hide. I don't know what that fool in the cab want with his ass, but I owe him and his cab big time for that light. I would've been driving around this circus for hours trying to find that damn van! Now it's ticktock on Terrell and that smart-mouth bitch from down at the hospital who just answered the door. Tick motherfucking tock." Elon opened the truck door. "Ticktock."

Chapter Twelve

Yankee's gunshot-wounded shoulder was starting to burn even more and stiffen, causing him to lose focus on the road. Even though the bullet was a clean shot, having gone in and out, he still was losing a huge amount of blood and needed some sort of medical attention other than an old T-shirt wrapped around it. *I need a fucking drink and a blunt!* Always keeping a stash of weed on him, dizzy and exhausted from the chain of horrific events he'd perpetrated at Stuff's house, Yankee decided that he needed to smoke at least to get his mind right and be able to continue to the Gates.

Damn! These streets is messed up! Why don't they hurry up and finish? With all the various ongoing detours and road construction projects in Michigan, Yankee was getting confused as hell. Miles out of his way, finally getting back on track and regaining his bearings, the youth, rapidly losing blood, soon realized he was at least a good four miles away from his exit.

Dang. Shit, it's burning like a motherfucker! He grabbed at his shoulder, complaining to himself as the once-clean T-shirt pressed to his open wound was now soaked. *Fuck Wahoo! I hope he burn in hell! That soft, pussy-built nigga should've just stuck to the goddamn program and manned up, and it would've been all gravy. But fuck his dumb crybaby ass and his sorry*

family, 'cause now I'm about to have it all. Shit, real talk,
I should call the State my damn self!

Yankee couldn't take the intense throbbing soreness
any longer and came up on the next exit he came to in
search of some liquor, preferably dark. Searching the
unfamiliar neighborhood, he finally found what he
was looking for. Seeing the yellow and red neon sign
indicating that they sold the sanctified potion Yankee
needed, he was relieved. After turning the new BMW
into the parking lot of the Southwest Detroit Party Store,
he removed the T-shirt from his shoulder and tossed it
out the car window onto the ground. Reaching over and
rifling through the pillowcases of stolen goods in the
passenger seat, Yankee took out one of Stuff's custom
button-ups with the initials KIS stitched on the pocket as
well as the collar. Although it was hot as hell and Yankee
was sweating like a whore in church, enduring the
pain, he slipped both arms in the wrinkled long-sleeved
shirt, opened the car door, and proceeded into the store.
Without any time to waste, lightheaded but still brazen
and extremely cocky in attitude, Yankee marched up to
the counter, acting as if there weren't a small group of
customers standing in line.

"Excuse me," an older lady interjected.

"Yeah, let me get a fifth of Hennessy, two cherry wraps,
and one of those lighters," Yankee ordered the young girl
behind the bulletproof glass as he tried flossing Stuff's
pinky ring he'd stolen. "And five packs of them extra-
strength Tylenols!"

"Yeah, dawg," added a clean-cut guy, who was dressed
like he'd just gotten off work. "You didn't notice we were
here in damn line?"

"Whatever," Yankee laughed it off as he tried this time
to show off with a small but impressive knot. "Slow y'all

roll, Hector, and go eat a taco or some bean burrito bullshit y'all fucks with!" he insulted the man, who was obviously Mexican. "It ain't that serious and shit, partner!"

Hoping to get the rude customer out the door as soon as possible before trouble broke out, the young girl hurried, giving Yankee what he needed and sending him on his way. Before he could get out the door, Yankee, eager to feel the liquor take over, cracked the seal open on the bottle, turned it up, and took a deep, long gulp straight to the head. Realizing that blood was starting to slowly seep through the threads of the shirt, he quickly made his way back to the BMW, which he was now officially calling his own, ripped open three of the five packs of Tylenol, and swallowed them all, taking another swig of Hennessy to wash them down.

Closing his eyes as the burning in his shoulder started to intensify, Yankee, totally off his game, didn't notice a dark Hummer parked across the street and watching his every move since he'd exited the freeway. As he used his teeth to tear open the clear plastic bag with his weed inside, the petty thief turned murderer felt his entire arm tingling and going completely numb. After rolling his blunt up, he lit it, taking several long, hard pulls before starting the engine, turning up the sounds, and taking off back en route to the Gates.

"'All eyes on me,'" Yankee sang along with the old-school throwback Tupac song as he got to the light, which had just turned red.

Sitting at the light, caught up in his thoughts of how his new life was gonna be as soon as he touched back down in Brooklyn, Yankee once again didn't notice the Hummer, which had now crept up alongside him. Suddenly a horn blew. Yankee looked over, nodding at the passenger and wondering what in the fuck these immigrant mother-fuckers from south of the border wanted. The driver of the Hummer blew once more, signaling for Yankee to lower his window. Glancing down at his gun, which was lying on the middle console, he turned down the sounds and cracked the window.

"Yeah, what up doe? What y'all need?" Yankee snarled with each word that passed his lips. "What it do?"

"Hey, homeboy, nice ride. Real nice ride," the man said. "Is this you?"

"Yeah, dawg." Yankee twisted his lip as he placed his hand on the steering wheel so the occupants in the Hummer could admire his ill-gotten ring. "This all me!"

"Oh, yeah?" the passenger questioned Yankee's response with a strange expression. "You don't know Kenneth?"

"Naw, I don't know no damn Kenneth. You got me mixed up, playa." Yankee hit the button to roll the window back up, and he sped off, getting a feeling something was wrong. *They asses probably some carjackers and shit trying to catch a brother slipping, but a nigga like me ain't falling for that bullshit!* Yankee glanced back in his rearview mirror as the Hummer continued to follow. *Not to-fucking-day!*

Running every other red light, Yankee floored the BMW, pushing it as fast as he could go and trying to shake the dudes in the Hummer. With Tupac still blaring from the custom sound system's speakers, he made two sharp lefts, a couple of rights, and unwisely another fast set of left turns before realizing he was completely lost in the heavily Hispanic Southwest Detroit neighborhood. Finding himself on a dead-end block, Yankee, whose one arm was now useless, threw the gear into reverse, trying to maneuver the high-powered, expensive vehicle off the block and to Fort Street, which he could see across the dense section of trees.

Blocking the pathway of the dark street, the truck in pursuit stood guard as Yankee came to the conclusion he was trapped. With the combination of the liquor, weed, and Tylenol, Yankee was feeling like he was Superman or some other old make-believe superhero bullshit like that. Taking his gun off the console and holding it tightly, he stepped out of the BMW, ready for whatever.

If they want this motherfucker, they gonna have to kill my black ass first! Yankee was prepared to fight for the car tooth and nail as if he'd spent six long, grueling months working overtime at one of Detroit's Big Three to scrape together the down payment to cop that son of a bitch.

Slowly the Hummer's passenger door opened, and a tall Spanish man exited the oversized vehicle. He fearlessly walked up to Yankee, who was half drunk and high out of his mind. Curious, poverty-stricken neighbors who'd come out of their homes after hearing the loud, disturbing sounds blasting from the shiny BMW turned away now, retreating inside after recognizing the man whose father owned most of the mortgages and deeds to their properties. Without fear of Yankee, he called out to him from about eight or so yards away.

"Hey, *pequeño pedazo de mierda,*" Juan Averez shouted to the guy he knew was driving his homeboy Stuff's new ride. "*Usted tiene una boca inteligente!*"

Not being able to speak Spanish, Yankee was at a total loss for what was being yelled out to him in the middle of the now-deserted street, but he could tell from the grim expression on the man's stern face as he approached him that it wasn't shit at all nice. "Look yo, I don't know what your problem is with me, but you might wanna go fuck with the next guy 'cause I ain't trying to hear that shit right about now!" Yankee raised his gun, showing Juan he was strapped and would most definitely shoot if he had to. "I ain't in the mood! I done had a long fucking day!"

"Okay, smart-mouth little black cotton-picking nigga! You sure you don't know Kenneth?" Juan spoke plain English. "Is that what you telling me?"

"Listen up, you fucked-up-speaking, rice-and-nasty-bean-eating motherfucker, I already done told you hell fucking naw!" Yankee spit through his teeth. "I don't know no Kenneth!"

"Damn, then that's real foul, you rotten piece of cow shit, because you about to get killed on the humble for driving a dead man's car!"

"What?" Yankee saw his short life on earth flash before his eyes as he went for his. "Go fuck yourself!"

Juan raised an Israeli-style Uzi he had concealed under his shirt, took aim, and let loose. "My sister's boyfriend, Stuff, said he owes you this! See you in hell!"

In a thunderous hail of one-sided bright gunfire sparks, Yankee's medium-built torso took in bullet after bullet as his body appeared to be dancing in the street until he finally dropped to the ground in defeat. Busting his head on the hard concrete then letting loose his gun, Yankee gave up, taking his last breath of the Detroit industrial-polluted air. The now-deceased Yankee, who always pestered, plotted, and schemed, wanting to meet Stuff and Terrell's connect so badly, had finally gotten his wish.

Juan had received the disturbing call about Stuff's untimely callous murder from his hysterical sister Marie. He thanked God for putting him in the right place at the right time, lucking out and seeing Yankee at the store he and his homeboys hung out at on the regular. After hearing Yankee's smart-mouth comments, it was more than a pleasure to let him have it.

As Juan drove off in Stuff's BMW to return it to his parents, who were both back at the house in mourning, Yankee lay dead in the litter-filled street, not to be discovered until daybreak by a couple of inebriated bums who searched his pockets first before calling the police, who of course took hours to respond.

Chapter Thirteen

"Okay, what happened to Stuff?" Once again, Terrell was back at his mother's throat, picking up where he'd left off before the interruption at the door. "I'm about to call him."

"Hold up." Simone pushed the cordless phone to the other side of the table. "Didn't Drake tell you he was on his way? And besides all that, you acting like you ain't hear shit I said about Elon!"

"Fuck what you talking about, Ma! I already done told you that if that faggot don't come see me soon, it really don't matter, 'cause I'm gonna go look for him." Terrell reached down, trying his best to keep his trembling legs to stop moving around from side to side. "Shit, I'm a grown-ass man. Despite what you think, I ain't no punk."

She cringed and shook her head at her son and the way he was in total denial about the severity of what was going down. Simone took a deep breath at the thought of what he'd gotten them both involved in because he wanted to prove a point. *Damn him for being Kamal's son.* "I should've just let you stay out there with Prayer when she called me begging my black ass to tell you that you wasn't welcome here," Simone fumed as she lit a Newport to calm her nerves. "But naw, instead I wanted for once to have the upper hand on her uppity, goody-two-shoes self!"

Li'l T couldn't believe his ears or what was coming from his mother's mouth. Rolling around to the other side of the gun-filled table and closer to Simone, Terrell felt his resentment level for both Prayer and her rise for using him once again as a human pawn in their silly and petty, jealous-inspired game. "Huh?" Terrell's mouth grew increasingly dry as he tried to speak. "What you talking about now?"

Seeing it as a way to get her son further away from Prayer and her overbearing, holier-than-thou influence, Simone vindictively decided she had nothing else to lose and went on to spill the beans about everything. *Okay, he wanna hear the real deal, then fuck it!*

That she really couldn't stand Joi, the reason being that her mother, Clip-N-Dip Moe, was known as the local setup queen and had gotten a lot of drug dealers, including Big Ace, damn near killed back in the day, didn't really come as a major surprise to the pissed-off Terrell. Then, finding out from his now-so-informative, whorish mother that throughout the years, on and off, she'd been sleeping with Drake in exchange for money and other gifts, despite his seemingly loyal and devoted marriage to Prayer, wasn't much in the way of a shock. Li'l T knew Drake was a man and was gonna get the pussy from any grimy bitch who opened her legs if he could, even if it was his wife's former best friend. And still, when Simone cruelly confessed the unthinkable, informing Terrell that she'd conspired with Prayer to keep a drunk, elderly Willy Dale, who was now confined to a nursing home and who was Kamal's biological father, making him Li'l T's grandfather, away from him so he wouldn't discover jack shit about that side of his family including an aunt who lived just outside of the Gates, he remained silent.

"You had enough of confession time now or what?" Simone lit yet another Newport, showing no shame for what she'd done and how she treated him throughout his childhood. "If not, I can keep it going!"

"Don't let me stop you," Terrell screamed out with the look of murder in his eyes as Joi emerged out his bedroom, alarming Simone, who up until this point was unaware that she was even in there. "You on a fucking roll and shit!"

"What in the hell she doing here?" Simone raged as a bruised and confused Joi wiped the sleep out of her swollen and puffy eyes. "She giving you and Big Ace's son the pussy and you got her all up in the crib! Is you crazy? I told you I saw this tramp with Elon last week, with your dumb ass!"

"Ma, damn all that." Li'l T rolled his chair toward Joi, who was now in tears with a runny nose after overhearing the awful things her boyfriend's mother was saying about Monique. "You was in the middle of 'Confessions of a Fucked-up Mother,' so keep going! Tell me how much other bullshit you done did to make my life miserable!"

Simone, having enough of her son's smart, disrespectful mouth, especially in front of a petty female who she didn't feel was fit to polish her shoes after stepping in a pile of dog shit, was set to really let him have it hardcore. With the final confession, which hit below the belt, on the tip of her tongue, a crashing sound from the rear of the house caused Simone, Terrell, and Joi to became panicked and instinctively take some sort of cover. Diving out of his wheelchair onto the carpet, Li'l T yelled for Joi to get out of harm's way and back into his room.

In the middle of all the chaos and confusion that was going on, spontaneously Simone grew instantly irritated that her son, her child, her first and only born, the little wide-headed baby who came crying out of her womb and stretched the motherfucker to twice its natural size hadn't even once screamed out to make sure she was safe.

Dig this ungrateful, crippled bastard seed of mine! Ain't this some bull! Drake is right! This one over there

*done forgot who feeds his sorry ass! He done let the
hot summer sun and that bitch's pussy fuck him all up!
That little ho Joi, who is acting all innocent and helpless,
gotsta go!* Simone, terrified herself, crouched down near
the side of the china cabinet and watched as she heard
another booming sound of wood and metal cracking.
When the kitchen door flew off the hinges and landed
on the marble floor, Simone had second thoughts about
running her mouth so much, not doing what she was told
by her sometimes fuck buddy, Prayer's husband.

Oh, Shit! Oh, Shit! Damn! Shit! She glanced up at the
cordless phone still on the table and unfortunately out of
reach as she held on tightly to the handle of her gun. *Why
didn't I just call the freaking police when Drake told me
to? Now that fool done kept his word and is in my damn
house! But I swear on every single dick I done sucked
and every ass I done kissed to get a bill paid, I'm gonna
blast that boy if he bend this corner! Big Ace can just
bury two sons instead of one!*

Terrell felt his legs still twitching as soon as he hit the
carpet after hearing the sounds come from the rear of
the house. Between all the yelling and arguing he and
Simone were preoccupied doing, he'd let his guard down
and had gotten caught slipping. Now, if what his mother
claimed was true, Big Ace's son, who was the same
coward who had raped his girl, was now inside his house
and ready to do battle.

"Joi, hurry up! Go back in my room and get out of
the fucking way," Terrell demanded as he gripped both
pistols and took aim at the direction the noises were
coming from. "I don't want you to get hurt," he shouted
as the young girl, nervous and still in tears, didn't know
which way to run. "Hurry up! Go!"

Seeing that his satanic-minded mother, who had given
birth to him under duress, was hidden behind the china

cabinet with a gun in her own hand for protection, Li'l T automatically knew she wasn't gonna go out like a bitch and just let Elon come in and run buck wild in the crib. His ol' girl wasn't cut like that, and all of Detroit knew it.

Good, she's over there near the other side of the room strapped up. And if I know my mama like I do, she'll nail Jesus back to the cross if it means her ornery ass will live to see another day. Terrell was confident. If the dude who was going around claiming I GO HARD wanted to make this their final night of reckoning, then so be it.

Chapter Fourteen

Elon didn't care if anyone saw him brandishing his weapon as he got out of his truck. His palms sweated with each step he took toward Terrell's house and the revenge he had planned. Still suffering from shock and denial about Donte and his critical condition, he paused as his cell phone rang. Seeing an unknown number flash on the screen, Elon shot the call straight to voicemail as he pulled up his sagging jeans and continued his small hike up the block.

"Excuse me, young man. Excuse me." An elderly woman, the Gates's own self-appointed busy body, poked her head out her front door after realizing she'd never before seen the teenager or his truck in their usually calm, tranquil neighborhood. "Can I help you? Are you lost?"

"What? Hell naw, I ain't lost." Elon sharply turned to face her eye to eye, raising his pistol from his side. Pointing it in the lady's direction, with his armpits showing heavy signs of perspiration, he dared her to say another single word. Then he gave her a direct order. "Now take ya old ass back into the house and shut the fucking door, or you gonna have a major problem on ya hands!"

With her old heart racing a hundred miles per hour, not waiting a moment more to see which way the outspoken thug was headed, immediately she did as she was told and slammed the door. After turning the lock, the woman then stumbled to her kitchen and grabbed the phone on the wall.

Picking up his pace, knowing full well the old lady was gonna call the police to the upscale neighborhood he was about to terrorize, Elon concentrated on his game plan. *I'm about to give that drag-along-leg nigga the true business!* He approached Terrell's van parked on the side of the house. Listening at the window to the array of voices, Elon once again paused as the strange number reappeared on his cell. *Who the fuck is calling me now?*

"Yeah, speak on it," he whispered so as not to be heard as he kept low and out of sight.

"Hey, baby, it's me," Auntie Eunice replied with a tone of sorrow. "Wherever you're at, you need to get back down here to the hospital."

"I will, Auntie, as soon as I take care of something first." Elon glanced over his shoulder, still hearing the voices inside the house get louder and turn into some sort of a shouting match as he made his way around the back. "Then I'll be on my way."

"Look, Elon," she said, keeping it real as she always had with her troublesome nephew, "your father told me to get in touch with you and tell you to get back down here ASAP because the doctors don't think your brother is gonna make it. Matter of fact, they've given up any hope."

"Naw! Naw! Naw!" Furious at the news he'd just heard from his auntie, Elon knocked over two steel garbage cans, smashing them against the house's frame. Then, in another act of rage mixed with grief, knowing his brother and best friend was barely clinging to life and about to die, Elon lifted his foot several times, kicking in Simone's back kitchen door and knocking it completely off its hinges.

"Show your face, motherfucker!" Elon demanded as if it were his house and not Simone's he was invading. "It's time to dance, you crippled bitch! So man up! Where you at?"

"All you gotta do is bring that punk ass out of the kitchen and out here in the open, and you can best believe the dance is definitely on and popping." Terrell lay spread-eagle on the floor by the couch, taking aim at the doorway separating him from Elon as he mocked him. "You done came this far, homeboy, so a few more damn steps ain't gonna kill you, coward. Or is that what you scared of?"

"Right! Come on now, dude, don't play yourself!" Elon quickly returned insults to his enemy. "You can ask your girl was I scared when I was pounding that bitch's pussy raw dog from the back!" he callously ridiculed with the blow-by-blow account of his tortured-filled evening with Joi. "Yeah, you can trust that fat, tender cat was tight as hell when I first stuffed this eight inches up in it, but after a few minutes, ump ump ump, I stretched that son of a bitch out just right for a brother." Elon continued shattering Terrell's world as he lay on the floor forced to listen. "And ooh-wee! I ain't gonna talk about the excellent head Joi got on her! Deep throat, swallow, the whole nine! She took it like a champ!"

He revealed even more as he scanned the room for any sight of Li'l T. "Shittttttt, she way better than that slut-ass sister of hers, 'cause in case ya don't know, Shauntae was a true bad bitch with hers, a real thoroughbred! Damn! What a shame I had to kill the ho! But oh, well." Elon laughed, shaking his head as he peeped around the corner. "Considering I'm here, you know it was only a matter of time before somebody got with her 'good to set up a nigga' ass!"

"Shut the fuck up, nigga! Ain't nobody trying to hear that bullshit," Terrell angrily yelled back across the room at Elon as his legs shook uncontrollably. "You gonna pay for all that shit you blowing out your grill!"

From the cover of the ivory-colored china cabinet and still out of harm's way, Terrell's mother sucked her teeth, knowing that she was 100 percent right all along about Joi's twisted intentions toward her son. "See, baby, I told you so! I told you this lowlife female ain't about nothing but some money and can't be trusted!" Simone let her feelings be known after hearing what'd obviously taken place between Elon and Joi. "Look at her dumb ass! Standing all over there trying to look like her fake behind don't know what's going on. She just like her sneaky, shady dead mama: not shit!"

"Shut up, Ma," Li'l T demanded as he glanced over, noticing Joi positioned in a corner near his mother. Trapped between the kitchen and bedroom doors, she remained motionless as she heard the allegations of what Elon claimed to have done to her, not to mention the last bombshell he dropped saying Shauntae was dead and he was her killer. "You don't know what the hell you talking about! Joi ain't nothing like that, so shut up!"

"Both you and her shut the fuck up, and let's get this party started." Elon brought a sudden halt to the family disagreement before it really got going. "Nigga, you shot my brother, and now he's about to die!"

Terrell felt a dark cloud loom over him, and his head started to pound. As a huge amount of sweat poured from the embedded worry lines across his forehead, Li'l T saw a flash of Kamal's face almost touching his. *I ain't scared of shit! And I ain't scared of you! You the reason my life is so fucked up! I'm crippled because of you! People think I ain't a man because of what you did!* He shook his head and tried to contain himself. The image reappeared this time, making him raise his gun a few inches higher than he was already aiming. The trigger was pulled. He let off three rounds into the stainless-steel refrigerator. "That fool was coming after me, so fuck him and you!"

The distinct smell of gunpowder filled the room as a speechless Joi and an evil-minded Simone watched on in disbelief at Terrell's fury and rage. Taking hold of the arm of the couch, Li'l T pulled himself up as if he were attempting to stand.

Elon, eager not to be outdone, returned fire, turning Simone's perfectly decorated home into a makeshift shooting gallery complete with her expensive furnishings serving as targets. Bam, bam, bam, bam. He came closer with each shot that echoed inside the house. "Donte is dead and so is you," Elon bellowed out with deliberate certainty. Bam, bam, bam.

Scared to death but still out for self, Simone felt that if she and Li'l T were lucky enough to make it out of this bullshit he'd got them involved in, there was no way in hell she was gonna put up with the likes of Joi being forced into her life. Without hesitation, the greedy mother wasted no time doing what came naturally to her and every other Detroit resident: self fucking survival, by any means necessary. In the midst of Terrell's vengeance concentrating on doing the unthinkable, standing on his own to get to Elon, Simone crawled over toward Joi, who was still in some sort of an emotional trance, not moved by the intense noise and chaos that was taking place before her eyes.

This little sneaky bitch got me and this game all fucked up if she thinks I'm gonna let my son be played by some ghetto project trash! She can join Monique and that smart-mouth sister in hell as far as I'm concerned! Simone got closer to her son's girlfriend as delusional thoughts took over her mind. *Big Ace was so worried about one of them remembering something about the day he killed they mama, shit, he gonna owe me big time for this one! And after my son kills his other son, then maybe he'll respect my gangsta and realize I didn't give birth to no ho-ass baby after all!*

It was back on. The bright sparks and earsplitting gunshots continued to engulf Simone's home. Cursed with a violent streak since birth, Simone stretched out her arms, yanking Joi by her wrist. With malice embedded in her heart, the devious mother then shoved the young, naive girl into the middle of the gun battle. Before Terrell knew what was happening, Joi's body had gotten struck by several rounds. Removing his finger from the trigger, Elon was the opposite, not caring who would ultimately suffer pain from his wrath. He continued to shoot, emptying his entire clip.

"Joi! Joi! Damn, Joi." Terrell dropped his gun to the carpet after taking a bullet himself in his lower calf. As the love of his young life fell to the ground with blood gushing from the huge hole in the side of her upper torso, tears flowed from his eyes. Placing his hand tightly around her throat in an attempt to stop or at least slow down the flow of the bright red, warm blood, Terrell cried out in anguish. "Nawwwww, Joi! Nawwwww!"

Simone was content, almost giddy with the outcome of her malicious act as her son swooped up a dying Joi in his arms, trying to convince her to live. *No better for the ho!* She showed no signs of remorse that the normal human being would feel upon witnessing a sight that was this heinous. Quickly realizing that Elon now had the advantage over her child and her, the scheming mother wasted no time making another harsh snap decision. *Now on to the other problem.* Simone grinned, not waiting for Elon to make the next move. *His ass!*

Chapter Fifteen

"Hell yeah! I hit that crippled buster in the leg and that silly chick of his." Elon's eyes grew wide after seeing Terrell drop his gun and fall to the ground. "I ain't new to this, young blood. I'm a hundred percent true to this! So brace yourself and say your prayers." He walked toward the doorway separating the kitchen and living room. "And goddamn! Tell that female to go 'head and die already. Nigga, I just hope you don't get to whining like her when I send you on your way!"

Holding Joi in his arms, Terrell listened to the muffled sounds of her gasping for air as she seemed to be gargling blood. With the moaning almost coming to a halt, Li'l T let go of Joi's body, laying her on the carpet. He assumed that she was dead and that he would one day see her on the other side. Terrell zoned completely out now, having nothing to lose. Licking some of Joi's warm blood off his hands while smearing the remainder on his face, he stopped fighting his father's never-ending presence.

With the distinct overwhelming, dry stench of death circulating in the room, mixed with sweat and gunpowder in the midst of the heavy, serious adrenalin rush of two individuals intent on creating more mayhem, Simone crept on her stomach near the leg of the dining room table with her gun still in her hands. What the hell is he doing now? *He crazy as his fucked-up, twisted daddy!* She shook her head, witnessing her son's bizarre yet familiar behavior. *I guess I'm on my own now, 'cause he done lost it!* Simone scanned the room as she noticed that Elon's footsteps were getting closer and closer to where she was now taking cover.

"All right, ya pussy! It's on now, big boy! So how 'bout it?" Elon disrespectfully spit a thick, nasty glob of saliva on Simone's kitchen floor and laughed. Revenge was about to fill his mouth. "Now you limp-leg faggot, can't walk, can't run, probably can't fuck, it's about that time! Look at you shedding tears over that slut bucket. You oughta be thanking me for putting you out of ya misery!" His grin widened with each step as his gun pointed directly at Terrell, who showed no signs of being worried about meeting his Maker.

"Your punk ass better kill me, 'cause if you don't, that's your and your father's life I'm gonna take!" Li'l T vowed with his hardened face dripping with Joi's blood. "There ain't nowhere ya gonna be able to hide!"

"Is that right?" Elon replied, still holding his pistol.

"Try me if you want to," Terrell said, glancing over at Joi's body. "But on everything I love, I'm gonna kill you!"

"Is that dumb-ass idle threat supposed to scare me or something?" Elon asked as he spit once more, keeping an extremely suspicious eye focused on a very prideful Terrell, who was making it perfectly clear that he had nothing else to lose. "Because if it is, you might wanna keep that shit moving!" Seeing that Terrell was fearless in the face of death angered Elon even more. He wanted to get the hard-dick satisfaction of having Li'l T at least beg for his life. "You and your little friends should learn that if y'all gonna run with the big dogs, there's big-dog consequences to the game! Me and my brother run these Detroit streets when it comes to trees, and not you or nobody gonna stop our flow! So take the lesson with you on ya way!" With a smile of satisfaction, Elon squeezed the trigger.

More gray smoke surrounded the room as the mirror on the wall fell off, shattering into a thousand small, sharp pieces. Another round was let loose, resulting in a hand-painted vase crashing into the side of the doorframe. Two more rang out. The dishes in the china cabinet broke, and the oversized picture window was shot out. Three loud screams of violent death once again overtook the household. When the smoke cleared and it was all said and done, the room grew eerily silent. Terrell's muscular body slumped over on top of Joi, who was passed out cold but still struggling to live.

Simone, who was full of arrogance because she'd just proved her loyalty to her son by pumping Big Ace's son full of several slugs from her .44-caliber revolver to save his life, slowly got up off the floor and made her way over to her deranged-looking offspring.

"Fuck that boy, Terrell, and all that delusional bullshit he was blowing out his grill!" She grabbed her son's bloody face as he stared off into the far distance like a zombie on crack. "Look at him now! He ain't jack shit but another dead-ass motherfucker in the D! And his daddy was talking all that family crap to me! Fuck 'em all!" Simone smiled as she went to get a towel to stop the heavy bleeding from the bullet wound in her child's leg. "Me and you can rule this goddamn city and shit! Between all the connects I got and that crazy-ass attitude and that trait you got in your bones of not being worried about getting killed, we can make some major bread!"

"Huh?" Terrell finally spoke, panting in a heavy tone as his mother shook him back into reality. "What you say?"

"I said since now Stuff is out of the way, those other two suckers you run with ain't got nothing coming." Simone got up off the floor after wiping the blood from her hands on Joi's T- shirt, showing no remorse for the innocent young girl her son loved.

"Out of the damn way?" He gave his mother a strange, bewildered look at what she was doing and what she'd just said. "What in the hell you mean out of the way?"

Simone acted as if what she was saying wouldn't mean shit to her son, since it obviously meant less than nothing to her. "Yeah, from what I assume from whatever happened out by his house, Drake said it didn't look good for your little friend. So one plus one, he's probably dead just like this tramp and ol' boy over there." She casually pointed across the room at Elon.

"What?" Li'l T felt a rush of indescribable rage take control of his entire being.

"Yeah, baby. I'm glad I pushed this two-timing skank when I did! No better for her ass! Cheating on you like she did with Big Ace's son and God knows who the fuck else. I told you a million times over that them project bitches ain't shit. Never was and never will be." She giggled in a roundabout way. "I don't know why they always step the fuck outta line."

Terrell, in denial, couldn't believe his ears and snapped. Acting as if his legs weren't physically immobile, once again he raised himself up, using the arm of the couch as a makeshift crutch. With his weak, underdeveloped legs trembling from the force of the weight of the top half of his body, he miraculously stood. "What you say?" As his upper lip curled over toward the side just as Kamal's used to when he was on the verge of committing one of his many unspeakable acts of violence, the teenager tried taking a step then fell back to the floor as his wobbly legs gave in. "Stuff is dead, and you pushed Joi? Is that what you fucking said?" Full of determination and fueled with rage from his mother's statements, he reached up for the chair, attempting to stand once again.

Before Simone could reply to her son's questions, Drake busted in the front door with the look of despair on his face. "Naw, man! Hell naw!" He squinted as he saw a female and a male sprawled out on the floor, in their own individual pools of blood, both presumably deceased. "Terrell, tell me you didn't." Drake threw his hands up.

"Damn, Drake," Simone answered for her son, brushing her pants off. "You's about a dollar short and a fucking dime late. Me and my baby done handled the situation now!"

"Why didn't you call the police when I told you? Maybe you could've avoided all this mess. Who are these two anyway?" Drake quizzed as he kicked the gun out of Elon's hand just in case he wasn't truly dead. He made his way to Terrell's side. "What happened in here?"

Seeing that Drake had her son preoccupied with a mini interrogation of what exactly had jumped off, Simone bent over to pick up Elon's cell phone, which was ringing. *Ain't this some fly shit?* After seeing it was Big Ace's number, she eagerly answered while resting her shoe on Elon's back. "Yeah, hello!"

"Yeah, hello," he yelled into Simone's ear, causing her to pull the flip phone back from her face. "Who this?"

"Don't tell me after all these years you don't know my damn voice," she cooed with amusement.

"Simone?" Big Ace raised the tone of voice even higher with each word. "Is this you? Where in the hell is my fucking boy at? Put him on the line!"

Simone smiled, pressing the heel of her shoe down harder into Elon's back before answering Big Ace's questions. "Dang, G! Yeah, it's me. You don't have to yell and shit. Your son is here at my damn house. Ain't that where he said he was going when he was selling all those wolf tickets at the hospital?"

"What, bitch?" Big Ace screamed at her.

"Nigga, you might wanna watch how the hell you speak to my pretty ass," Simone suggested to the rude Big Ace.

"Look, you dumb bitch, put Elon on the phone and stop playing games with me," Big Ace demanded, still yelling. "His brother just died, and your crippled-ass son is at fault. You lucky I don't come over there and kill both y'all sorry asses!"

"Boy, you and what damn army?" Simone snickered, applying more pressure to Elon, her new footrest. "If you come out to my crib with that bullshit, you gonna get the same damn treatment this buster over here got."

"Say what?" Big Ace asked.

"Yeah, you heard me." She was on top of the world. She glanced over at Drake, who was still talking to Terrell, as the piercing sounds of police sirens seemed to be getting closer. "Your 'wanna go for bad' kid over here dead as a motherfucker!" Simone teased. "I guess he the real sorry ass, not me and my son. You talking that crap about checking me and Terrell, well, checkmate on your punk ass. The game is over. I stay winning."

"Dead?" Big Ace bellowed into the phone. "I know that ain't what you said!"

"Tsk, tsk, tsk," Simone callously continued, ridiculing his loss. "I guess that's me and my seed two, your family zero!" After hearing the line go dead, Simone could only assume that Big Ace was on his way over. *Oh, well. That's on his black ass! Shitttt, instead of coming over here fucking with me and Li'l T, he needs to be planning a double funeral! Maybe the people can hook him up with a two-for-one special!*

Chapter Sixteen

Holding his head up with no shame, Terrell seemed not to sit still as he practically burned a hole through Simone's face with his eyes. With his legs vibrating and his heart racing, the angry teenager's hands opened and closed repeatedly as they itched to deal with what his mother had said pertaining to Joi's injuries. Throughout the rambled and jumbled conversation, Drake finally found out that Joi was Li'l T's girlfriend and also the daughter of Monique, whom he vividly remembered from back in the day. Then as if that revelation weren't enough, he found out that the other body was the son of Big Ace, also a veteran from back in the day.

After Terrell divulged that unsettling news to his surrogate father, Drake had some information of his own as the police sirens got closer. He disclosed to the shocked Li'l T that his supposed cohorts, Yankee and Wahoo, had double-crossed him and murdered Stuff. It was more than the young man could stand. Finding out that they were both now dead gave him no comfort. Terrell clenched his fists and pounded them on the floor in denial.

Flashing lights, along with the screeching sounds of several police vehicles swerving into the driveway and in front of Simone's house, halted any more confessions of incredible bullshit for the evening. Knowing there would undoubtedly be plenty of questions, accusations, and blame to go around, Drake decided to go out and try his hand at informing the authorities that he, Terrell, and

Simone were going to come out peacefully, and of course, aid them in any way they could. Upon hearing one of the cops yell, "Police," from the front grass, Drake looked at Li'l T, who once again appeared zoned out and focused on Simone.

"Listen, Terrell." Drake leaned in to make sure he was being heard. "I'm gonna go outside and explain to these folks what's going on in here. In the meantime, get yourself together, because the shit is really about to hit the fan."

"Fuck the damn police," Simone blurted out.

"Naw, Simone, fuck you and all that foolishness you always feeding him." Drake shook his head. "Now, Terrell, you always claiming you a grown-ass man. Well, this is part of walking the walk, facing up to the hard times as well as the good. So even if this bullshit kills you, be a man for just one fucking minute. Ya hear me?" Drake headed toward the door to deal with the law. "Be a man for one minute, and after that don't nothing else matter!"

No sooner than Drake exited the door, he was grabbed by the police and immediately handcuffed then searched.

Left alone in the house, the mother and son were now face-to-face. Terrell, his face still covered in blood, turned to Simone with the look of contempt.

"Now," he hissed, "back to you. Did you say ya no-good, fucked-up ass pushed my girl out in the middle of that gunfire?"

"Yeah, and so what about it?" Simone showed no remorse whatsoever about her actions or the tragic results of them. "I did your behind a goddamn favor, so why in the hell you tripping? Just boss up and get ready to talk to these damn police out front!"

"All my life you ain't been shit to me but trouble." Li'l T struggled once again to stand on his own. "From day one you ain't care about me and only used me as bait to lure them dudes to your bitch ass! Then after that ho nigga Kamal fucked me over, you ain't come around for years!"

"Look, Terrell," Simone tried cutting him off, not wanting to hear his insults, but her baby boy was having no part of it whatsoever.

"Look my ass, Ma." He actually took a step on his own before falling to the ground. "I loved Joi, and now she's gone! And you standing over there telling me that it was by your hand!"

"Grow up and stop bugging. I did what I did for you, and all I get is your lip." Simone was amazed he'd taken a step. "Now like I was saying before Drake's suddenly square ass came up in here trying to turn you back into Dudley fucking Do-Right, we can run Detroit! Both of Big Ace's sons are out of the way, and even though he my people, he can get it to!"

"Are you just that selfish and messed up in the brain?"

"Selfish?" Simone fired back at her son. "Listen, you ungrateful bastard! Everything I did from day one was to keep your ass in new clothes and sneakers even though you can't even walk! I could've just let them put them orthopedic, thick-soled bullshit on your feet, but I didn't!"

"Oh, yeah?" Li'l T got angrier as he crawled over toward his mother. "Is that right?"

"Hell yeah, it is. Matter of fact, while you playing, I'm the one who signed the papers so Prayer and Drake could keep your silly-acting ass out there with them." Simone watched her child heading in her direction, looking like a wild dog. With his face bloodied and eyes that seemed to be glowing, Terrell was almost within grabbing distance before she took a few steps back from his reach. "Now I'm trying to turn you on to a new hustle and put your crippled ass on kingpin status so me and you can eat good the rest of our lives, and you tripping the hell out!"

His temper was at a boiling point as he listened to his supposedly beloved mother preach to him about all the sacrifices she'd made for him over the years. It was as if he were in one of those heinous dreams he was used to having, as he crawled past Joi's body and then near Elon's corpse. With his nostrils flaring, inhaling the foul, rotten odor of both that'd released their last bodily fluids, Terrell licked his lips, tasting nothing but Joi's blood on them. "I'm tired of you and everything you stand for!"

"What? 'I'm tired of you and everything you stand for,'" she mocked, laughing out loud at his statement. "Damn, little nigga," Simone taunted him. "All this time I thought you was Kamal's son and you had some of his gangsta pumping through your veins, but the way you up in here acting, maybe you are Joey's punk-ass seed!"

Terrell reached up on the dining room table, bracing himself for the pain that his gunshot wound was causing him as he stood once more. "Stop praising that fucked-up motherfucker like he some sort of a god! You acting like he ain't the reason I'm like the way I am now. Get off his dick." He fell to the floor as his mother walked over to him, seemingly amused at his failed attempt to stand.

Simone poked Li'l T in the middle of his forehead as he continued to struggle to stand. "Listen up! I ain't never been on no nigga's dick. Niggas be on mine. And believe me, Kamal got his for what he did to you."

"Bitch, stop lying." Li'l T yanked her finger and twisted it.

In pain as she felt her bone start to come out of its socket, Simone openly confessed something she'd never ever told anyone before. "I killed that motherfucker Kamal that night, trust. I'm the one who stopped his ho ass from breathing, and I did that bullshit for you."

"What is you lying about now?" Terrell kept twisting her finger, bringing Simone down on her knees so that she was face-to-face with him on his level.

"I'm not lying. I'm not." She tried unsuccessfully to snatch away from his muscular grasp and postpone the inevitable from occurring. "After he killed Joey, he was still alive, begging to live. But I cut that shit short. Me. And I did it because that fool had fucked over both of us. I gave Kamal the straight-up business."

"Yeah, well, you can walk, can't you? Your ass can run. You ain't pissing on yourself sometimes and had a damn shit bag on your side for years that all the kids in school dogged you out about. If you had stopped playing all them games you famous for playing, my life would've been better." Once again Kamal's face seemed to materialize to him and command him on what moves to make next. As he watched his mother's lips move, Li'l T heard his father's devious voice whispering in his ear.

"There are always casualties of war, Negro. And what's done is done, you pathetic, crippled-ass, ungrateful little bastard!" Simone made one last attempt to manipulate her son's way of thinking by shaming him. "You act like you special. Like you the only one who was affected by that night. But fuck what happened in the past, and just man up now."

"Oh, you think it's that damn easy?" he snarled, applying more pressure.

"Hell to the yeah, it better be," Simone proclaimed in agony. "Remember what Drake just said. Be a man for one fucking minute. Because when you sitting in that dirty, filthy-ass jail cell fighting that murder case for both Big Ace's sons and charges for all this weed you got stashed around here plus these guns that your smart behind got out my closet that got your fingerprints on them not mine, you gonna need Mama to hold you down, 'cause you know good and damn well Prayer's uppity ass ain't visiting no prisons. You gonna need me."

"Are you freaking nuts? Me need you? Me depend on you?" His body started to shake as he mumbled his words.

"Yeah, and let's just hope I'm in the mood to do that after the way you treating me now." Simone was in pain but had suffered enough ass kickings over the years to never let a nigga see her sweat. She could talk her way out of anything if she followed that rule.

Terrell let go of her finger as he swiftly raised his other hand, taking a strong, tight grip of Simone's throat. "I'm tired of you, bitch!" Still hearing Kamal's voice, he closed his hand and increased the pressure on her neck. "It's always been about your ass and what you want!" Getting intense enjoyment from watching his mother squirm trying to fight him off was adding to his hot-flash adrenalin rush and fueling his murderous intent. *I owe you this! I owe you this!* he repeated in his mind as if he were speaking for himself and Kamal and possibly even Joey. The police started yelling for them to come outside with their hands up. *For all the years you fucked me over, I owe you! Now it's my time to shine!* Terrell smiled as Simone's eyes started to slightly roll toward the back of her head as her arms flung down to the floor.

Not ready to die, the strong-willed mother continued to fight to survive her son's attack, which was sudden but a long time coming and well deserved. "Your crippled ass ain't about shit," Simone managed to speak, gasping for air. "No wonder Joi gave dude the pussy. Ya probably can't even fuck. You ain't a man." She smugly smiled as Li'l T's hold tightened. Her hands searched the carpet for anything she could use as a weapon. "I bet ol' boy beat that pussy up, too!"

Choking Simone, trying to make her pay for all the sins she'd committed against him and for what she'd just said, Terrell yoked her up even more. "Shut up, bitch," he screamed as spit flew into her face. "Shut your motherfucking mouth!" He twisted up on her throat as he felt her neck start to make crackling noises. "Shut up! Shut up! Shut up!"

"This is the police. Come out with your hands up!" rang out over a speaker. "You won't be harmed if you do as we ask."

Watching his mother lose the battle to take in any more oxygen, Terrell finally felt like he was going to be free of her once and for all. Even if it meant spending the rest of his life behind bars, he was willing to face whatever consequences he had to incur to have Simone lose and for him to have the last laugh. "Die, bitch, die." Li'l T kept at it as he became completely unstable. "I won this time!"

Once again, the trigger was pulled. A half second after hearing the last, triumphant snap of the bones in Simone's neck, signifying he'd broken it, the thunderous blast of a solitary gunshot went off. Feeling the burning force of an apparent gunshot wound to his head, Terrell barely could focus on the .44-caliber pistol that was still clutched in his now-dead mother's hand. With the heavy flow of blood that was gushing out of his temple, he knew his time on earth was nearing the end. *That dirty bitch! How could she kill her own seed? Did she hate me that much?* Terrell started losing consciousness rapidly as he crawled into the other room and leaned over toward the wall, waiting patiently to die.

Several minutes later, heavily armed Detroit police officers from the SWAT unit, accompanied by Drake, stormed Simone's house, where they found the deceased bodies of Elon and Simone sprawled out on the dining room floor. An innocent Joi Richards was lying in a pool of her own blood. The young victim of circumstance had somewhat regained consciousness. Delirious, she was in excruciating pain from both the brutal rape she'd endured and the various bullet wounds her small frame had taken in. The officers signaled that they had at least one person who was alive and needed transport to a medical facility. Indeed, she looked in bad shape, but if there was fight in her, there was hope.

Keeping their guns drawn, they lastly discovered Terrell Harris barely clinging to life. Like the love of his young world, he struggled to live, although he didn't want to. As the ambulance technicians feverously worked on the teenager, knowing his survival changes were bleak, Drake saw some sort of bloody writing on the wall where they'd found Li'l T lying. Squinting in disbelief and utter sorrow, Drake slowly read the words his adopted son must've written: I am a man! Seconds later, Drake heard them pronounce Terrell dead. He'd left this earth just as his father, Kamel, had before him: in pandemonium.

Chapter Seventeen

It had been months since the ill-fated night. The gossip and true awfulness of what had taken place behind the Gates had long since perished. The headlines of the news had moved on to other crimes equally as terrible in the crime-ridden city of Detroit. There were no more tears from friends or protests for added security from neighbors. For most, life had returned to business as usual. However, for the lone survivor of the bloodbath, Joi Richards, life could never go back to how it was. Already having lost her mother years prior, and seeing her younger brother taken into the system, now she was faced with more harsh reality. Her sister was dead. The love of her life, Terrell, was dead. And here she was, still lying in a hospital bed, fighting to recover from several gunshot wounds.

To make matters worse, the young girl, her face now disfigured, was told by the doctors that she was pregnant. Joi knew she'd been raped by that monster Elon. Clinically depressed and on just about every pain pill the hospital could legally prescribe without possible injury to the unborn fetus, she sobbed. At this point, Joi didn't know who the father was. She couldn't be sure. Whereas part of her wanted to believe it was a love child belonging to her and Terrell, her mind told her differently. The mother-to-be fought hard with her mental demons. They persuaded her that the soon-to-be bastard belonged to Elon. At this point, both potential fathers were deceased, so any way it went, she'd be a single mother.

Knowing she was with child, Prayer came to visit Joi constantly, trying to figure out if Terrell was indeed the father. Drake and Big Ace made several visits as well during the first few weeks, trying to find out what truly jumped off that day at Simone's. Each man wanted a blow-by-blow account of what had happened that left them without their sons. Since Joi was the only live witness, she was the key to that puzzle.

However, Joi was a different person. Her normally bubbly personality was now gone. Her upbeat attitude toward life had vanished with her injuries. Her face was sunken in, and she had horrible scars from all the surgeries she'd gone through. Half out of her mind and not wanting to relive that day, Joi blocked everything out. She refused to speak to any of the three: Prayer, Drake, or Big Ace. After a while, they gave up seeking the information. They moved on. Joi, deranged and addicted to prescription pills, and whoever's baby she was carrying were on their own.

When Joi was finally released, the pregnant female did everything she could to get her next fix. The baby she was carrying was nothing more than a nuisance. Having turned into a mirror image of her mother, Joi had no conscience. In the pursuit of money, she cruelly stabbed an elderly man walking home from the bank. He'd just cashed his first check of the month, and Joi wanted, no needed, that cash. In her twisted mind, her baby was telling her to do it.

Thankfully she was arrested. He later died from his injuries, and Joi was sent to prison. There, behind bars, she gave birth to her son. Joi refused to name him, so the court-appointed social worker gave him the name of Justice, hoping one day the small infant would receive some. There was no father listed on baby Justice's birth certificate, and no one was left who wanted to step up and claim him. He was then entrusted to the system.

During one visit to family court, Joi said, "Yeah, this circus is getting on my last nerve. You got me all the way twisted around here. See, it makes no motherfucking difference one way or the other. You can take his lazy-eyed, freak-looking ass away from me. I'm good. I swear to God I'm good. It's his fault I'm in here in the first place. He told me to do what I did. I'm innocent!"

"Calm down, Miss Richards. Think about what you're saying." The social worker held the infant, swaddled in a sky blue blanket, protectively in her arms. "This is your flesh and blood. He's your child. How can you be so cruel and unfeeling?" she said, rightfully passing judgment.

"Get that damn kid away from me," Joi loudly demanded, showing every yellow tooth she was fortunate enough to still have lodged in her mouth. "If you so worried about him, then why don't you take his retarded butt home with you? I told all y'all I'm over it. Damn!"

"You are a disgrace to mothers everywhere. Don't you have any shame about your actions? How can you sleep at night?"

"Listen, lady, fuck you and that baby over there too. Just because you a social worker don't make you no better than me. When your old ass was my age, you used to bleed once a month just like me and get it in."

"Excuse me, Miss Richards." The gavel slammed down on the oak bench. "Are you telling the courts you want nothing to do with your son?" the newly elected judge to family court calmly intervened, asking the hysterical, handcuffed new mother. "Is that your final decision?"

"Damn, lady! What part of 'I'm good' don't you under-stand?" Joi sucked her teeth. She twisted her body as she spoke, still disrespecting the courtroom and its many occupants. "Unless you gonna let my ass out of here right now, what difference do it make what happens to my baby or what I say? Shitttt, y'all gonna do what y'all wanna do just like any other time. Fuck!"

"Watch your crude tone in my courtroom!" Judge Curtis cautiously advised before lowering her head and reading over Joi's long, detailed file. With her wire-rimmed glasses on the tip of her nose, she soon came to her conclusion. The defendant standing in front of her was indeed 100 percent correct. The court was going to render the final decision in the case of two-month-old Justice Richards, who was sadly born addicted to pills behind the steel bars of Wayne County Women's Correctional Facility. He would be returned to foster care, pending possible adoption.

"Listen up, Judge, Your Honor," a stone-faced Joi said, "if you can just hurry up and sign them papers, I can get back to my cell before lunch."

"Is that truly the only thing you care about, Miss Richards?" Judge Curtis lifted her head, making eye contact once more with the street-seasoned Joi. "Are you really in that much of a rush to sign your son over to the system and risk the chance of never seeing him again? Is that what you want, all your parental rights terminated?"

"Oh, my God! Are you people deaf? This don't make no freaking sense!" Joi squirmed, trying to loosen the tight restraint of the handcuffs as she looked over at the hands of the clock on the wall. "Like I said, just come on so the guards can take me back before I miss lunch."

With three or four signatures on several documents, the life-changing deed was done. The future of baby boy Justice Richards, aka case number M7-5461S8, was determined. From this point forward, pending adoption, he was officially a ward of the State of Michigan and would undoubtedly turn out like most of the other Detroit throwaway crack babies, as a true menace to society.

"I hope this baby doesn't turn out like her," the judge whispered to the social worker as the guards removed his deranged mother from the courtroom. "Because if he does, all of Detroit is going to have a huge problem on its hands. But as they say, only time will tell. I only pray I'm not alive to see that day."

Chapter Eighteen

"Come on, guy, and stop worrying about how your pretty ass look. You's a street soldier in the D, not a model," Justice, a grown thug, yelled back at his partner in crime, Cree, who was busy wiping the crumbs off his shirt from the breakfast his girl cooked. "You act like this shit a joke out here. Let's go!"

"Damn, slow ya roll. Trust when I tell you them crack-heads gonna be roaming the streets all day searching for a blast. Five minutes ain't gonna stop shit." Cree jumped down off the porch of the four-family flat he, his girl, and his granny called home. He joined a fast-walking Justice.

"Dude, fuck what you talking about." Justice banged his fist on his chest as they crossed Davison. "I'm out here alone and have been for years. I ain't got no stankin' bitch to be frying my black ass no bacon. I came from nothing."

"Yeah, well, if you went on the east side, I bet your girl Greedy would hook you right up!"

"Yeah, well, I ain't trying to hear shit Greedy saying. I ain't got no time for that 'in love' garbage. Besides, thangs about to get hard around these parts when it come to slanging. Them boys about to start cracking down. Especially near election time. Like, look at this." He paused on the corner and stared down at a copy of the *Detroit Free Press*. "Oh, hell naw! Please tell me they clowning." Justice hocked, spitting a stream of saliva through the huge gap in his front teeth. "I been living in the city my entire life, and ain't nothing ever happened good in this bitch to me! Ya feel me! Just poverty and hard goddamn living, but this here is outrageous! Reporters around here ain't got jack else to do but blow that shit out they grills about any stupid-sounding mess they make up! They need to focus they asses on something else. They're worried about the next man's dick!"

Cree nodded in agreement. His boy kicked over the rusty red newspaper box, causing the cheap lock to pop open and a thick stack of Saturday's thin edition to blow down Linwood. "Who in the hell you telling? Not only did them crackers shit on our ex-mayor and send him to the county for damn near a hundred and twenty days for lying about some dumb mess, but they wanna lynch the brotha." Cree pulled up his sagging jeans as the pair kept it moving. "And oh, yeah, let's not forget trying to charge him for conspiracy in killing some wild yester-year G-string dancer who supposedly had the nerve to come to that man's crib and not expect a damn serious, class double A beat down when wifey ran up on that dis-respectful ass. Now the damn Feds wanna stick they nose in city business and label our stomping ground the num-ber-one impoverished bloodthirsty spot around!"

"Look , it's Malcolm X's third illegitimate son!" Justice mocked, having heard enough of some crap neither he nor his homeboy could change. "I know where you coming from with ya wilded-out political ass, but right about now our only focus should be getting our pockets lined proper, not giving a damn about a stack of papers in an old-ass metal box or what some whitey sitting behind a desk done made up. Now let's get this dough!"

Standing around the corner liquor store for a few hours, letting the hot July sunlight beam down on their heads, caused the young men to sweat buckets as they tried slinging the rest of the twice-over stepped-on powder they'd copped on credit from Moe Mack, the so-called neighborhood big fella. Each wearing wife beaters from straight out of the pack and Tigers baseball caps turned to the back, they waited patiently for dopefiends to find their way to them and make that shit happen. Only weeks prior they were clocking major figures with the package they were selling on their territory of the hood, DLA, but now the tide had turned, and they couldn't seem to catch a damn break. It was downright ridiculous and an insult to dope sellers all across Motown what custos were saying. "Naw! Next time! I pass! We good! Nigga, please!"

Being forced to listen to complaint after complaint from crackheads gave them all the proof needed to bug out on their weak-ass connect, Moe Mack. Considering that the blow they'd originally nicknamed Head Banger wasn't strong as a crushed-up baby aspirin, the word had definitely gotten around the west side Detroit neighbor-hood, bringing once-flourishing sales down to practically nothing. The arrogance of their clientele was unbeliev-able but still expected. For a group of broken down, poor, pimping drug addicts who roamed the Motor City streets, lived in vacant houses, and didn't have jack shit to call their own, they were some of the hardest hustling, trash-talking, money-getting heathens around and picky as to what they sniffed, snorted, smoked, or stuck into the open wounds of their often-infected veins. That's how life was in Detroit: serious.

"We should give the rest of this garbage back to that fake-ass baller!" Cree turned up an ice-cold Faygo Redpop and threw the bottle into an empty field. "That fool knew this was straight-up trash when he pawned it off on us!"

"Word! And now he wants us to pay him that high-ran-som ticket on the package." Justice lit a cherry-blend Black & Mild. He blew the smoke out and up into Detroit's already-polluted air. "See, that's exactly what I was talking about earlier. Ya boy Moe Mack supposed to be such a hellava mover and shaker around this piece, and look how he fucks over the little man! He foul!"

Cree cracked his knuckles, sticking his chest out as he watched a group of young females drive past, blowing their horn and flirting with him. "I feels ya, dawg! For real! We out here on the regular, pounding the pavement in the scorching, desert-ass heat trying to do the damn thang, and he playing us like two virgin pussies! We might as well grab some dresses and ride with them sluts, 'cause he straight fucking us over!"

"Yeah, Cree, but a guy like me can't say I'm surprised. People from the D is so cutthroat with it. You know like me, they'd stab they own baby in the neck with a dull screwdriver if they thought there was profit in the outcome!" Justice chewed down on the plastic tip of his cigar. "But real talk, I'm 'bout tired of getting dry ground in the game! The next time we do business with ol' boy gonna be that buster's last time disrespecting our hustle if he don't come correct, because I ain't feeling this half-ass shit no more!"

As if on cue, Cree and Justice both looked up the block to the left, just in time to catch a glimpse of the red taillights of Moe Mack's car bending the corner, sounds blasting, heading toward the freeway. Then, enviously leering at one another with a stare of contempt from their hearts for their supplier, they sighed, obviously thinking the same thought: *look at this nigga. One day he gonna pay for fucking over us!*

Hearing the loud rattling metal sounds of a shopping buggy barely held together, the two associates then glanced over to their right to see Last Chance, a smelly, dusty, seasoned head coming down Linwood Avenue. He stopped dead in front of the liquor store's entrance.

"What up doe, Last Chance, my nigga? Holler at ya boy! We got that sho'nuff package for ya!" Justice proudly spoke up, putting bass in his voice and still chewing on his cigar's tip. "Two for ones all day, baby! How 'bout it?"

"Naw, young blood." Last Chance confusedly riffled through his buggy in search of a few returnable bottles so he could buy a loosie. "I'm good on that."

"Come on now and give us a play." Cree threw his hands up, practically begging. "I see you straight proper 'cause you got damn near every piece of metal from the lamppost sticking out of this cart!"

Last Chance finally found what he was desperately in search of. Snatching five or six of them from the bottom of his buggy, clutching the semi-smashed, unclean bottles under his musty armpits, he smiled. Now satisfied he would soon have a smoke to calm his nerves, he was ready to talk shit.

"You right, youngster." He grinned, showing off the four and a half crooked, rotten teeth he had left in his mouth. "I been at it all night. This here is about to be my third trip to the scrapyard! Detroit gonna go dark tonight!" he joked.

"That's what's up!" Justice nodded upward.

"Yeah, that's what I'm saying!" Cree laughed, anticipating a much-needed and hard-sought sale as he rubbed his hands together. "So spend some of that bread with me and my manz! Share the love!"

"Can one of y'all playas do me a solid and watch my buggy until I get me a cigarette and a shot?" he grunted, changing the subject.

"Go on and handle ya business, old man! We out here on post!" Justice waved him off. "Ain't nobody about to mess with ya moneymaking buggy. We got ya!"

Eagerly approaching several other crackheads, aka potential customers, the sad-faced partners on the come-up struck out with each sales pitch they delivered. Both depressed, with empty pockets to keep them company, Justice and Cree stood to the side of the bulletproof glass door as the irate owner of the store suddenly strong-armed a defiant Last Chance out to the sidewalk, warning him to never step foot inside his establishment again.

"I'm not playing around! You go!"

"I swear to God, if you didn't have that bat in your hand, I'd teach you a good old-fashioned lesson from back in the day for putting ya hands on me, raghead!" Last Chance vowed, staggering backward into his shopping cart.

"Get out of here! Get out of here! You people make me sick!" The first-generation immigrant started yelling in his native language at Last Chance, who was caught stealing two honey buns, a can of Spam, and a quarter-sized grape juice.

"Speak English, you dirty sand nigga!" Last Chance caught hold of the side of the cart to keep his balance.

"I'm dirty? You's dirty, you old man!" he fired off loudly in response. "Get a job, you bum, instead of stealing all my stock! Stupid, dumb people!"

As the red-faced Arab disappeared back inside his store, still furious that one more black person was taking advantage of him and his family's good fortune to own a business, Last Chance got himself together. Pissed at getting caught, he lit his Smokers Choice cigarette, which was now broken in two pieces. "They come over here from freaking Baghdad or wherever and think they own the world! Them honey buns wasn't gonna kill they stankin' asses!"

Cree wanted nothing more than to intervene and weigh in on the foul-ass choice of words the foreigner used, but he changed his mind when he realized Last Chance was rolling off without copping so much as a single pack from them. "Damn, guy! What's up? You wanna holler or what?"

"Naw, youngster, I don't want none of that," Last Chance decisively mumbled. "I done heard it's weak and ain't gonna halfway get me where I need to be."

Hearing that crucial statement was the last straw, making Justice pissed. Since Moe Mack had them so royally fucked in the game, right then and there on the spot, he decided he and Cree had to get revenge much sooner rather than later. Realizing that Last Chance was probably getting more money hustling copper than them, the down-and-practically-out Justice couldn't wait to have a face-to-face sit-down with their supplier. Moe Mack was riding good, eating good, sleeping good, and even tricking good while they damn near starved. The time for payback was now! Giving up any more useless attempts to move the rest of the dope in their possession, the duo walked down Linwood, hit Davison, cut across the gas station lot where Reverend Marvin Winans got jacked, and went into the forever-crowded Coney Island Restaurant to grab some grub and politick.

"What up doe? Let me get a cheeseburger deluxe," Cree said to the token black young girl they had working the cash register.

"And let me get an order of chili cheese fries," Justice added. "Plus throw some chopped onions on them bad boys."

"All right." She smiled, handing them separate tickets. "Give me about ten minutes."

After receiving their food and purchasing a few bootleg movies, both guys headed to the rear booth, where they plotted their devious revenge on Moe Mack. They vowed he was gonna give them their just due whether he liked it or not. In less than thirty or so minutes, the plan was totally calculated and minutes away from being put into full play. Unfortunately for Moe Mack and the rest of the residents of Detroit, after nightfall, the city would never be the same.

"Yo, my dude! Get two pairs of gloves and a couple rolls of duct tape," Justice reminded Cree as they stood outside the local dollar store. "Matter of fact, you better get at least five or six rolls."

"You right," he agreed, thinking well ahead as he glanced at his watch. "It ain't no telling how many wannabe heroes gonna be posted at that house, or how long we gonna have to wait for Moe Mack to show his face."

"Bet money, but no matter how long we do end up waiting, when dude do show up it's definitely gonna be on and popping!" Justice schemed as his lazy eye twitched. "I'm done messing around!"

"Say word!" Cree smiled before entering the store's sticker-covered double doors. "Say motherfucking word!"

Chapter Nineteen

"Dang, G. When you stopping by the house? Me and your son miss you," NayNay whined, finally getting an answer from her baby's daddy after a rampage of blowing up his phone all afternoon. "Plus I need some diapers, some wipes, and a pack of Newports."

"Come on, NayNay! You don't miss me so stop with all the games! What ya really miss is this here knot in my pocket and some of this big, fat dick in my hands!"

"Oh, yeah?" NayNay sucked her teeth but didn't deny his statement. "You really think so?"

"Hell yeah! And PS, instead of trying so hard to manipulate a brotha, what you need to do is potty train that li'l bad-ass nigga!" Moe Mack taunted as he twisted the top off a cold beer. He took a quick swig before swerving his wide-body BMW to avoid a few teenagers who were riding mopeds. "That's why he don't hang with me now!"

"You a man, so why can't you just teach him to piss in that damn pot? He don't wanna be listening to me!" NayNay scratched roughly at her head with a wide-tooth comb as huge white flakes of dandruff fell onto the shoulders of her black T-shirt.

"Girl, fuck you!" Moe Mack ridiculed as he continued to bend corners. "What the hell I look like, the nanny or something? Just fall back, go easy, and I'll be through there in a few. Me and Keith just gotta handle some business first."

"Yeah, Moe, but I'm serious. Maurice needs some damn diapers, so come the fuck on!"

"Bitch, watch ya mouth and just chill out." Fed up with all the back-and-forth, his tone changed. "I said I'll be there! Now peace!"

"Okay, but don't forget my Newports!" NayNay, who'd spent all of her welfare check the moment it touched her greedy hands, managed to blurt out once again before hearing the line go completely dead.

Removing several hairpins that were barely holding her $9.99 synthetic burgundy and blond streaked pony-tail in place, a stressed-out NayNay, desperately in need of a cigarette, headed toward the kitchen sink. Of course, it was overflowing with filthy dishes, pots, pans, and two skillets with burnt bottoms. The fact that she, her sister, and her sister's grown daughter were living there, plus all their kids combined, still didn't help matters any when it came to keeping the household clean. All three women had one main agenda, and that was begging men for that revenue, not being Holly Homemakers.

Rinsing out a red plastic cup to get a drink from the pitcher of cherry Kool-Aid in the refrigerator, home alone with her sick baby, she started thinking about her life. *That punk-ass Moe gonna miss me when I leave him the hell by himself.* Disgusted, NayNay swore she meant it, looking out the cracked living room window, which had sheets tacked up that doubled as curtains. *I ain't gonna be sitting around looking stupid while he do whatever with the next chick. I'm better than all that! He must not know who the fuck I am!* She searched through the ashtray, hoping to find a butt with at least one or two more pulls on it.

As time ticked by, NayNay fell asleep but was almost immediately awakened by several quick knocks at the front black steel gate. *Damn!* Assuming that it must've been Moe or one of the kids since her sister and niece were out of town, she felt at ease. Wiping her eyes groggily, she twisted the lock, swung the door open, and turned away, walking back to the couch.

"Oh, my God! Oh, my God!" Before the single, young, unfit mother knew what hit her next, she was ruthlessly shoved flat on her stomach with her face smushed down into the worn-out carpet.

"What in the hell?" She tried struggling as the stinging feeling of a huge carpet burn across her forehead kicked in. "What you want? Oh, my God! What in the fuck?"

"Shut ya big mouth before I body ya ass!" Her assailant's hot, onion, stank breath filled her ear. "Calm the fuck down or else! You hear me? Calm that ass down!"

"Why is you doing this?" NayNay continued to speak as if his threat were idle and she was in control. "Is you crazy? Do you know who my man is?"

"Listen, ho! I said calm ya ass down! You must really want me to put these paws on you!"

"You hurting me." She yanked, still attempting to break free.

Justice had no choice whatsoever but to apply more pressure to her neck as his knee pressed deeper into her spine. "Look, I ain't playing around with you! Don't make me snap this son of a bitch in two!" he threatened as he ripped a long piece of duct tape off the roll. He wrapped it forcefully around her mouth and head. "Now shut up! I mean it!" He pushed her on her side. "And FYI, fuck ya man!"

After securely binding her wrists and feet together, Justice removed his gun from his blue jean waistband. He then started easing his way through the rest of the house. Cautiously lurching around each corner, his heartbeat increased with every passing step. Luckily discovering room after room empty, he finally stumbled across NayNay's sleeping son on a fluffy pallet of blankets on the side of a twin bed. Knowing the small, diaper-clad child didn't pose a threat to his and Cree's game plan, he sympathetically chose to let the little boy be as he went on his way to secure the rest of the perimeter.

After finally reaching the side entrance located off the driveway, he unlocked the three security deadbolts on the flimsy door with a set of keys that were conveniently hung on an old rusty nail. He quietly allowed his partner in crime Cree to enter the house so they could totally put the scheme of revenge on Moe Mack into full force.

"What up doe? Is we good? Is the coast clear?" Cree quizzed, looking around to see if any neighbors had seen him perched by the door.

"Yeah, dawg! We good for sure," Justice affirmed. "Ain't nobody here but Moe Mack's ho and her baby."

"That's what's up," Cree nervously responded. His palms dripped with perspiration as he held his pistol at his side. "But we still need to get ready in case any of the rest of them decides to come back before ol' boy shows."

"Okay, let's do this! Ol' girl in there." Justice pointed up the stairs. "Come on!"

Cree followed his boy's lead, finding NayNay bound and gagged on the living room floor. Hopelessly still squirming in an attempt to get free, she'd somehow managed to knock over the coffee table and tip over a bottle of warm, half-drunk Pepsi. Realizing the one intruder who originally attacked her had now multiplied to two, her eyes widened with fear in anticipation of what exactly they had in store for her.

"Yo, bitch! When that fake baller of yours coming through to check dat ass?" Justice yanked at NayNay's hair, which was now tangled and all over her head. "Huh? What damn time?" Obviously not getting an answer, especially since her mouth was covered, he callously pushed the barrel of his pistol to the side of her temple. With his gun clutched in his sweaty hand, he dared NayNay to mutter one solitary word. "I don't give a damn if this shit hurt like a motherfucker! You better not scream or else!" he ordered with authority, roughly snatching the gray duct tape off her mouth, which also ripped her hair out by the roots. "Now answer my damn question," Justice repeated with anger. "When that dude Moe Mack gonna be here?"

"I dunno." NayNay trembled, fighting back the tears as it dawned on her exactly what this blatant and sudden invasion of her home was about. "I dunno."

"Don't lie to us and you won't get hurt!" Cree furiously advised, looking at his watch to check on the time. "We ain't come here on no dummy mission!"

"I swear I don't know," she whimpered from the floor as both guys towered over her.

Justice found NayNay's Metro PCS cell phone on the couch and flipped it open while still gripping the handle of his gun. "Well, guess what, dumb bitch? You about to call that guy and tell him there's a damn emergency or some shit like that with his bastard son. And then you need to tell him to rush his punk ass over! Ya feel me?"

"But he ain't gonna answer," NayNay said, trying to talk her way out of calling her child's father. "He's busy doing some stuff."

"Well, you better hope he answers, because if he don't, then trust that's ya ass!" Cree was trying to go in extra hard informing the now-hysterical, crying female, hoping to intimidate her. "So ya best get ya game face on!"

Justice scrolled down the long list of names in her address book, and he finally came up with the letter M. There he found what he was looking for: Moe.

"All right, trick," Justice fumed with the cold steel pressing into her jawbone. "I'm about to call this faggot!

And when he pick up, you better play it off, or I'm gonna let one of these hot ones loose right into the side of ya face! Ya follow?"

Just as Justice was about to push the button calling Moe Mack, the doorbell rang, and the sound of three knocks on the gate followed. Cree's, Justice's, and NayNay's eyes all met, and the room grew silent. Whoever was at the door waited no more than a good five seconds before they knocked once again. Scared half to death that the scheme they'd so quickly planned was going down so fast with unforeseen obstacles, the guys froze, not knowing what move to make next.

"Yo, is you expecting company?" Justice pushed his gun deeper into her jaw. "Who at that door?"

NayNay shrugged while praying that whoever it was would come to her rescue. As the mailbox slot opened up and a couple of small pamphlets were pushed through, hitting the floor, it became apparent to all of them that it was no one of any great importance or any detriment to the ongoing crime.

"Them motherfucking Jehovah's Witnesses gonna get killed one day coming to niggas' houses with that dumb shit!"

"Yeah," Cree agreed. "Why they be coming on them dummy missions anyhow? Ain't nobody in the hood be listening to that shit!"

Getting back to the business at hand, Justice once again focused on his hostage. "Okay, bitch, get ready to make that call. And remember, no slick shit!"

NayNay was terrified but managed nodding, indicating she understood what he was saying. After a series of rings, the voicemail continued clicking on each time they placed a call. It soon became painfully obvious that Moe Mack had no intention whatsoever of accepting any more of his worrisome baby mama's calls. Oh, well. Too bad!

So sad! Unfortunately, neither Cree nor Justice had any idea that the whore they picked to use as human bait was infamous for pestering their connect so bad that even if she called a hundred times, Moe Mack wasn't gonna pick up that motherfucker until he got good and damn ready.

"Man! Didn't I just hang up from that good-begging NayNay a little while ago?" Moe Mack turned the head-banging sounds down as he headed toward the far east side of Detroit to meet up with some of his crim-inal-minded cohorts. "Now she back calling like there ain't no tomorrow! I swear if she didn't have my seed, I'd stop dealing with the worrisome bitch! A brother sure hate the rubber busted that night!"

Keith posted back low profile in the passenger seat. Seriously as he could be, he preached, schooling his boy on art of training renegade hoes. "Dawg, kid or not, what ya need to do is chin check her ass. Don't call back or go around for a week or so. She'll straighten up and fly right then! That's the recipe for putting a li'l act right on 'em!"

"You's about right, my dude! I might just do that on the real if she keeps blowing my cell up!" Moe Mack consid-ered as he hit the IGNORE button on his phone once more then pushed the steering wheel's side switch, increasing the radio's volume again.

After devouring something to eat at a Greek Town pizzeria along with a couple of stiff drinks, soon the pair, born and raised on the west side, were pulling up at an apartment building near the corner of I-94 and Harper. They had a meeting scheduled for four o'clock with a dude from Ohio whom Moe Mack had previously purchased some weight from. It seemed the connect unknowingly sold a couple of kilos to a few major ballers from the D who were, of course, understandably pissed off about the quality of the dope, which was weak as hell. And needless to say, the streets were talking. Not wanting to suffer the inevitable wrath of their retaliation or sever business ties, the connect wisely decided to make things right, blessing Moe Mack, Flipper, Chase, Big B, Li'l Tone, and of course Keith with a new, fresh, strong, uncut package for half the regular price.

The entire time Moe Mack and the rest of the fellas were at the meeting counting money and making sure the weight was correct, NayNay never once let up on calling her son's father. *This chick is really bugging out over a pack of Newports.* He shook his head in deep thought as he and Keith discreetly pulled out of the rear of the building's trash-littered alleyway and headed toward Jefferson Avenue. *As soon as I get back around the way, I'm gonna go over there and stomp a mudhole in her ass.* Trying to keep his baby mama off his mind and concentrate on safely transporting the dope stashed in his car, he turned his constantly ringing cell phone to silent.

As he drove back to the neighborhood, he and Keith unanimously decided to look out for each one of their loyal crew members who had ridden the bullshit out, from the mid-level hustlers directly under them who bought big eighths to the small-time street soldiers who sold double-ups to survive on a day-to-day basis to feed their families and put new sneakers on their feet. They'd all been forced to weather the storm of having bad product, but now in a matter of hours, Lady Luck herself was about to shine her light directly on their asses. That no doubt included his new-school moneymaking team of Justice and Cree, whom he'd seen earlier up on Linwood trying to do their thang.

But as Maurice Javon Johnson Sr. drove down the Lodge Freeway dirty as hell feeling generous to the troops, little did he know the brazen renegade duo didn't have time to wait for a blessing from him or any more runaround blasé explanations about this or that they'd heard in the previous weeks when they complained. Justice and Cree were going for what they knew right now, in real time, and they definitely planned on getting that shit how they lived, which was like most Detroiters who were 'bout it, 'bout it! Rowdy! Rough! Raw! And without a bit of doubt un- motherfucking-cut!

Chapter Twenty

Cree calmed down, regaining his composure after he and Justice forced NayNay to call their ultimate intended victim a few more times. They still got no satisfaction of him picking up or confirming he was on his way. Kicking two or three good-size holes in the house's walls, then stomping some toys that were scattered around the filthy home, relieved a little tension for Cree, but not much. Pacing the floor, trying to figure out what their next move would be if Moe Mack didn't show up soon, was causing him to sweat and get thirsty. Not to mention that NayNay's light green contact lenses seemed to be glowing, throwing him all off his square. *Damn this is some real fucked-up bullshit.* He swallowed a lump in his throat, realizing it was now a quarter past six and he was late taking his pregnant girl some food. *We should've been outta here by now.*

NayNay, who was still on the floor, was now in an upright position, leaning by the fireplace. Seeing Cree's rage firsthand and the promise of Justice's bullet, she opted to do as she was told in hopes of living to see another day. "Excuse me, but can you please check on my son?" She was humble in her request. "Or bring him to me?"

"Ain't nothing wrong with that li'l dude," Cree reassured her, trying his best not to make eye contact after closing all the open windows in the house. "I was just back there and he still sleeping on the floor."

"Yeah, but—"

Justice came from the rear of the house with NayNay's jewelry box, her bootleg Coach purse, and an armful of men's clothes, which had to belong to Moe Mack. "But what, bitch?" he cut her off, spitting on the carpet as if he were outside. "Don't make me put that tape back over that complaining mouth of yours!"

Still tied up, praying for nothing except her and her child to survive this ordeal, NayNay didn't argue. Even when Justice dumped the contents of her bag onto the floor, rummaged through her wallet in search of cash, then called her several broke-ass hoes, she still refrained from her customary rude and most times obnoxious outburst of putting a person in their place whether they be young or old, black or white, or even male or female. Yet, this was a much different circumstance from the normal controversial, petty crap the self-proclaimed Linwood Hood Diva found herself usually caught up in. This time around, Miss NayNay losing control of her well-known short temper could cost not only her life, but also that of her small son. She had no choice. Seething as her baby daddy's formerly insignificant worker stuffed his pockets with her many ten-karat rings, three pair of gold hoops, and a diamond tennis bracelet she received for a birthday present, NayNay still kept quiet.

"Hey! Where's all that other gear you and your wide-assed sister be flossing, acting all high profile?"

"Excuse me?" NayNay timidly spoke, trying to loosen the tape that was cutting off the circulation in her hands. "You got my stuff!"

"I mean hey, let's keep it real. All the time when you was riding down Linwood past me and my boy, acting all stuck-up and high post and ya black ass is broke as we is!" he vindictively teased. "My bottom bitch be all on my back trying to get me to buy her outfits like she see you rocking at the club, and your house looking like this!" he cruelly judged, turning his head from side to side. "No wonder my man ain't picking up checking for you! How in the hell he end up with a baby mama cut like you? If his ho ass ain't owe me and my manz some loot, I'd kinda feel sorry for him!"

"Go fuck yourself," she arrogantly mumbled under her breath as she burned a hole through him with her bitter stare.

Justice lifted his head from searching through the pile of men's clothes, trying to find something he liked, just in time to hear NayNay's annoyed voice speak. "Did you say something to me?"

"Yeah," Cree blurted out, heading toward the window to investigate the noise of some kids walking down the block. "She said for you to get naked, go in the closet, chop ya dick off, then fuck ya self in the ass!"

"What?" Justice dropped a shirt he was checking for the size and raised his hand, rushing in the defenseless female's direction. "Bitch, I should smack the fire outta ya mouth!"

"Naw, naw, naw, hold up, guy. I was just clowning." Cree quickly stopped his boy, defusing the situation before a strong-armed meeting with Moe Mack turned to something much worse. "Slow down. She ain't say shit! But real talk, y'all, two little kids is coming up this walkway. Do they stay here or something?" He directed his question to NayNay.

She took a deep breath, trembling with fear. "Yessss," she stuttered. "Those are my nephews. I'm watching them until my sister gets back in town. Please don't hurt them!"

"Shut up, bitch!" Justice demanded, rushing up on her.

"Yeah, just be quiet." Cree raised his gun barrel up against his lips. "Ain't nobody here to be hurting no little kids, so chill!"

The roguish kids' laughter and boisterous voices imitating old Last Chance, whose buggy they'd just maliciously flipped over, echoed throughout the silent house as they pounded their small fists on the gate. "Somebody open the damn door!" The children had no respect or regard for the elderly neighborhood busybody Mrs. Perkins, the long-time block club president, as they cursed loudly, acting as if they didn't even care she was in her front yard working in her garden.

Peeping out the window from behind the dirty sheet, Cree made sure the kids were alone. He then gave Justice the signal to open the door, letting the boys, too grown for their own good, into the home and what would soon be remembered as their worst nightmare. Used to seeing different men around the house all times of the day and night caused the boys to not give the stranger who'd opened the door a second thought as they playfully breezed past Justice with not so much as a glance. It wasn't until the two got all the way into the living room that they noticed something was wrong.

"Dang, G! Why you on the floor taped up?" the eldest asked his aunt as the door slammed shut. "And why is the table flipped over?"

"Yeah, why?" The little one wiped snot from his nose as Cree unexpectedly snatched him up, tossing him onto the couch.

Realizing what was going on, the older boy tried to backtrack bolting toward the door. Instantly, he was stopped by Justice grabbing his wrinkled T-shirt up by the collar, dragging him across the room over to join his brother, who was now in tears.

"Please don't hurt them!" NayNay pleaded with a face full of tears. "Please, please, please."

After a few eerie seconds of silence, the older boy locked eyes with Cree as if he were grown, then once again tried unsuccessfully to break free and run for the door. "Forget y'all!" he screamed at them both. "Y'all ain't shooting me!"

"Ya better go sit ya motherfucking, bad li'l behind down!" Justice stuck out his arm, clotheslining him. Laughing, he proceeded to smack the child across the face twice before brutally body slamming him to the carpet, knocking all the wind out of the young boy. "Don't make me really beat that ass! Now stay the fuck down!"

As NayNay's one nephew lay balled up on the living room floor with a small gash above his eyebrow and a rapidly swelling lip, begging for his mama, the other was now posted at her side with his arms wrapped around her neck, terrified. "I'm scared, Auntie Nay. Make him stop hurting my brother!" the littler one begged, turning his face away. "Make him leave!"

"Stop it! Stop it!" she repeatedly shouted, fighting to break the gray duct tape still holding her captive. Still out of control, Justice towered vindictively over the youngster. "He ain't nothing but a kid!"

"Yeah, ya right, a kid with a smart-ass mouth who can't follow directions." He kicked the boy in his leg then kicked NayNay. "I get enough of that bullshit at my girl's crib!"

"What's wrong with you?" NayNay hollered, still fighting a losing battle to break free. "Who in the fuck does that to a kid? What's wrong with you?"

"What's wrong with me? Bitch, what's wrong with you?" Justice took one of the rolls of tape off the fireplace mantle. Half out of his mind, he yanked the boy from the floor, throwing him in the oversized chair in the corner of the room. "You need to teach these little bastards some damned manners before I do, 'cause that ain't a problem."

"Calm down, guy. Damn." Cree saw things were quickly getting out of hand as he watched his partner demand that the other child sit in the chair with his brother. "And you shut the hell up." He pointed his pistol at a hysterical NayNay. Confused, they both watched an enraged Justice start peeling the tape off, wrapping both kids tightly to the chair before stuffing sweat socks in their mouths.

Cree couldn't believe his eyes and what the hell he'd gotten himself into. This definitely wasn't what he'd planned when he and Justice decided to have Moe Mack make their package right. He'd just played *Madden* all night, kicking back with the fellas getting high as hell. Earlier he'd thought about what outfit to buy to go with the new Jordans that came out Monday. And damn, the usually mild-mannered small-time drug dealer planned on going to the doctor come morning with his girl, who was seven months pregnant with his firstborn. Now here he was, just like that, caught up in breaking and entering, kidnapping, child abuse, assault, and from the looks of things, possibly murder. *Why did I even think this bullshittin' plan would work? Things don't ever work out for me! Justice is nutting all the way up! Damn this shit going too far!*

Moe Mack drove down Joy Road, heading toward Dexter Boulevard. It was now close to six-thirty in the evening, and the hot July summer sun was still beaming as if it were high noon. With plans of meeting back up with his boy Keith, hanging out at one of the strip clubs on Eight Mile, he smiled. Celebrating their latest strong product that was sure to take their crews off of craps was in order. He had only a few more deliveries to make to some of his street teams before finally going over NayNay's, who by this time he knew was beyond irate.

I should do what ol' boy just said and teach her trifling butt a hellava lesson. Shoot, out of all the females I deal with, she the only one who acts up. If that crazy, out-for-self whore wouldn't go down to put me on child support, I'd dip! Flat out! Matter of fact, a guy like me needs to make a trip to go see Maury.

Taking his cell off silent, he couldn't do anything but shake his head in utter disgust over whom he'd ultimately been cursed with as his alleged child's mother. Each time he'd try using his phone to place a call, he was met with the annoying sound of NayNay's assigned ring tone, "Bust It Baby," along with several urgent voice messages where his son's mama was practically begging him to come over. *Damn this chick is really bugging out! Eighteen back-to-back calls in a row! She needs to be medicated! Bad! Now she texting me! Stupid bitch!*

Cruising the violent inner-city neighborhood, he reclined deep in the seat of his chromed-out Beemer. Moe Mack turned on his favorite jazz CD in a much-needed attempt to drown out NayNay's relentless tirade. Still amazed at the sometimes-ruthless, poverty-driven behavior of the Motown residents and the things they did to survive, it was soon utterly clear to him why Detroit was number one in crime. "Bust It Baby." *I'm gonna call her back as soon as this song go off and cuss that bitch all the way out! She done lost her rabbit-ass mind! Don't nobody need a pack of Newports that damn bad!*

"Why you doing them like that?" NayNay questioned with contempt, no longer holding back her anger. "You ain't about nothing, you punk-ass, broke nigga!"

"Broke?" Justice grew more outraged, practically smacking the dog shit outta her. "If the hell I am broke, it's because of ya baby daddy and his shady, stepped-on dope!"

"You just a jealous hater," she alleged, taking the hit to the face like a trooper.

"Jealous of what? A little nappy-headed slut like you? Bitch, please!"

"Yeah, well, why you all up in my crib taking the next person's property?"

"'Cause the fuck I want to! Now shut up! I don't even wanna hear you breathe!" Justice reached for NayNay's cell phone, once again calling Moe Mack, who obviously shot the call immediately to voicemail. "It's probably that smart mouth of yours that's making dude not even wanna deal with you. I mean real rap, ya sitting over here with his seed in the back sick and no doubt that nigga somewhere posted up with his true wifey, a bitch who can probably cook and clean!"

"Whatever." NayNay arrogantly twisted her lips, rolling her eyes in denial as if she weren't tied up on the floor of her filthy, unkempt rental house, looking like a certified stank-a-dank, "girl why don't ya get yourself together," hot ghetto-ass mess. "You just wish a female like me would deal with your lowlife ass! Boy, you need to buy a clue. Don't nobody, especially me, want your crazy-looking ass!"

"Is you high or something? Shittt, what you been smoking?" Justice taunted, leaning over in her face as the two traded insults. "I need some of that weed! That must be some of that purple!"

"Naw, you need to brush ya motherfucking teeth! That's what in the fuck you need to do!"

Tuning the silly bickering out, a concerned Cree was in his own world worrying about the young, frightened boys and the horrified expressions that graced their tiny faces. "Can y'all breathe or what?" he sympathetically asked, removing the dirty sock from the smaller child's mouth.

Moments later, interrupting NayNay's last comeback, Justice and Cree were both amazed when her cell phone rang. It was flashing Moe Mack's name and number across the screen. The living room was motionless as if this weren't the moment they'd all been on pins and needles waiting for.

"Oh, shit! It's that guy," Justice panicked, grabbing his pistol, which was now on the mantle.

"Y'all kids better not say anything, okay? I'm not playing around." Cree acted as if they had a choice in the matter.

"Yeah, that goes for you too! I'ma put this shit on speaker, and you better not say no dumb shit or else!" Justice shoved the gun into NayNay's ribcage as Cree stood guard near the two boys. The cell rang once more.

"Hello."

"Yeah, NayNay, what the hell is so important that you keep calling me like you crazy?" Moe Mack went straight into flip-out mode.

"I . . . I . . ." She fought to get her words out. "It's the baby. Maurice got a high temperature."

"And?"

"And I need for you to come over." She felt the pressure of Justice's huge gun stab her side as she tried convincing her son's father to show up.

"For what? I ain't no damn doctor!" Moe Mack wasn't showing any signs of sympathy for NayNay and her fictitious tale. "And even if I were, I still wouldn't stop what I was doing because your trifling ass called! You doing too damn much, Nay! Matter of fact, I don't think I'm coming that way for a couple of days!" Moe remembered what Keith said earlier.

NayNay momentarily glanced over at her young defenseless nephews taped to the chair. With the eldest slowly losing a battle fighting to breathe as a sock still blocked his airway, she gave Maurice's father her best "nigga, please come help a ho" routine.

"Look, sweetie," she said, trying to come at him from a different angle as Justice's rough, ashy hand held her cell up to her trembling lips. "I'm sorry for keep calling you like I did, but I didn't know what to do or who else to call. You know my sister and 'em is out of town and the boys are with me. You know how they be getting out of hand!"

"Oh, yeah, I forgot." Moe Mack slightly let down his irritated demeanor as he slowed his expensive car down, letting an older woman carrying several bags of groceries cross the street. "But dang, still. Calling a Negro that much is outright ridiculous. I told you earlier I was about to take care of some business, and ya pesky ass was still out of pocket. Embarrassing me in front of all my boys like you's a stalker! You got a nigga not wanting to deal with you at all!"

"Baby, please, I said I'm sorry." NayNay's eyes shut tightly as she hesitated but reluctantly continued trying to lure her son's father to her house and to what could very well be his last day on earth. "Can you just come see me? I need you. I'm begging!"

Knowing he was gonna give in sooner or later, Moe Mack let his baby mama off the hook, saying the words Justice and Cree were waiting so desperately for hours to hear come out of his mouth. "After I make a few more runs, I'll be on my way. So now you can stop perpetrating like my son is over there dying, okay?" Moe Mack checked the time, informing her to expect him about eight o'clock.

Abruptly he ended their conversation.

"Good." Justice sinisterly grinned, leering at NayNay while flipping her cell closed. "And when ol' boy get here, he better come correct!"

Chapter Twenty-one

Although Cree was to some extent relieved, there would soon be a conclusion to the long, drawn-out day of terror he and Justice had perpetrated. Along with the fact that by the time the sun went down his pockets would most likely be on swoll, he still couldn't shake the cold, eerie feeling that somehow, someway, things wouldn't go as planned. Shit never did for him. That would be too much like right in his forever-corrupt, fucked-up existence. If it wasn't one thing, it was sure a goddamned other where Cree was concerned.

Hell, keeping things a hundred, since the first day his heroin-addicted mother suddenly abandoned him, when he was only seven, his two sisters, and their matted-hair, three-legged, flea-infested dog on his granny's front porch in search of the ultimate high, an ongoing cloud of doom seemed to follow him on a daily basis. From the word go, Cree felt it was always him against the world. Now lately, from time to time, just as he'd ended up mercifully putting a BB gun to Ava's head, putting her out of her never-ending misery of catching the short end of the stick when it came to a dog's life, he himself was contemplating checking out. Fortunately, the only thing keeping him sane and thinking rational was the thought of becoming a new father.

Watching the small boys squirm around in the chair and hyperventilate with panic, not knowing what was gonna happen next, made him have flashbacks to being hungry, being mistreated, and also being left night after night alone with his sisters to fend for themselves. Cree remembered those horrible days he was consumed with vulnerability, scared of his own shadow. It was those very memories that made him stop resenting his mother so much for giving them away and more thankful to his granny for saving their lives.

He was indeed a drug dealer. So what? Big deal! That was an accepted and expected line of work in Detroit, but fuck the rest of what was transpiring. Cree's granny didn't raise him to be no baby killer, and there wasn't no way in sweet, hot hell his homeboy Justice was gonna persuade him otherwise. Knowing right from wrong, Cree was taken over by compassion. With compassion, he removed the sock still stuffed in the older child's mouth so he could at least breathe, despite Justice's disapproving frown.

As NayNay mouthed the words "thank you," Cree made a mental note to tell his grandmother he loved her. Maybe Sunday morning he would even go to church with her.

Suddenly he heard a noise in the rear of the house that captured his full attention.

Finally free from gagging for air, the two usually talkative, mischievous brothers sat immobile, duct-taped tightly to the chair, sharing the same thoughts while staring at their auntie Nay begging the men who'd intruded their once-secure home to spare all of their lives. The one man who'd taken the socks out of their mouths seemed like he was the nicer of the two and would maybe let them go if they did as they were told. Even at a young age, the boys weren't fools. They were hood raised and knew the odds weren't in their favor. It was apparent to them that the other man, the one with the gap in his teeth like Florida Evans's from the *Good Times* reruns they watched every day, was the leader and called most of the shots. He didn't play and meant business. So for the time being, they followed instructions. Yet in the back of the older boy's naive mind, he still plotted to escape and beat up the man who'd slammed him to the ground.

NayNay closed her eyes for a few seconds, trying to restore her self-control. Thankful to Cree for taking the sock out of her nephews' mouths, she felt some sort of momentary connection with him. There was something in his expression that seemed familiar. It was a look she'd seen plenty of times in the mirror herself while growing up in a single-parent household with a neglectful mother who cared more about partying, fucking, getting blown, and running the hardcore Detroit streets than her own children. Maybe that was the true reason she and her sack-chasing sister turned out the way they did. Nevertheless, NayNay didn't have time to figure out the strange link she and Cree appeared to share or rehash her tragic past. Right now, she had to try to bargain with the both dudes into letting the kids free, letting her loose, and lastly, letting her son's daddy live.

Lost in thought of the speech she was going to try to concoct to convince Cree and Justice to leave, she was soon brought back to the present reality of the awful moment as her small son Maurice, who was whining, made his way from the room he'd been sleeping in. Luckily the summer cold he was suffering from, along with the Children's Tylenol drops he was given, had blessed him with avoiding the life-lasting nightmarish sights and sounds of his mother and cousins being tortured up until now. Once again looking up at Cree as he was her personal savior, a still-restrained NayNay hoped he would shed one more act of kindness toward her and her family in the way of allowing her innocent baby to come to her side.

Look at these suckers, Justice reflected as he watched his boy and NayNay share some sort of magical dumb-ass moment in time. *I oughta take that slut in the basement and put some of this hot lead up in her ass,* he considered. Peeking out the front window, he saw an old lady in the yard across the street handing Last Chance a few empty bottles to add to his collection. Glancing back, he saw NayNay's son, clad only in a diaper, emerge from a rear bedroom, wiping sleep out of the corners of his eyes. Listening to the child repeatedly call out for his no-good mother, Justice felt a sudden surge of hate come over him.

Born addicted to prescription drugs, with a lazy eye, Justice was seemingly cursed from conception. He'd been told his mother was serving prison time and he came into the world behind bars. Suffering from a severe learning disability, he learned to fend for himself. By hook or by crook, Justice had to make it happen. The forever-heartless alleyways, pimps, whores, drug addicts, and old-school, real-life gangsters from back in the day were his parents and the sole reason he was alive today.

Justice was 100 percent a product of his environment, not believing in any consequences to his often-outrageous actions or savage lifestyle. He was Detroit! The only thing he was loyal to daily was his own survival. Whether it meant robbing, killing, or stealing from a human being from eight to eighty, if it put food in his stomach, clothes on his back, and a roof over his head, it was all fair game.

The fact that Justice allowed Moe Mack to get away with giving him and his boy Cree a weak-ass package twice in a row without some sort of a fatal confrontation jumping off was nothing short of what Detroit homicide detectives down at 1300 Beaubien jokingly referred to as a motherfucking miracle in the hood.

After three or four grueling minutes of the irritated baby unsuccessfully trying to get his still-restrained mother to hold him, Cree couldn't take it any longer. Finding out that the child was probably hungry, as well as wet, he went into the filthy kitchen. Shortly, he returned with a small cup of milk and a couple of saltine crackers to soothe the baby's cries. Picking the boy up, he took him back to the room he'd been sleeping in, changed his diaper, and placed him in a playpen instead of on the mattress he was originally asleep on. Making sure the little boy was content, Cree then rejoined NayNay, Justice, and the two older children in the front room of the house. There he was met with different comments from each adult.

"Listen, I appreciate you helping my son." NayNay choked back the tears after seeing a man who wasn't her child's father or even someone whose dick she sucked be so nice to Maurice Jr. "I would've done it myself but—"

Seeing her trying to manipulate his boy with that yin-yang bitch shit hoes tried to run on niggas, Justice intervened, throwing major salt in NayNay's game. "Stop playing! You wasn't gonna do jack shit. That li'l bastard probably been running around here heavy in the diaper for hours with your trifling, no-good ass!" He then turned his verbal assault on Cree. "And damn motherfucker! Who the hell ya ass trying to be, the stepdaddy or something? Bet money, if this trick weren't tied up, she wouldn't have no words for ya gullible ass!"

"Nigga, chill." A fed-up Cree shook his head. "What you want me to do, let the li'l fella starve? What you got against kids anyway? Damn!"

"What?" Justice's head tilted to the side. "Fuck a kid! Them motherfuckers ain't shit but another mouth to feed and a child support case waiting to happen! You'll see when ya girl drag ya ass down in front of the judge and they gang rape ya pockets! Talk that shit then!"

"Whatever, dude." Cree laughed. "Ain't Greedy over there on the east side with a big belly?"

"So fucking what? It ain't mine, and even if it were I ain't claiming the bastard! Trust that! It's every man for himself in Detroit, nigga!"

Almost seconds apart, interrupting their little disagreement, both guys received text messages from none other than their intended target for the evening, Mr. Moe Mack himself. He informed them both to meet him up on Linwood and Davison at the KFC, seven forty-five sharp to grab some new work.

"Ain't this some shit! No, that faggot ain't trying to push no more of that weak garbage on us!" Justice fumed as he paced the floor with malice in his heart and revenge in his mind. "He got me all fucked up!"

Cree felt the same way when it came to his money. That was one issue he and Justice definitely had no problem with. "You right! I know ol' boy don't think we about to pay him off so soon on this garbage!" He tossed onto the table a brown paper bag filled with the rest of the pathetic dope they couldn't sell to a rookie undercover cop trying to arrest a nigga for jaywalking. "Fuck Moe Mack in the ass! I ain't 'bout to take no more losses! Shit! I got people to feed too!" He looked at another incoming text, this time from his pregnant girlfriend.

Chapter Twenty-two

"Oh, well, fuck it! I guess when they finish tricking somewhere or shooting dice they'll get back so they can get their package tightened up."

It was nearing 8:00 p.m. and Moe Mack had sent texts to Justice and Cree three more times, not receiving a reply from either. Before heading to NayNay's, he stopped at the liquor store to grab, of course, her pack of oh-so-important Newports. He also needed a bottle of Grey Goose. He knew he'd need it to take the edge off of him having to suffer the headache of hearing NayNay's complaining voice the rest of the evening until he hooked back up with his homeboy Keith. Not being able to get out the car, he was met by a drunk but sincerely pissed-off Last Chance.

"Those bad-ass nephews of yours knocked my buggy over earlier, and the big one spit on me!"

"Look, I done told you a hundred different times them kids is my baby mama's family, not mine!"

"It's the same thang to me, Maurice!" a still-aggravated Last Chance slurred rebelliously, following him into the same store he was thrown out of just hours earlier. "Them boys ain't got any kind of respect for old people like y'all did! Just because I'm messed up now ain't no call for them to treat me like I ain't still a man!"

Moe Mack, knowing Last Chance ever since he was a small child himself growing up across the street from where his own son lived now, gave the old man the decency to listen to his complaints. In all actuality, back in the day, before he got smoked out, Last Chance, who used to work the midnight shift at Chrysler, had a wife and a son, who was Moe Mack's best friend until he went away to college. It was for that trip down memory lane and that reason alone he even entertained any sort of conversation with the dirty, unshaven, drug-addicted alcoholic.

"Listen, I'ma tell you what." Moe Mack grabbed his bag after paying for his items and headed out the door toward his car. "Come by NayNay's later and I'ma hook you up with all the empty bottles they got." Satisfied that a few dollars would be adequate payback for the humiliating act of getting spat on and bested by two kids young enough to be his grandchildren, Last Chance agreed as Moe Mack, whom he'd taken on his family vacations years ago, bent the corner and went out of sight.

Cree and Justice had been arguing for what seemed like hours. NayNay and her nephews, who were all suffering from the agonizing torture of their circulation being cut off by the tightness of the duct tape, were forced to listen. As the clock slowly ticked, the two drug dealers turned kidnappers realized it was nearing eight. Knowing Moe Mack should be on his way, they put their petty beef to rest so as to concentrate on the real reason they'd spent their afternoon posted in a house with a loudmouth, perpetrating ho and three kids: money.

It was five after eight and the target was right on time. Turning his car into NayNay's driveway, Moe Mack switched the loud, bumping music off, throwing the car in park. Reaching over, he snatched the bag off the passenger seat and was on his way to the front porch when he was stopped by nosy old Mrs. Perkins signaling for him to come over. *Damn, now what she want? First Last Chance then her! Old people be tripping!*

Gun in hand, Justice nervously peeked out the window when he heard Moe Mack pull up. When he stepped out of the BMW Justice always admired and was envious of, his eye twitched, and his wife beater became drenched with sweat. Eagerly he informed Cree the shit was about to go down and to get ready. "All right, nigga! He all by himself. So when he come in, I'm gonna hit him with this motherfucker"—he waved his pistol—"then bum-rush dude to the ground."

"Don't worry, dawg! I got ya back!" Having no choice but to cover his ass, Cree apologetically stuffed socks back in each child's mouth, ensuring they wouldn't scream out when their little cousin's daddy came in the house, warning him that something was wrong.

"Please, y'all! Don't do this!" a teary-eyed NayNay begged, causing Justice to rush over, covering her mouth once again with tape before immediately returning to the sheet-covered window.

Seeing his supplier finish talking to the gray-haired lady across the street, Justice's heart raced rapidly. His adrenalin rose with each step Moe Mack took toward the stairs of the house. "Get ready, Cree!" his raspy voice loudly whispered as he crept behind the door, posted for whatever. "He on the porch! Let's make this lame pay!"

Damn, what am I doing? was the only thought racing through Cree's mind as he started realizing what was about to go down and what could ultimately take place if Justice had his way. *Damn. Damn. Damn! I'm tripping! Why did I listen to this crazy motherfucker?*

Listening to the key turn the lock on the steel gate and then hearing the main door slightly crack open, Justice took a deep breath, as did everyone else in the hot, stuffy, closed-in house.

Seconds before Moe Mack stepped inside the house, a tan and black minivan packed with teenagers roared up in the driveway. Screeching its tires, it stopped only inches away from Moe Mack's parked BMW. Much to the disgust of old Mrs. Perkins, when Yak and his boys swung open the doors, offensive music filled the entire block.

"What up doe?" Moe Mack left the porch to see what was up with several of his loyal crew.

Yak, the driver, turned down the sounds, already reading the expression on his boss's face. "What up doe? I ain't wanna say shit, but good looking out on that hookup! We about to head out to Chandler Park now. You should hang!"

Staring back at NayNay's, his first mind wanted him to jump back in the ride and hang out for the rest of the night, but he knew good and damn well he'd have to beat the brakes off his baby mama if he didn't at least give the trifling female her pack of Newports. "Nah, I'm good. Y'all go get fucked up for a brother."

"You sure?" Yak finished off his open beer.

"No doubt. I'm about to go in here and chill with this." Moe Mack held up the brown bag he was holding.

"All right then, but yo, I need to take a leak. You think ya girl would mind?" Yak held his dick in his hands as his boys jumped out of the van, claiming the same.

Perched down by the door, Justice didn't know what to do next. *Shit, if Yak and all 'em come in this motherfucker we done! Fuck, fuck, fuck!* He almost wanted to run to the back door and bust out. Even though NayNay and her nephews had seen his and Cree's faces and could easily identify them, at least they'd both be alive and have a fighting chance. *Oh, shit, here they come! Damn! Ain't this a bitch!*

"Yo, real rap!" Moe Mack really ain't want all his workers inside his girl's house, so he stopped them dead in their tracks. "There's way too many of y'all, and Yak, you already know how NayNay be tripping!"

Agreeing with Moe Mack, much to Justice and Cree's relief, Yak and the crew drove around to the alley to take a leak then headed off to the park.

After apologizing once again to Mrs. Perkins for the noise, Moe Mack made his way back up on the porch. Chirping his alarm on the Beemer, he pushed the door open, stepping inside NayNay's where all hell broke loose. Snatching Moe Mack, completely caught off guard, inside the entranceway of the house by his expensive shirt, Justice simultaneously slammed the side of his 9 mm twice against his temple, knocking him to the ground. Justice smiled with excitement as the small boys looked away in fear.

Dazed by the traumatic force of the hard blow he'd just taken to the head, Moe Mack was unable to resist or fight back. Cree automatically removed the gun from his waistband before quickly wrapping his hands and feet with the remaining rolls of duct tape.

As Moe Mack lay on the floor, trying to come to grips as to what exactly was going on, a violent, obviously mentally unstable Justice followed his initial attack with stomping him in the upper stomach area, no doubt cracking a few ribs. Even with suffering the horrifying pain he was experiencing, the strong-willed, always-polished Moe Mack refused to give his assailants the pleasure of hearing him yell out in agony.

"What up doe, playboy?" Justice sarcastically questioned as he leaned over in his face. "Did you text me earlier or what?"

"What the fuck?" Moe Mack coughed, throwing up the food he'd eaten for lunch. "Have you lost ya damn mind, motherfucker?"

"Naw, Negro, New World Order! I'm the one asking all the damn questions up in this bitch!" Justice laughed, holding his nut sac. "I'm the boss and you taking the loss! So deal with it!"

Cree stood way over to the side of the room, almost ashamed to make eye contact with Moe Mack, who up until a few weeks ago had been plenty stand up with both him and Justice. "Go easy, dawg! We ain't here for all that." He finally stepped out of the shadows, revealing that he also was in on the ambush. "You bugging out! Slow ya roll!"

Dragging him by his legs, Justice got Moe Mack near the fireplace where his baby mama was sobbing uncontrollably. "Aww, look at the happy couple. Ike and Tina in this motherfucker!" He continued to prove he had the upper hand.

"Straight up! You better kill me, faggot, 'cause if y'all don't . . ." Moe Mack swore, still remaining strong.

"Miss me with all that," Justice laughed.

"On my word! Y'all faggots done walking around Detroit! The streets gonna run red with motherfuckers hunting y'all down!"

"Whatever you say, boss hog." Justice dismissed the empty threat. "That ain't a problem at all! I'ma have to take that chance!"

Cree halted any further back-and-forth arguing and wisely tried getting down to the real reason they were there. "Look, Moe, it's like this here." He shamefully paced the floor, still avoiding direct eye contact. "You done gave us a bunch of garbage the last few times we copped. And straight up, we still been out there trying to make that shit happen, but there's only so much one nigga can take, ya feel me? I got a baby on the way and bills to pay!"

"Damn, dawg!" Moe Mack spit a clot of blood from his mouth that'd dripped down from a nice-size gash Justice had made with his pistol. "Is that what the fuck all this bullshit is about?"

"Yeah, ho-ass faggot," Justice angrily interjected. "Don't you think we wanna ride around Big Willie style, flossed-out, stuntin' on fools?"

"Real talk, if y'all pussies would've answered y'all cells, y'all would've found out what was going down, but y'all held all up in my baby mama house making the worst mistake of y'all life!"

"Nigga, what?" Justice raced over, smacking Moe Mack like he was his woman who'd just gotten out of pocket. "Who the fuck you talking to like that? You owe us!"

"I swear, boy! You's damn lucky y'all caught a brother slippin' on the humble, but it's all good and gonna be only better in a few! Remember what I said. The streets gonna run red!"

"What, you trying to get tough?" Justice raised his hand again as Moe Mack refused to flinch. "You might need to step up or step off!"

Cree yanked his boy's arm back and stepped to Moe Mack like a man. "Dude, what is you talking about?"

"I'll tell you crab-ass niggas what," he said, eye fucking them both as blood continued to drip down. "Why don't y'all holler at ya boy Denard or Bama Bob or Yak, who just pulled off? They'll let y'all know what's really good out in them streets."

Following Moe Mack's suggestion, Cree flipped open his cell, calling Bama Bob as Justice held his gun on the duct-taped couple. "What up doe?"

"What it do, playa?"

"I was just calling to see what y'all had popping for the night and shit." Cree chose his words carefully, trying to peep the situation out.

"Shittttt, me and my people 'bouts to party and get fucked up as hell behind that shit ol' boy hooked us up on!" Bama Bob joked as he lit up the biggest, fattest blunt he could roll. "Two and a half goddamn free ounces of uncut, un-stepped-on powder and our old tickets all squashed! Moe Mack really showed us love this time around, making up for that bold shit he had us out here pushing! We heading out to hook up with Yak and the crew in a few. Hit me up if you hanging!"

Cree was dumbfounded, realizing the man they had tied up on the floor was right. He and Justice had made the worst mistake of their lives. *Shit! Shit! Shit!* Now the only thing was how in the hell could he make things proper? *Ain't this a bitch!* Ending the call, he stood silent until Justice nudged him with his elbow.

"Well, guy, what Bama Bob's good country ass say?"

"Yeah, Cree." Moe Mack spat once more as NayNay nuzzled her body close to his for comfort. "Tell us all what ol' boy said."

Cree took a deep breath, rubbing his hand down the front of his face. "We done fucked up!"

There wasn't much that could be said after Cree repeated what Bama Bob had said. He was in way too deep to turn around now without fear of retaliation from Moe Mack, but he couldn't bring himself to go any further. Although in denial, Cree racked his brain to find a way out, yet all seemed lost. What to do? Now as he dropped his head, confused, he had to worry about either catching a case or a bullet if Moe Mack had his way. *Shit, maybe both.* Let alone the rest of the fellas' vengeance for taking such a good connect out the game if they ever found out what they'd done. *Why did I listen to this dude? He always dragging me into some dumb shit! Now I'm fucked!*

Against Justice's wishes, Cree, full of regret and remorse for all his unwarranted actions, took the socks back out of the petrified kid's mouths so at least they could breathe and their untimely deaths by means of suffocation wouldn't be on his conscience.

Still going hard and true to the mission, Justice, on the other hand, didn't seem to give two hot damns in hell what Bama Bob had said. "Okay, so this nigga wanna make thangs right! Big fucking deal! That still don't erase the fact that he gave us the bold shit in the first place!"

"You right, dude, but—"

"But nothing." Justice roughly placed a piece of duct tape over Moe Mack's mouth to stop him from putting any more sabotaging thoughts into Cree's weakening mind. "Stop being such a pussy!"

Noticing the effect the long day was having on Cree, Justice opted to slow his roll to make sure he and his boy were still on the same page and knew what had to happen next. Reaching down for the bag that was in Moe Mack's arm when he came in, he took out the bottle of Grey Goose and took it to the head before passing it to Cree, who was sweating like a Hebrew slave.

"Come on, guy." Justice gave Cree a half smile. "Relax for a minute, take a swig, and think. You and me like brothers. Don't let this cat get inside ya head!"

Chapter Twenty-three

Deciding they would ride it out in the crib until the summer sun completely went down and then sneak out unnoticed, the duo, opposite as night and day, had to make the best of the rest of their time there. To Justice, bottle still in tow, that meant ransacking NayNay's house, room to room, stuffing pillowcases with whatever else he thought he or his on-again, off-again girlfriend nicknamed Greedy wanted. Relieving a still-bleeding Moe Mack of his cash, jewelry, iPhone, and of course keys to the Beemer, nothing was off-limits as he gathered the kids' PlayStation along with all their games.

It was now a little past nine, and needless to say, things had gotten way out of control. Buzzing from finishing off the majority of the liquor, a drained Justice kicked back on the couch in one of his infamous zoned-out trances. He had no idea whatsoever that he had all the rotten DNA characteristics of three generations before him: Terrell, Kamal, and even his great-granddaddy Willy Dale. His tainted bloodline ran deep. With his lazy eye closing even more, he soon took on the strange appearance of a monster to the exhausted children, who had both urinated on themselves over an hour ago when he halted Cree's sympathetic attempts to free them.

"Dawg, at least let me fix them something to drink and loosen that tape. They lips is dry and cracked as a motherfucker," Cree argued, heading into the kitchen, searching for a glass. "What if they was ya family, dude?"

"Do what ya do," Justice slurred out with a loud, non-chalant tone. "I'm tired of all you whining pussies around here, especially her!" He pointed at NayNay, who was setting him on fire with her eyes as her injured baby daddy lay slumped over, semiconscious on her lap.

Setting a huge ghetto-style pitcher of Kool-Aid onto the crowded countertop, Cree was just about to pour a glass for both kids to share as he was interrupted by the sounds of the radio being turned on. That was followed by NayNay's muffled screams coming from the living room along with the boys yelling for help. Taking his gun out of his waistband, not knowing what to expect next, Cree cautiously bent the corner and was instantly pissed at what he was seeing.

"Dude! Have you fucking done lost your mind?" Cree ran over, snatching an almost-salivating Justice off of a hysterical NayNay. He now had her T-shirt ripped down the middle, exposing her breasts. Shoving him as hard as he could across the room into the closet door, Cree stuck out his chest. "Ain't you got us both fucked around enough with all your bright-ass ideas? Now you want me to catch a charge for taking place in a rape? Nigga, please!" he ranted with anger, wishing he could turn back the hands of time. "You got me all the way twisted! You going too far!"

Stumbling backward, Justice shook it off but got on balance quickly, returning several accusations and insults of his own. "How the hell I get your ass in this? You the one need extra cheese all the time, not me! Your ass always the one be giving your old granny some bill money! And bet! You the one with a kid on the way you always whining about buying bullshit for who probably ain't even yours!" Justice spitefully alleged, finally going too far with the stuff he was saying. "Your girl probably somewhere right now sucking the next nigga's dick! Matter of fact, I might hit that pregnant pussy later!"

"I'll tell you what, guy." Cree shrugged his shoulders, having dealt with his homeboy's outburst time after time when he was faded beyond his limit. "I know you high right about now, so I'm gonna let that last remark about my girl slide and give your punk ass a pass! But what you really need to do is go splash some water on your face and chill the hell out! You must be off your meds!"

Justice wasn't in the mood to deal with his boy's holier-than-thou attitude. He was past being forced to hear one of his long-winded speeches about his mental state or one of the many prescriptions he was supposed to be taking. Deciding he did need to get back on top of his game and pull the rest of the plan together, he took off his now-torn wife beater. Disappearing into the kitchen, he removed a gang of dirty dishes from the sink, turned the cold water on full blast, and let the flow from the nozzle cover his head. Leaning up, he used a soiled dishrag to wipe his red, shaded eyes. As he went to the doorway, overhearing Cree in the living room talking slick about him behind his back and then apologizing to that slut on his behalf like he was some sort of a monster, Justice felt his blood boil.

Who in the fuck this nigga Cree think he is turning on me like we ain't been boys since back in the day? This ho done got this nigga sprung and he ain't even had the pussy! He in there acting like he better than me! Me and him came up together and now he tripping! I swear niggas be fake as fuck!

Feeling betrayed, Justice tried maintaining his composure as he ducked back in the kitchen, pounding himself on the forehead with the palm of his still-damp hand. Trying desperately to figure out what his next move would be, Justice stared down at his bare chest and all the wounds from cigarette burns one of his many foster mothers had inflicted upon him. *Another person against my black ass! They all out to get me!* Mistakenly assuming Cree had overplayed his position flipping the script, he now wanted nothing more than to get revenge on NayNay for her apparent mind games that he'd believed manipulated ol' boy to turn his back on him. Justice then glanced in the far corner of the kitchen counter, seeing his opportunity staring him right in the face. *Hell yeah! This'll teach that manipulative bitch a lesson!*

Cree covered NayNay with a towel that was on the arm of the couch. "Like I said, we ain't mean for things to turn out like this. And Moe Mack always been all right with me! That's real talk!" Trying to convince her of his sincerity, Cree then told her he was about to give her sniffling nephews something to drink and untie them so they could get out of those wet clothes and at least go in the room where her baby was sleeping. Bumping into Justice coming out of the kitchen, Cree noticed an expression on his face that was stranger than usual, but he attributed it to the bottle of Grey Goose that obviously still had a tight grip on his emotions. "You good?"

"Yeah, dude." Justice grinned, sitting at the table across from the horrified kids. They dared not mutter a single sound as they saw the hideous vision of his disfigured chest and the various demonic jailhouse tattoos that covered his arms. "I'm more than good! And what y'all little niggas looking at? Y'all ain't never seen a true hood warrior?"

Shortly thereafter, Cree returned with a big glass of cherry Kool-Aid, holding it up to each child's dry lips. As they happily gulped it down, Justice watched like a hawk. Suddenly, like a ticking time bomb destined to explode, each child started suspiciously coughing, gagging, and throwing up, followed by some sort of weird convulsions. Seeing the look of enjoyment grace Justice's face as their bodies grew increasingly limp, Cree immediately concluded his best friend and road dawg had done something sinister.

Hurrying in an attempt to save each child's life, Cree bolted into the kitchen, grabbing a huge butcher knife to cut the duct tape shackles off NayNay's small nephews. *Awww, hell naw! He didn't!* Realizing what Justice had callously done, Cree couldn't believe his eyes. In a rush to pour the cold drink for the once-playful boys, he'd failed to notice an open bag of green pellets on the stove next to a spoon that was clearly used to crush them up. The label read: DANGER RAT POISON.

"No, the fuck you didn't, nigga," Cree belted out, running back in the room just in time to bear witness to each little boy shake and jerk once more before taking their final breaths. As they lay slumped over, still taped to the chair, totally unresponsive, Cree finally decided he'd had enough. The street thug was sick to his stomach. "You done messed around and killed some kids! Hell naw! That shit is fucked up! Some fucking little kids!"

NayNay struggled, kicking her feet the best she could, trying to break loose and somehow miraculously save her sister's kids' lives, but it was too late. No more summer days running through the sprinkler on the front grass or swinging at the playground. No more arguing over what cartoon to watch or who won the video game they constantly played. Old Last Chance would never have to worry about them knocking over his buggy again. The young boys were gone. Justice had murdered them just like that.

"Fuck them li'l bad-ass motherfuckers!"

"Naw, fuck you, Justice! I'm 'bout to bounce, guy!" Cree was in shock, not believing his own eyes. "I ain't gonna be a part of killing no kids! You gonna catch that case yourself! I ain't nothing like you!"

"Oh, it's like that? Now you wanna break out?" Justice jumped to his feet, turning the radio up louder. Stepping across NayNay, who was still fighting to break free, he zoned out. Running his tongue across the front of his teeth, he spat before snatching a throw pillow off the couch. "You think that shit is that easy?" He held the multicolored pillow down on Moe Mack's head, whipping out his 9 mm. "I don't give a fuck about nobody!" Unemotional and cold, he pulled the trigger, putting two hot slugs in his unconscious supplier. Justice's adrenaline rose. "You all up in this bullshit, and who the hell you think you talking to? You just like me!" He pounded his clenched fist to his chest.

Cree, seeing his road dawg had officially snapped, losing his damn mind, had no other choice but to bum-rush Justice if he wanted to get out of the house alive himself. So bracing for the fight of his life, he made his move, knocking the gun out of his boy's hand. Instantly he started delivering blow after blow to his midsection. As the two locked up, they fell to the ground, landing on top of Moe Mack's dead body. They then rolled toward NayNay, who was sweating buckets of perspiration still bucking to get free and out of the madhouse she was trapped in.

With the radio continuing to blast out the sounds of Jay-Z, no words were passed between the two as they battled relentlessly. A few punches later, Cree finally got the ups on a shirtless Justice. Wrapping his hands around his throat, he started strangling him, causing Justice's lazy eye to open wide. In an effort to get Cree off of him, Justice stretched his arm out. Finally searching for anything he could use as a weapon, he found what he needed to win the battle and took the opportunity. Grabbing the bronze fireplace poker, the crazed corner boy tightened his grip. NayNay watched in dismay as Justice raised the metal poker, stabbing the young father-to-be repeatedly in his skull, killing him almost instantaneously.

Pushing Cree's heavy corpse off him, a victorious, out-of-breath Justice stumbled to his feet, nursing a bloody, possibly broken nose and a chipped tooth. *Look at what you made me do,* he thought, looking down at Cree, who was flat on his back with his eyes wide open. *Why couldn't you just stick with the game plan and ride it out with a nigga? We would've both been on easy street.*

Things had gone all the way to the south in her once-perfect, sack-chasing life. At this point, NayNay could only pray for Justice to spare her and her baby's life, but she knew the odds weren't good. Horror-struck, seeing her sister's kids, her son's father, and the only man who could've stopped Justice and his murderous rampage all lying in their own bodily fluids, which were released when they took their last breaths, NayNay prepared herself for the worst.

Justice wiped the thick, mucus-filled blood from his nose, smearing it against the living room wall, and he laughed. Slowly he raised his foot up then slammed it down into the young mother's chest. "Ho, you done ruined everything!" Watching NayNay fall back, striking her head on the imitation marble floor surrounding the fireplace, Justice's manhood started to rise. Wanting to hear her last words before she left earth, he ruthlessly snatched the duct tape off her mouth, allowing her to speak.

"Why! Why! Why!" she questioned as she cried, squirming around on the floor with blood pouring from the rear of her skull.

Not having an inch of remorse for the murders he'd just committed, even his best friend Cree's, he unzipped his pants. Still zoned out, he took out his hard dick and started beating his meat to the rhythm of NayNay's petrified, erratic body movements. When he couldn't take it anymore, he busted a thick, hot stream of cum all over her face. Then without a second thought, he once again raised his foot, stomping the life out of NayNay, taking her out of the game for good. *Oh, well, fuck all they asses!*

Chapter Twenty-four

Not caring about who was looking or who might've heard the two fatal gunshots that'd claimed Moe Mack's existence, Justice brashly loaded all his stolen goods into the trunk of his newly obtained Beemer. Excited, he found the small duffle bag containing the work that must've been for him and Cree. For him, things couldn't get any better.

Justice now had cash, dope, expensive clothes, a new iPhone, a pocketful of NayNay's jewelry, three guns (counting Cree's and Moe Mack's), and a new ride. Best of all, he didn't have to share it with anyone. What could be fucking better? He thought he was finally about to live the black American Dream. *But I still need to handle one more thing before I'm ghost!* Strolling back into the house one last time, heading to the room where NayNay's small, innocent son was still sleeping, he focused in on the child. Trying to prove the point to no one but himself that he wasn't a total animal, completely out of character, the maniac took a couple of dollars from his pocket and placed it in the playpen next to the boy.

"Stay up. You might need this shit later on because Detroit definitely ain't got no type of love for a broke motherfucker, let alone a li'l dude with no parents!" He thought about his own disastrous childhood before turning the loud radio off and going back out to the car. He peeled out of the driveway.

"Who in the world is that child driving Maurice's car all fast and carrying on?" Nosy Mrs. Perkins asked her ex-husband, who was standing in the front yard begging from her as usual. "I just told him about all the noise and traffic that girlfriend of his has coming in and out."

"I dunno for sure. I'll ask him when I go over there to get the bottles he promised me." Last Chance looked across the street at NayNay's house. "But it sure looked like one of them corner boys!"

Damn, it's crowded at this motherfucker! Justice, now wearing one of the many outfits once belonging to Moe Mack that he'd stolen out of NayNay's house, proudly swerved the Beemer, with its custom license plates and chrome rims, up to the downtown club's front entrance. Stepping out stuntin', throwing the valet an extra twenty dollars outta Moe Mack's bank roll to park his shit up front, he went inside to get his party on, broken nose, chipped tooth, and all.

Flossing up in VIP, surrounded by two bad bitches and not once caring about the deadly deeds he'd committed, Justice popped at least three bottles, getting his big shot on. Flicking up, taking seven or eight pictures of himself with various females, he felt he was a motherfucking boss to the tenth degree. With one of the huge plasma televisions mounted throughout the club broadcasting breaking news of several different homicide scenes in a range of locations within the city of Detroit, the ruthless killer seemed he couldn't care less. He was deep off into his zone.

Without warning, a gang of police came bursting through the front door of the crowded club, asking the bouncer several questions while showing him what Justice thought was possibly a snapshot. Checking out every inch of the club's interior with his eyes, he quickly realized Detroit's finest were blocking all visible exits to the street.

Shit! I swear on everything I love, I damn straight hope these busters ain't here for my black ass, 'cause a nigga like me ain't in the mood to go back to jail! Not tonight! That ain't part of the plan! Pouring himself another drink from the bottle, the intoxicated murderer watched the police like a hawk while the females he was sitting with got scared, never being in a raid before. As the police made their way up the stairs in his direction, Justice ran his tongue across his chipped tooth then smiled. Calmly he sat back in the booth, listening to the beat of the loud music vibrate in the club, waiting for what would fucking happen after what fucking came next. In the meantime, the once-petty street hustler turned murder made a toast to his childhood friend he was forced to body, Cree.

No hard feelings, my nigga. You how the game go! If you hadn't been such a straight pussy, you'd be here with me getting your drink on and not stretched out in the city morgue!

Last Chance, desperate for the returnable bottles promised to him for being spit on, made his way across the street full of potholes. After watching one of the corner boys from earlier speed off in his car, Last Chance knew for certain that Moe Mack was still indeed posted inside of NayNay's house. Hopefully, he was still in a generous mood. With every step he took, the alcoholic copper hustler kept looking over his shoulder, ensuring no one was messing with his raggedy buggy, which was now stuffed with nothing of any true value to anyone other than himself.

"Maurice! Maurice!" Having been barred from ever stepping foot on NayNay's front porch, he shouted out Moe Mack's government name at the side window located near the rear of the driveway. "It's me! I came for those bottles you said I could have!" Even with his ex-wife standing on her porch, spying on his every move at the home that was always packed with commotion, Last Chance refused to give up his plight to get those much-needed bottles, even as he heard the blaring sounds of a baby's cries come from the house. "Maurice! It's me! Maurice!" he yelled louder, trying to drown out the baby's piecing screams.

"Are you crazy, old man?" Mrs. Perkins hissed with contempt at his over-the-top actions. "Hush!"

"Yo, Moe Mack." He switched up names, seeing if his son's friend answered to that. "I hear the baby crying, so I know you probably busy tending to him," he reasoned. "So whenever you get a chance I'll be out here waiting!"

"You need to stop all that hollering and carrying on!" Mrs. Perkins insisted loudly enough for Last Chance to hear as he marched from the back toward the front of NayNay's. "It's a sin and a shame how you out here behaving for some plastic! There oughta be a law!"

The one-time love of his life was 100 percent correct. Last Chance knew he was definitely out of order in his behavior and had been for some time. Nevertheless, at this point in his pitiful life, he had no pride left when it could possibly come between him and a drink or a blow. He had no limits.

"Well, do you think you can you do me a favor, honey?" He tried pouring on the charm in the hope that she would show some mercy on him. "Maybe just a dollar or two?"

"I tell you what," she bargained, trying to shut him up. "You take these bags of top soil around to the backyard and spread it evenly on the lawn, and when you finish, I'll give that few dollars to you."

Knowing he didn't want to run the risk of Moe Mack leaving and missing out on the bottles, he opted to help his ex-wife out so he could stay close to NayNay's without hearing her nagging him to death.

Chapter Twenty-five

"Yo, Bama Bob, What up doe?" Keith nervously questioned as he checked his watch.

"You got it, playa, what's the deal?" Bama Bob answered in his down-deep country dirty-South accent, which was his trademark with the city boys and females who were easy to impress. "What it do? What you need pimping?"

"Yeah, listen. I've been trying like a motherfucker to get in touch with that nigga Moe, but he ain't picking up."

"Oh, yeah." Bama Bob repeatedly rubbed down on his unshaven beard. "He was by here a couple of hours ago tightening us all up."

"Yeah, I know." Keith's voice was noticeably nervous as he spoke. "When that guy left me we was both dirty as a fuck. That's why I'm trying to track his ass down. Ya feel me?"

"No doubt, no doubt." Blazing up a blunt, Bama Bob then remembered Cree calling him about an hour or so ago, and from the conversation he knew that he and Justice still hadn't been blessed yet with the new package. "I'll make a trip back to the hood in a few, but in the meantime, call that nigga Cree or Justice. I think they still haven't hollered at dawg!"

"All right, that'll work," Keith agreed. "And, real rap, hit me once you get over around the way. He probably just laid up with that no-good baby mama of his and she done turned off his phone."

"That's a bet. One."
"One."

Getting finished as quickly as possible, Last Chance snatched the three one-dollar bills out his ex-wife's hand, stuffing them deep into the front pocket of his filthy pants. Not once forgetting about the bottles promised to him, he wasted no time heading back across the street as a proud, holier-than-thou Mrs. Perkins watched on in embarrassment. Even though Last Chance stayed drunk and high, after the half hour he spent slaving for his former better half, his entire buzz was totally killed. So he knew it wasn't his mind playing tricks on him when he heard crying sounds still coming from the rear bedroom window of NayNay's house.

It's been over a good hour or so and they still letting that baby cry? Last Chance stood silent, listening to the child seem to walk from the front of the house to the back of the house, never once letting up on screaming out for his mommy. *I know this child's mother ain't no good, but Maurice wouldn't let his son just cry this long.*

Sarcastically Mrs. Perkins taunted, "Why you over there begging and carrying on? What's wrong? Are you too exhausted from doing some real work?" Not receiving an answer, suddenly she felt a strange feeling come over her that caused her to come off her porch and onto her front perfectly kept grass. "I said what's wrong? Why on God's green earth are you just standing over there like that?"

Walking toward the front of the house and NayNay's stairs, Last Chance was then joined by his nosy ex-wife, who soon heard the sobbing as well. "You know I ain't supposed to go on this girl porch, but I think something is wrong in there. That baby been crying since earlier.

Why don't you go up there and ring the bell or knock on the door?"

Hearing the deafening sounds of the baby boy crying coming from her young, irresponsible neighbor's house was nothing new to Mrs. Perkins. She'd had it out with NayNay on more than several occasions about just that very subject, not to mention that of her two nephews' rude, obnoxious behavior. However, being a mother, as well as a grandmother, Mrs. Perkin's maternal instinct kicked in, realizing these cries she and Last Chance were hearing were like those of a child in agony and pain, not a baby needing a mere diaper change or a bottle. With her ex-husband leaning on the handrail, now truly in desperate need of a drink, Mrs. Perkins bravely made her way up the stairs, knocking on the black steel gate.

"Hello, hello." Her voice rang out as the baby's cries got louder. "Maurice, do you hear me? It's Mrs. Perkins! NayNay, I know y'all hear that baby of y'all's!" Hearing nothing but the child, she glanced over her shoulder at Last Chance as if to say, "Watch my back." She then eased over to the other side of the porch. Slowly crouching down with her hand on the concrete windowpane, she tried with no success to see through the sheets. *This girl needs some serious home training. Sheets for curtains. Hmph! Hmph! Hmph! It just don't make no kind of sense.*

"Well?" Last Chance asked as his hands started to shake. "What you see, huh? What you see?"

"Shut up, old man!" was the only reply he got before a worried Mrs. Perkins knocked again, only this time on the glass.

Almost immediately after knocking, she and Last Chance got the shock of a lifetime as the small, whimpering toddler pulled back the dirty sheet, revealing himself.

"What the hell?" Last Chance didn't care about NayNay's house rules as he came stumbling up the stairs onto the porch by his trembling ex-wife's side.

"Oh, my God! Good Lord!" Mrs. Perkins screamed out, seeing the little boy's face and body covered in what appeared to be blood. "Somebody, call the police!" she frantically yelled as the small child's hands banged on the other side of the window in an attempt to get out. "Somebody call the police! Oh, sweet baby Jesus, help me! Help me!"

As the sobbing tot continued to snatch at the sheets while leaving his petite bloody handprints on the glass, Last Chance got a much better look inside of the usually lively house. In clear sight he observed NayNay's motionless body laid out on the living room floor in a pool of blood near the fireplace. Moe Mack's legs were sticking out from behind the coffee table. A third person appeared to be lying in the corner, but Last Chance couldn't quite make out who it was.

In a matter of minutes, sirens were blaring, and a multitude of red and blue lights were flashing. Detroit's finest swarmed NayNay's house. With weapons drawn, as neighbors looked on, they kicked the door in, practically snatching it out of the frame.

"Son of a bitch!" was all the neighbors heard one officer say as he exited the horrific crime scene, shaking his head in unreserved disgust. He had a bloodied Maurice Jr. clutched in his arms.

Chapter Twenty-six

"Good evening, residents of Metro Detroit. The bloodshed and body count continue to rise tonight. I'm here on Fullerton Street between Linwood and Dexter Avenue, which is located on the city's west side. Sadly, tragedy has once again struck our economically stressed and crime-infested town. After several frantic 911 calls were received, police burst through the doors of the home located behind me." The reporter pointed up toward NayNay's taped-off house as a crowd of shocked neighbors gathered around.

"What they found behind those doors, no one, including many veteran officers with as many as twenty years on the job, could stomach. The victims, three young adults, were found brutally murdered. Two of them were bound and gagged, and one was killed seemingly execution style. However, what makes this crime scene more heinous and heart-wrenching than the other breaking-news homicides we've reported on this evening is that unfortunately there were two other victims, both children of elementary school age."

The angry, concerned crowd continued to grow as the lights from the camera shone bright. "Our sources tell us both small children were found duct-taped together in a chair and possibly poisoned. The older of the two boys also appears to have been beaten. Identities are being withheld pending notifications of families. But joining us live we now have newly appointed Detroit Police Chief

Evan Warrington, who has just arrived on the crime scene. Chief, what can you tell us?"

"Yes, well, um, it has indeed been a night, or should I say a day, of complete chaos in Detroit. Within a short twenty-four-hour span we now have at least seventeen confirmed homicides and more than nine or ten shootings that have resulted in non-life-threatening injuries. Our prayers go out to the victims' families, and I also want to reassure our law-abiding citizens that the department is working over-time to regain order and diplomacy in the streets." The chief then gave a long, cold stare into the camera as he made his point clear. "These criminals will not take over our city! These savage, senseless acts will definitely not be tolerated, and those responsible will be apprehended and swiftly brought to justice. All available manpower has been called to duty, and no stone will be left unturned. Everyone breaking the law tonight in Detroit, I'm putting you on proper notice. We'll be coming for you in full force."

A group of elderly neighbors clapped as the camera continued rolling and the reporter shoved the micro-phone into the chief's face, holding him there. "Thank you, Chief. One last question: this has proven to be the deadliest day in Motown history. Do you have any suspects in any of the crimes as of yet?"

"At this time all leads are being aggressively followed, and we encourage the public to contact us with any information that will assist in our efforts. Thank you."

"Well, there you have it. The chief has ensured us that he and his officers will restore peace to Detroit. Live on the west side, Jayden James reporting for Channel 7 Action News."

Stepping out of the thick crowd of gawkers, Bama Bob, even though he was as gangster as the next nigga, couldn't believe what the hell was going on as the whispers of the victims' identities spread. His homeboy and connect, Moe Mack, was dead as a son of a bitch. He shook his head, coming to grips with the news. *I just seen that guy. He was good peoples. Whoever did this shit is gonna pay! It ain't gonna be over just like that!* He remembered exactly what Moe Mack had told Cree and Justice just hours earlier before dying.

"Follow my orders!" Chief Warrington instructed the head of the Gang Squad and SWAT units as Bama Bob and other residents listened to him bark out orders. "Kick in the doors of any and every suspected dope house in the city limits. I couldn't care less about warrants. We'll deal with the legalities later! I need some arrests made! If you see a stray dog or cat jaywalking, bring them in for questioning!"

Knowing he had to make sure he handled his business, warning everyone in his crew to shut down operations until things cooled off as well as spreading the bad news about Moe Mack's untimely demise, Bama Bob discreetly separated himself from the onlookers. Pulling his cell phone out, he was interrupted by Last Chance, who'd also emerged from the crowd.

"What up doe, old man?"

"Hey, Bama Bob." Last Chance's hands shook. "I know this ain't the time or the place, but can you spare a few dollars? I need a drink bad!"

"Come on now, dawg. Miss me with all that begging." He watched the medical examiner bring out black body bags. "My boy is in one of them motherfuckers!"

"I know." Last Chance lowered his head out of respect as each one passed. "Me and my wife called the police. We were the ones who found them."

"What?"

"Yeah. Maurice said I could have some bottles. So after that crazy corner boy drove off in his car, I went over there."

"What corner boy?" Bama Bob irately quizzed Last Chance, giving him his undivided attention. "Which one? Do I know the motherfucker?"

Last Chance continued to shake as two small body bags were brought out, undoubtedly housing the children's corpses. "I wasn't snitching or nothing like that, but like I told the police, it was the one with the lazy eye who be up there on Linwood. The loudmouth one." He shook as he spoke. "He put some stuff in Maurice's trunk and left. I thought he was going to the car wash or something. But now when I think about it, he was dressed too fancy to be washing any car."

"Justice." Bama Bob grew angry at the thought of knowing who might've killed his homeboy. "Is that who ya talking about? Justice's bitch nickel-hustlin' ass?"

"Yeah, that's his name! His eye stay half closed all the time." Last Chance nodded. "I dunno what happened inside of that girl's house, but his running buddy with the gap was in there dead right along with the rest of 'em." He looked puzzled. "And I thought they were friends."

"Who, young Cree?"

"Whatever his name is." Last Chance then sadly mumbled, "Or was."

Bama Bob tore Last Chance off a couple of twenties from his knot for the valuable 411, and he sent out a text exclusively to everyone he dealt with in the game. 187-187 shut down 187-187, he typed three or four times in a row, before sending out a different mass text that read that if anyone saw that nigga Justice on the streets or Moe Mack's Beemer, anywhere, to hit him up immediately with the location of both. After that he scrolled down his list of contacts, placing a call to Keith to deliver the tragic news of their fallen comrade.

Sitting in the car after delivering the devastating blow to Keith, Bama Bob starting receiving replies to his texts that his spots were shut down and all the workers had gone home until further notice. *Hell yeah, at least that's done!* In the barrage of incoming texts, one was more interesting than the others. It was from his girl from around the way, Ariel, telling him that she and her friends had just gotten turned away from the club downtown because the police had raided it. *And? Big deal!* He waited for the rest of the message to download. *Oh, shit!* was all he could think as he looked at a picture of Ariel posted up on the hood of Moe Mack's BMW.

"Yo, shawty!" Bama Bob wasted no time calling Ariel back. "Do me a solid and stay put. I'm on my way to you now, and real rap, keep an eye on Moe's car. Ya feel me? I'll be there in ten, fifteen minutes tops!"

"Not a problem, honey," Ariel replied as she and her half-dressed friends flirted with the many officers around the club's front entrance.

Calling back an enraged Keith, then all his crew, and telling them to meet him down at the club, Bama Bob started his engine just as NayNay's older sister and niece returned home from their trip out of town. Heartbreakingly, as the confused pair pushed through the crowd approaching their house, they would soon find out their lives would never be the same.

"Damn!" Bama Bob reached for his blunt, watching the two hysterical females break down in his rearview mirror as he drove off. "This shit is fucked up! I swear to God, that dusty-ass nigga Justice is a dead man when I see him!" He blazed up, bending the corner, heading toward the freeway. "A fucking dead man!"

"Damn, now I wish I hadn't texted that country fool back." Ariel tugged down on her baby T-shirt so the officer guarding the front entrance of the club could get a good view of her breasts. "'Cause a bitch like me could be getting all of ol' boy over there city paycheck or trying to push up on Moe Mack's fine ass when he comes outside, especially if he ain't with that stank-ass baby mama of his! Now Bama Bob gonna be cock blocking."

"Yeah, probably so, but we gotta wait for Stephanie to come out anyway," Ariel's friend smartly replied, anxious to get their mournful drinking started. "And you know since her man Tre just got killed on the west side, she's gonna be needing us to stay by her side no matter what."

"You right," Ariel conceded, knowing Tre's body wasn't even cold yet, and they were out getting their drink on. "It's just, damn! There's so many dicks around this motherfucker!"

Still flirting with the officer, just as Ariel leaned back on the hood of Moe Mack's BMW like it was hers, from around the side of the building her girl Stephanie eased up, clutching her purse with a look of panic and determination. Ten minutes later Bama Bob, followed by a small team of street soldiers, drove up, parking across the street from the heavily guarded nightclub.

"Yo, shawty," he yelled into her cell as soon as she answered his call. "Bring ya ass!"

Prancing across the traffic toward Bama Bob, Ariel was immediately met by a thousand questions being thrown at her at one time, right off rip.

Chapter Twenty-seven

"Turn that music off immediately," one of the many officers demanded of the DJ as soon as the interior of the club was surrounded and the exit points were secure. "And hit all the house lights!"

Justice continued to calmly sip on his drink as small cubes of ice clinked on the rim of the glass. With every step the police made in his direction, each female sitting in the booth got closer underneath him as if he had some type of invisible potion or a magic carpet that could get them out of there without static. *I knew I should've just dipped over to Greedy's damn house!* He thought about his bottom bitch, who had four different baby daddies, as the glass sweated in his hands. She was a whore, but Justice claimed she had the best head in town. *A nigga just wanted one, maybe two drinks, and then I was gonna be out and getting my dick sucked!*

"All right, big pimp player!" the white officer loudly addressed Justice. Yanking the table back with one hand, he caused the half-drunk bottle of champagne to go crashing to the floor along with all the photos they'd taken. "You and these girls all need to raise the hell up. Now!"

"Yessss, sir," both females replied, standing while tugging down on their overly tight minidresses.

"Hey, homeboy! Did you hear me talking to you?" The plainclothes cop coldly eye fucked Justice, who hadn't flinched a muscle in the way of complying. "This ain't no goddamn game! I said move!"

As the glass from the broken bottle sparkled off the strobe lights shining from the club's ceiling, an insubordinate Justice felt his temperature rise and his anger kick into full gear. "Yo! What the fuck! I just bought that damn bottle!"

"So what, tough guy? You think I care?" After smacking the glass Justice was holding out of his hands, the cocky officer aggressively snatched him up by his collar. "Get your punk ass up and against that wall!"

Justice's first mind was to react with violence and try fighting the officer of the law like he'd done so many times before when the Po-Po called themselves getting fly. Those irrational actions always resulted in him getting beaten down by a gang of cops, plus at least ninety days locked up and a huge fine. Normally the mad-dog killer would be up for the challenge, but considering the long, grueling afternoon he'd had and the hard-fought life-or-death battle with Cree, Justice's energy level wasn't up to feeling the barrage of different fists or the harsh feeling of boot soles stomping down on his back if he swung at Officer Smart-ass.

"Damn, dawg," he responded as he felt his already-battered, bruised face being smashed against the club's freshly painted walls.

"I ain't ya dawg." The officer quickly patted him down for any hidden weapons that might've gotten past the bouncers and the metal detectors. "So just watch your mouth and follow instructions!" he hissed, finding nothing but two cell phones, one which belonged to Moe Mack, a small wad of cash, mostly tens and twenties, and Justice's ID.

After being thoroughly searched, Justice, who was ready to surrender without a fight, and the now-crying females along with everyone else from VIP were roughly led downstairs. Looking around the club, which was almost packed to capacity, Justice realized that maybe they weren't there for him. Maybe his luck hadn't run out. Maybe no one had discovered the dead bodies of Moe Mack, NayNay's tramp ass, them two meddlesome kids, or, regretfully, his best friend Cree.

Shit, if they came in here looking for my black ass, then why is they checking everybody else? This bullshit don't make no sense. He started to feel a bit of relief.

"All right, people! Be quiet! Calm down!" a stone-faced officer stood behind the DJ booth with the microphone in hand. "Everybody, follow instructions and do what you're told, and you'll be out of here and tucked in ya little beds before you know it!"

"Why y'all always ruining shit?" someone's random voice shouted out of the irritated crowd while a few more partygoers concurred. "Y'all foul as hell!"

"'Cause that's what we get paid to do!" the officer smartly fired back. "So just do what you're told so we can all go home!"

Standing packed like sardines at the bottom of the staircase, Justice felt the vibration of Moe Mack's cell phone. Slowly removing it from his pocket, he saw a small envelope icon located in the corner of the screen, signifying that someone had sent several text messages. *Damn, dis nigga don't never stop getting that bread.* He assumed the call was business related until he pushed the combination of buttons and proceeded to read the two messages to himself:

Nigga, we hot on dat ass! We don't die, we multi-fucking-ply!

You can run, but ya can't hide!

Justice was no fool. He knew at that point there was no way in sweet hellfire that Moe Mack's boy Keith would be sending those texts unless he knew for certain Moe was dead and the murderer probably had his phone. "Fuck!"

he mumbled just as his own phone vibrated. Reading the text sent from Bama Bob—*If you see Moe Mack's car or Justice, blah, blah, blah*—further reassured him that the shit had indeed hit the fan. Now hustlers from one end of Detroit to the other, not to mention the police if they knew his true identity, would be hunting his black ass down. *Fuck 'em!* he reasoned as one of the police officers started telling people which line to get into in order to get out of the club. The only problems facing Justice were that he didn't know what exactly was waiting for him on the other side of the nightclub's doors, and his gun was stashed in Moe Mack's car, so he was definitely at a total disadvantage when he did step out.

With the lines growing longer, stretching on each side of the club's front mirrored entranceway, Justice kept his composure even though he had several checkpoints to clear before he was home free. Not knowing exactly who or what the police were looking for, he merged with the other partygoers, trying to act as if he hadn't just slaughtered five innocent people. Detroit's true hustlers and top-notch bitches who also had valet tickets like he did were posted on the left, while the others were to the far right. The fact that the line he was in was much shorter and moving more quickly only added to his anxiety.

"Everybody have your IDs out by the time you get to the front!" one of the many officers instructed as he marched in the middle of the aisleway. "And those of you who don't have IDs, step to the middle and make your way back to the middle of the club."

"They act like they run the city!" one guy told another. "This lame just like me and you except the pale face got a badge! He probably got his ass kicked as a kid! You know how that shit go!"

"Yeah, most police are some ho-ass homos anyhow!" his boy agreed. "Especially this Andy Griffith buster!"

"Shut your damn mouth and do what you're told!" the officer snarled back, overhearing the comments made about his manhood.

"Man, fuck you!" the first guy responded. "You might have the rest of these people in here buffaloed but not me! I ain't got no tickets, no warrants, and I got a pocket full, so you can fall the hell back on all that big-man bullshit you blowing out your mouth!"

As the officer snatched both guys out of the valet line and had the cop checking IDs shut it down for fifteen minutes or so to inconvenience the rest of the people, everyone grew inpatient and much more irritated.

"This is some straight-up bullshit!" Justice listened to the girl standing in front of him mumble underneath her breath as she shifted her weight to one side.

"Hell motherfucking yeah!" he quietly concurred as his eyes roamed her entire well-dressed body. Forgetting for one second his main focus was to get out of the club and hopefully drive away in Moe Mack's stolen BMW, Justice's dick instinctively jumped. *Damn, I'd tear this trick's pussy up!*

"I wonder what the fuck this is about." The mystery girl glanced over at Justice as if he really knew the answer to her million-dollar question. Then, as if she were the mayor, she shouted out another question. "Hey, how long we gonna be in this bitch?"

"Damn, ma, slow ya roll!" Seeing what'd just happened to the loudmouth guys standing a few feet ahead of them, Justice's dick grew limp, knowing that homegirl's rowdy demeanor would draw attention to them both if she didn't shut her fucking grill. *Shit, here this whitey come! Fuck! Why the fine females always got them fly-ass smart mouths on 'em! Damn!* Justice rubbed his hand on his chin, bracing as the white officer headed in their direction, undoubtedly having heard what Miss 2 Fine had just said.

"Tell me why you people just can't follow simple instructions." The cop leaned over in the female's face close enough that their noses almost touched, then he walked away without giving her the opportunity to reply.

Obviously furious she'd been chin checked, the girl turned to Justice, still flapping her gums. "Did you hear that shit?"

"Yeah, ma, I heard him, but don't let that shit faze you!" Justice was just glad the cop had kept it moving as he kept a careful eye out of the club's lighted glass front windows.

"It's just I had a pretty fucked-up day, and I'm just ready to get the fuck outta here!" She didn't care who heard her.

"I feel you." Justice stopped as several familiar cars pulled up across the street from the club and parked. "Oh, hell naw!" he softly spoke before tossing his valet ticket into the nearby trashcan. "My day been pretty fucked up too!" Justice finished his thought as the girl seemed to be on her own mission. *And it's about to get even more fucked up as soon as I hit the street!* he thought, watching Bama Bob get out of his car as some hoodrat ran over toward him. *If I can just get outta here, maybe I can at least make it to the east side and over to Greedy's and grab one of my other guns.*

Just as a confused Justice thought matters couldn't get any worse, the boisterous female was back at it, calling another police officer over in their direction. *Is this bitch nuts or something? She fine as a motherfucker and all, but fuck getting caught up on the humble behind her wild ass!* Trying to keep an eye on Bama Bob as the line started to move again, Justice kinda eased over to the side as if he weren't paying attention to the girl at all. After a brief exchange between the female and the cop, Justice realized she must've known the dude on a personal level

since he called her out by her name, Bonita. Then when
he told her to come with him and he'd escort her to the
door, Justice knew the chick had the hookup.

"All right then." She smugly smirked, glancing over her
shoulder at Justice while waving.

"Damn, homie!" Justice blurted out while slightly
pulling on the girl's arm. "I know you ain't just gonna
leave me hanging like that. Hook ya boy up!"

Turning around, seeing the obvious look of desperation in Justice's face, the female he'd just met showed
him some mercy. "Hey, wait a minute," she said to the
cop, shrugging her arm back from Justice's touch. "Can
you get my cousin out too? We met up down here, and
I'm his ride," she lied.

After sizing up Bonita's supposed relative, making sure
he knew who was boss, the officer gave in to the girl's
wishes, signaling for them both to follow him toward the
front.

"Good looking out, Bonita!" Justice happily stressed
every syllable of her government name, knowing he was
about to be given a free pass out the door.

"You straight, ummm . . ." She leered at him as they
breezed past all the agitated people stuck in line.

"Justice," he whispered in her ear so the cop wouldn't
catch on that they weren't really cousins.

No sooner than Bonita had gotten her keys from the
main officer checking IDs were the club's steel double
doors pushed open. *Shit, I need them keys to Moe's
whip!* With the sudden feeling of the still-warm summer
breeze hitting his face, Justice's heart raced, not knowing
what was gonna jump off as his stolen Gucci Loafers
touched the pavement. *Damn, this is it!*

In the midst of all the chaotic commotion, the eyes
of the child killer stretched, even the lazy one, trying to
watch the magnitudes of police posted everywhere. He

was also still monitoring Bama Bob's every move. The tension he was feeling mounted. *Look at these sack-chasing-ass hood rats posting up on my motherfucking car. I swear to God if all these ho-ass cops wasn't out here, I'd smack the cow shit outta all they asses!* Justice's mind raced a mile a minute as if he'd really worked hard himself to pay for the BMW the stray females' behinds were calling home.

Dang, I hope this nigga don't look the fuck over here now! His thoughts went in another direction as he saw Bama Bob and a gang of other dudes he once called his homeboys appear to posse up, undoubtedly plotting his demise.

"Yo, I know this next shit is way beyond the call of duty, but can you give a nigga a ride?" Justice zoned in, noticing that the so-called meeting of the minds Bama Bob was holding seemed to be breaking up, and nine outta ten their focus would be back on Moe Mack's BMW.

"Yeah, I guess so." The girl frowned up at him while keeping her sights on the same group of hoes who were on the Beemer. "Damn, where to?"

As some of Bama Bob's cronies waited for traffic to pass so they could cross the street, Justice had to think of any place to go other than where he was at now. "East side," he stammered, answering her question. "Or better yet, how about the casino?"

"All right, cool." Surprisingly she reached over, hugging up on Justice's arm as a burly plainclothes policeman instructed everyone standing on the front entrance of the club's sidewalk to break it up and keep it moving. "See you later." Justice watched Bonita smile at one of the females sitting on Moe Mack's car as they quickly walked to a Hummer.

Hearing the chirp of the truck alarm go off and seeing the lights flash, Justice hopped up in the passenger seat, still looking back at Moe Mack's car he was just forced to abandon. *This is some fucked-up bullshit! Why the damn police had to bring they asses up here raiding this son of a bitch tonight? If I could just get inside the trunk for five minutes, I'd be straight for life!*

"No offense, but I don't know you."

Justice was sadly yanked out of his remorseful thoughts of taking such a huge loss as Bonita removed a gun from the glove compartment, placing it on her lap. "Damn, Bonita!" He once again stressed every letter in her name, tugging down on the crotch of his pants. "You straight gangster! You can get to know me!"

With his eyes tracing every inch of her body, she eagerly offered him some advice. "Look, don't make me change my mind. And quit calling me Bonita. To you, my name is just Bo!"

"Yeah, all right, damn! Excuse the fuck outta me! You's one of them high-class broads!" Justice then stared over in the sideview mirror as she drove out of sight of Moe's car and any chance he had of getting that dope or the guns.

Complete silence took over the truck's interior as each one of the occupants obviously had their own troubles on their minds. Five minutes later, Bo was pulling up almost in front of the MGM.

"Be safe!" She offered encouragement, knowing that if his day was as half as fucked up as hers, he'd need it.

Justice was still coming to terms with what had just happened to him on the humble, but he thought he'd give it one more shot before shutting the truck door. "You sure I can't go with you?" He hoped she wouldn't reject him, but deep down inside he knew she would. That was the story of his life.

"Boy, bye!" She hysterically laughed in his face before skirting off, causing the truck's door to shut on its own.

I should've at least tried to rob the stuck-up bitch since she wasn't giving up the pussy, or at least taken that gun.

As Justice, hard dick in hand, stood on the side of the casino's entrance, watching the Hummer drive out of sight and the taillights bend the corner, his emotions took over, and his anger intensified. What had started off as a typical day of standing on Linwood with Cree, putting in work on a bold package, had now turned out to be nothing more than a complete waste of time. With multiple criminal charges sure to be pressed against him, Justice by force had abandoned everything he'd plotted, kidnapped, robbed, murdered, and betrayed for. All three guns he was cherishing earlier were stashed along with the dope in Moe Mack's trunk, which he couldn't get near. The clothes he'd stolen from NayNay's closet for Greedy, not to mention all of Moe's high-priced gear, were stuffed in the back seat. Removing the vibrating cell phone from his front pocket, Justice saw he had one missed call from a random female, one from Cree's pregnant girlfriend, and lastly another text message, this time from Bama Bob: Ho-ass nigga, we know you inside of the club. When you come out, you's as good as dead!

After twice reading over Bama Bob's promising death threat, Justice smiled. He was going to get such a head start on getting out of dodge and lost in the city as they waited it out. *This dumb country Bama all posted back at that club, and I'm long gone.* He smiled, taking in his surroundings. *But now what? Maybe I should go in this motherfucker and hit the craps table!*

With more vehicles than he could count entering the casino parking structure, Justice knew they all had money they'd be more than happy to part with if he had his pistol on his side. At least he could make some sort of a come-up and the evening wouldn't be a total loss, seeing how that black American Dream he was living as he pulled up in valet a few short hours ago was gone. Just like that, Justice was back where he'd started: zero, bitter, broke, and again on the prowl.

It was like one of his many foster mothers had repeatedly yelled out to him in the middle of her harsh beatings he suffered: "You were born to be a sorry loser!" He'd feel the sting of the long brown extension cord being slammed across his damp bare back. "No one wants you, little boy, not even God! If I didn't get a check from the State of Michigan once a month, I wouldn't even want your ugly, no-good ass!"

Chapter Twenty-eight

Allowing three or four elderly people to go inside the casino, then at least ten or eleven more, Justice could never find the right moment to snatch a purse or hit a man over the head with the huge rock he was holding in his hand while crouched down behind a candy-apple red Ford F-150. Eavesdropping on all the white, pasty-face people talk shit about the Negroes who lived in Detroit and the many police sirens that were roaring by, Justice couldn't take it anymore.

Dropping the black piece of stone to the ground, he reached in his pocket, taking out the small knot of money he had left from partying, counting it up. "$386 ain't jack shit!" he reasoned as another set of headlights entered the structure. *I know I should've just bought a few shots of Rémy! Damn, what was I thinking tricking with them hoes?*

Deciding it'd be in his best interest to just catch a cab to Greedy's crib so he could come up with a game plan, Justice emerged from the parking garage. Checking the block for signs of anyone he knew, he jumped in one of the many waiting yellow taxis.

"Yeah, dude, Devonshire and Mack." He slammed the door as the driver disapprovingly looked back. "Then I'll tell you where from there."

"Look, umm, sir, sorry. I'm only taking airport runs tonight."

"So damn what?"

"Well, I can't go that far east," the driver of Indian descent explained. "I try to stay on this side of town for airport runs only."

Justice wasn't in the mood to argue with the driver, whose head was wrapped in a purple turban. "Look, Ali Baba, just take me where the fuck I wanna go. Why y'all gotsta be so difficult? My money spends just like everybody else's! If I were white—"

"I'm not saying that. I just do—"

"Look," Justice stopped his protesting, holding up money to the bulletproof partition. "Are we gonna ride or what?"

Seeing that his disrespectful passenger had cash in hand, and taking into consideration that the night was slow, the driver opted to follow instructions, carefully pulling away from the casino and into traffic. "Okay, you win. We go. But I need money first."

"Damn, fool, just keep driving," Justice angrily advised. "You'll get ya loot!"

"Okay, okay."

"I thought so." Justice lowered his head, going through all of Moe Mack's texts. "Money talks and bullshit walks!"

"They done let a gang of motherfuckers out of that joint." Bama Bob reached up, banging his hand on the green street sign. "And ain't none of those dudes Justice's ho ass. If that faggot would've come anywhere near Moe's ride, we would've peeped him out."

"Yeah, you right," one of the angry crew said. "Unless he somewhere in there hiding out."

"Come on, dude, use ya brain," Bama Bob reasoned. "There ain't no way the cops gonna be letting that retarded son of a bitch post up nowhere in there. I just hope he ain't got no warrants and they arrest his ass on the humble before we get a hold of him! But just in case,

I'm gonna get in touch with my girl Jazmine and see if she's on duty tonight. If she is, I know she can get me the 411 on what her people know so far."

As the clock ticked by, Jazmine finally called Bama Bob back. She informed him not only was she on duty the deadliest night in Detroit history, but she was actually inside of the nightclub, helping to clear it out before moving to their squad's next designated hot spot to raid.

"Hey now." Her voice rang out rapidly in the midst of all the loud commotion going on in the background. "I'm kinda busy right about now. It's a madhouse in this bitch! But what do you need, and can it wait?"

"Naw, it can't wait! I need some info, baby girl, real quick, fast, and in a hurry," he demanded in a rough tone. "I don't know if you heard yet, but OG Moe Mack took a fall tonight. So this shit right here is top priority, ya heard!"

"Hell naw. You lying? Are you sure? His car is parked right out front. I saw it when we stormed the club!" Full of questions, heading toward the front of the crowded building, Jazmine exhaled, peeping out the window. Seeing the Beemer definitely still parked in valet made her continue to question the tragic news she'd just heard. "Moe? Gone? You sure?" Jazmine sucked her teeth in denial. "Where was this at? What side of town? What happened? Damn!"

"West side, Linwood and Dexter," Bama Bob sadly responded as his soldiers stood tall, watching the club's entrance for any signs of Justice. "Ol' girl NayNay and them bad-ass kids of her sister's got the business too! That's why I'm calling. I need to know what ya might've heard about what ya people think went on inside that crib. Plus, I need you to check for the snake-ass motherfucker who did the deed! He the one who's pushing Moe's whip!"

"That was Moe and his people?" Jazmine shook her head, almost gasping to breathe. "We heard that bullshit on the radio on the way here. That's fucked up! I mean real fucked up!"

"Yeah," Bama Bob solemnly agreed. "Ho-ass corner boy!"

"Y'all know who it was?" Jazmine trembled with a mixture of sorrow and anger. She tried to remain on her square after hearing her boy from way back when, Moe Mack, had left the world that most called hell. The young narcotics squad officer had been raised in the hood and had experienced death often in her line of work, even being behind the gun of several justifiable police shootings herself. Yet anytime her own left this place it was a sad day, to say the least. Momentarily paralyzed and stunned, Jazmine came to her senses, searching the room as her trigger finger itched with anticipation. "Fuck it, what y'all need me to do? Y'all think he in here? Now? What that fool look like?"

With Bama Bob giving her Justice's description, Jazmine got another officer to take her line duty, and she started her hunt. Quickly discovering that no one had an obvious lazy eye who had processed a valet ticket, her police skills kicked into full gear. Eagerly taking two steps at a time, Jazmine got up to the VIP section, finding it completely empty. *Where could this nigga be?* She kept her hand on her pistol just in case of any unexpected surprises. With each footstep the grief-stricken cop took, broken glass barely penetrated her thick-soled combat boots. Kicking bottles of beer and champagne out of her path, Jazmine's eyes soon became glued on a few scattered snapshots on the floor near one tossed-over table. Shining her department-issued flashlight on the trampled photographs, one in particular stood out. *This that one-eyed bastard right the fuck here! Ugly-ass, jealous motherfucker!*

As her adrenalin rose, she rushed back down the flight of stairs, eye fucking every nigga she came across who had on an outfit similar to the one Justice was wearing in the pictures. Still having no luck on her own, she tried calming down and thinking with her head and not her heart. Showing the picture to several of her fellow officers, Jazmine found out from one of them that he'd given the lazy-eyed Negro and some hot-in-the-ass female he claimed to have known a pass earlier to skip the line and leave.

"One day you and your dick gonna get you kicked off the force!" Jazmine ranted as if she herself weren't on a mission for the dope-selling dudes she ran with after work. "That was the kid-killing psycho from the west side bullshit!" *Damn, now I gotta call Bama Bob back and tell him, then the sergeant. Shit!* She clutched the Polaroids in her hands.

In the meantime, outside, receiving several text messages from Keith, who was furiously waiting for any updates, Bama Bob and his fellas had no choice but to wait it out, even if it meant staying posted across the street all night. Moe Mack was their comrade, and if that meant doing just that, they were all ready to put in the work in his honor.

With the radio blasting the continuous breaking-news updates, Justice tried his best not to pay attention when the driver shook his head in shock over each report in the crime-ridden city he was forced to work in.

"It makes no kind of sense," the driver casually remarked.

"What?" Justice lifted his head from searching through Moe Mack's various text messages. "You talking to me?"

"No, I was just talking to myself." He hardly glanced back over his shoulder at the black youth.

Realizing they were getting closer to Greedy's house, Justice dialed her number and got shot straight to voicemail. "Yo, bitch! Pick up the phone," his voice barked out before he ended the call and immediately placed another. Still hearing Greedy's musical recording, Justice's patience was starting to wear thin. "All right, bitch, if ya think I'm playing with you, trust ya mistaken! I'm on my way over there and—" Before he could finish his violent threat, his phone beeped, indicating that he had an incoming call. Double-checking the caller ID, he saw it was Greedy.

"Hello," she managed to quickly get out before the cursing began.

"Is you fucking nuts or what? I know ya seen the first time I called ya ass!" Justice was on the warpath as the cab driver turned up the radio in an attempt to drown him out.

"Dang, boy, I was in the bathroom. Is that all right with you?"

"Who the fuck you getting smart with? Don't get that ass smacked! Tonight ain't the night!"

"Nobody, I was just saying," the young mother replied, also not in the mood for hearing his bullshit. "Stop tripping!"

"Anyway, I'm about to fall through there, so make sure all them bad-ass bastards of yours is in the bed! You understand me? I need to figure some shit out!"

"Justice, all the kids is already asleep. But my cousin is spending the night over here. Me and him is chilling smoking a blunt."

"What you say?"

"Come on, Justice, don't trip!"

"Listen, I done had a fucked-up day and ain't in the mood for no more dumb shit. Send that li'l sissy packing. Plus, why your stupid ass over there pregnant and smoking anyhow? You unfit as hell!"

"First of all, Cuzzo already here chilling, I told you. And second, why is you tripping on me smoking? It ain't even that serious. Don't let me find out your hardcore ass really give a shit about this baby." She rubbed her stomach while blowing smoke up into the air.

"Damn, bitch, don't play yourself! That's your baby, not mine!" Justice had just about enough of her flip mouth. "Just clear the crib out! Shitttt, you act like y'all two over there banging. Now unless that fool ready to stand tall when I get there, send his fuck-boy ass on his way!"

"Boy, bye! It's too late for him to go home now." Greedy lit another blunt, hoping Justice's threats were just that: threats. "I'll just see you whenever you get here! And just for the record, it's your baby too!"

Hanging up the phone, Greedy was lost. She had no idea the guy who'd been her fuck buddy on and off over the past year had snapped, her new baby daddy was one of the many killers the entire Detroit Police Department was so desperately searching for, or that her young, innocent homosexual cousin would soon be another one of his victims by sunrise.

Chapter Twenty-nine

Unfortunately, as the cab driver drove down the long city blocks, each broken-out streetlight made it more difficult for him to see the road. If it weren't for the bright, illuminated neon signs that read LIQUOR, LOTTERY, or BEER AND WINE every other corner, Detroit would've been pitch-black in some parts. *These people in Detroit won't be happy until they've all killed each other. They behave like animals.* The driver was lost in his thoughts, trying to get to his destination as soon as possible and back to the casino. *They tear up and destroy everything they touch. Detroiters are poison to their own neighbors, thugs, thieves, crackheads, bums, and hooligans. Now listen to this unfortunate tragedy.*

With the radio giving details of each suspected culprit in crime after crime, the one that proved to be the most heinous finally made its way to the airwaves. When Justice heard the news announcer mention NayNay's street and that two kids had been found murdered, he knew that not only were Bama Bob and 'em looking for him, but the police were also.

Damn, shit's getting tight. I gotta make a move. He hoped the cops didn't have a complete description of him, let alone a name. *I need to get out of Detroit somehow, someway.* Holding his and Moe Mack's constantly vibrating cell phones in his hand, Justice had to get himself a drink and quick. "Yo, my manz, pull over at the next store you see," he ordered up toward the front like he was in a limo. "And make sure they sell liquor in that motherfucker, ya feel me?"

"I already told you I have to get back to the other side of town. I cannot do."

"It ain't gonna take you but five minutes, damn!" Justice leaned up, banging his palm on the partition as he insisted the driver pull over. "There go a liquor store over there near them hoes! Now pull the fuck over. I need to get a taste!"

Demanding an extra ten-dollar deposit, the driver finally pulled over, parking next to the bus stop where several females were standing. Justice grabbed the handle, swinging the rear door open. Stepping out and onto the curb, his animal instinct took over as he approached the girl who he thought was the prettiest of the pack.

"What's up with you, sexy?" He eased over in her personal space. "Why you out here so late in these Detroit streets?"

"Excuse you." She leaned back, holding on tightly to her bootleg Coach purse considering the rough physical appearance of Justice. "Do you mind? I'm not interested in holding any conversations with strangers."

"Why you gotta be acting all stuck-up and shit? A guy only trying to be nice to your high-yellow ass!"

"Okay, look." Her eyes shot daggers as she turned up her nose to block the strong smell of hot liquor that was blowing out of Justice's mouth. "I got a man, all right? And trust, even if I didn't, I wouldn't wanna bang with you. So kick rocks and go find a stray alley rat that likes your kind!"

Before Justice could get a chance to verbally respond or at least smack the cow shit fire out the tramp, he heard the loud, annoying sounds of the cab driver blowing his horn then yelling out his open window. "Hurry up in store! You hurry up, or I leave!"

What the fuck? Justice, caught in his emotions, stared over at the cab then back at the smart-mouth female who was now laughing. "All of y'all got me fucked up! Do you know who the fuck I am?" His chest stuck out as he marched back over toward the cab without even bothering to go inside of the store for that drink he was so anxious to get. The closer he got, he heard the radio disc jockey giving another breaking-news alert. This time, he gave a general description over the airwaves of the child killer, including what he was last seen wearing.

"Once again, if you see the man who matches this description, do not try to apprehend him yourself. Be advised he is considered armed and dangerous."

Damn! How in the fuck they know what a nigga got on his back? Justice paused, glancing down at his shirt, then locked eyes with the taxi driver.

It took all of five seconds for the driver to put two and two together, realizing his unruly passenger was the coldhearted lunatic most of Detroit would grow to hate by daybreak.

"You go away from this cab now! Take your money! Take it! I don't want trouble!" Throwing the cash onto the pavement, the terrified man with a family at home rushed in an effort to manually roll up the cab's window and pull off. Violently, he was stopped by the brutal force of Justice's already-battered fist socking him in the jaw once, then twice in the temple. His head bobbed to the side as saliva flew out of his mouth, followed by a thick stream of blood that splattered across the dashboard and onto the inside of the windshield.

"No, no, please, please!" In excruciating pain, the man begged for his life to be spared while attempting to defend himself against Justice's vicious, unwarranted attack.

Taking notice that he was now the center of attention, a glory-hound Justice grinned. He was accustomed to being shunned and rejected by most women, starting with his own mother the day of his birth. He wickedly laughed while the group of girls with their cell phones glued to their ears looked on. Despite knowing that at least one, if not all, called the police on his black ass, the melee intensified, with him not missing a single beat.

"Don't nobody tell me what the fuck to do! Nobody! I'm grown around these parts! NFL, Niggas From Linwood, all day and all night!" Justice shouted as the long list of crimes he'd committed in less than twenty-four hours continued to grow. "I run this!" Leaning his upper body inside the cab, his hands wrapped around the throat of the now-defenseless man who'd lost all hope of ever seeing his wife and four small children again. Beating the innocent cab driver was not enough satisfaction for Justice. He callously snatched the man's body out through the open window of the cab before kicking him in his face then in the rear of his head, causing his turban to unwrap. "Foreign-ass immigrant motherfuckers coming over here! Y'all ain't running shit! Especially in Detroit!"

With police sirens not too far away, Justice opened the cab door, jumping inside. Before he could pull off, the strong-willed driver made one final attempt to save his leased taxi from becoming another stolen car statistic in the Motor City. Raising his sore, beaten arm, he held the rusty bottom of the automobile's door.

"Please don't," the man managed to say before an evil-minded Justice slammed the door shut, smashing his right hand against the taxi's steel frame, making the entire car rock.

"Noooooo!"

"Fuck you and anybody who looks like you!"

Throwing the cab into gear, Justice then pushed his foot down on the gas pedal, ripping the driver's fingertips from his hand. If that in itself weren't enough brutality for the growing group of shocked spectators to witness, as the cab's wheels turned, the screaming man's religiously worn purple turban was now tangled in the tires, dragging him along the pothole-filled streets for four or five good yards until his bloodied body broke free.

Almost losing control of the vehicle, Justice continued to show no remorse for his violent acts as the yellow cab jumped the concrete curb. He purposely barreled into the one female, killing her instantly. *Fuck you, that tramp NayNay, the high-post-acting chick who gave me a ride, and my ho-ass mother! All you bitches ain't shit!* Justice's mind was racing nearly as fast as the taxi, which now had only one working headlight. He regained control, skirting off into the darkness of Detroit. *Greedy best have her shit correct, too, 'cause if she don't, her ass gonna be next to see what's ready good! I'm tired of motherfuckers talking and acting reckless! I don't owe the streets. They owe me!*

Chapter Thirty

"There are dead bodies turning up left and right in each section of the entire freaking city. We've got murders happening damn near every hour on the hour! What in the hell are you and your men doing in the way of controlling this bullshit? Can you tell me that? Please!" The mayor of Detroit was at the end of his rope, losing patience in the late-night conversation he was having with his chief of police.

"Channels two, four, and seven are on my back for comments. Those damn hypocritical religious ministers of every faith keep flooding the phone lines demanding answers. And now that fucking CNN is calling!" He banged his fist on the cherry-oak desk in the office he'd been confined to since the early morning hours trying to get a grip on the high-profile, chaotic town he was in charge of.

"Don't worry, sir, we have every available man on duty working double shifts," the chief promised, driving past Tiger Stadium with sirens blasting and lights flashing. "The description of the suspect in the multiple-victim homicide has been just sent to the media. And we're making headway on some of the other murders, but you gotta know, Mr. Mayor, as soon as we get a decent hold of one crime scene, another one is jumping off. It's as if something is in the water!" he tried to joke to ease the tension.

"Look, ain't nothing funny! I don't wanna hear that 'something in the water' bullshit, you understand? I want some arrests made. I need some goddamn faces of criminals in shackles to flash across these television screens and in Sunday's paper to show everybody we mean business in Detroit when it comes to crime!" Frustrated, he stood up, pacing the floor as his loosened tie swung from side to side. "I got a lot of major deals hanging in the balance. If those white, rich motherfuckers think I'm all right with having the highest homicide rate in the damn United States, including a psycho who murdered two innocent kids like that, their asses definitely won't do business!"

"I understand, sir! I'm on it, Mr. Mayor."

Ending the dreaded call from his boss, the chief finally arrived to console the family of a teenage female who'd just been deliberately rammed into the side of a liquor store after some lunatic carjacked a taxi cab, also killing the immigrant driver. Grabbing his hat off the passenger seat, exhausted, he prepared himself to give the same speech to the victim's family he'd given countless times throughout the day.

Abandoning the stolen, damaged taxi a number of blocks over from Greedy's house, Justice, still feeling no pain, took off on foot. Creeping throughout the back alleyways, cutting across several vacant lots, then taking a shortcut that only nearby residents were aware of, he hit Greedy's front door, drenched in sweat, but without further incident.

"Yo, Greedy." He banged on the torn screen once or twice before she flung the wooden door open, big belly and all, blunt hanging from her lips.

"Be quiet before you wake them up." Shushing Justice, she motioned toward the back room where her kids were fast asleep. "And damn, what happened to you? You look like death!"

"Don't worry about all that! And get the fuck out of my way before I kick that baby out of your dumb ass!" He shoved by, making his way into the air-conditioned living room. Inside, he found Cuzzo still there, chilling watching music videos with his perfectly manicured feet resting up on the glass coffee table.

"Hey, Justice." Cuzzo waved his hand like he was a true diva. "How you doing?" He mimicked Wendy Williams.

"Damn, Greedy! Damn!" Justice turned back to face her as his upper lip curled. "Didn't I tell your stankin' ass to put this mixed-up faggot out before the fuck I got here? Is you deaf?"

Cuzzo was all of five feet four, weighing barely 120 pounds naked in his thong. Wearing his hair in a shoulder-length streaked-blond bob since the age fourteen, and wearing eyeliner since twelve, the homosexual, frail teen was used to being called everything except a child of God. So Justice's evil insults rolled off his back like it was nothing. Besides, he secretly had a crush on him. "Oh, please. Boy, bye! This here my cousin's house! How you look coming over here, calling shots whenever you wanna get your little dick wet?"

"Nigga, what?" Justice lunged at him no sooner the last words escaped Cuzzo's candy-apple red lips.

"Stop! Stop! Damn!" Greedy quickly intervened, shielding her cousin, preventing him from getting a beat down. "Get back, Justice! You bugging!"

Bringing extra tension to the situation, two of Greedy's older children were now wide awake, crying, begging for Justice not to hit their mother and to leave their favorite older cousin alone.

Suffering the once-again annoying sounds of sobbing ghetto kids gone wild, Justice fought back the strong urge to give Greedy's children the same lethal Kool-Aid/ rat poison mixture that'd tragically ended NayNay's young nephews' innocent lives.

"All right, all right, shit!" He snatched his forearm back from Cuzzo's throat, shrugging Greedy's hands off him. "Yo, I'm good! I'm good!"

Almost hysterical, Cuzzo had huge crocodile tears flowing down his face. Slowly rubbing the sore rainbow-colored butterfly tattooed on his neck, rolling his eyes, he struggled to speak. "You ain't right! That shit is foul as hell. I ain't even do nothing to you!" he protested, screaming like a woman instead of bossing up like a man. "You wrong! You wrong! You wrong!"

Feeling the vibration of his cell phone ringing, Justice didn't react to Cuzzo's female tendencies and emotional breakdown. Instead, reaching in his pocket, he read another threatening text message from Bama Bob: Know u left da club. Still on dat azz! After reading the text, Justice had to seriously reflect on what his next move would be if he hoped to avoid the ho-ass police, Bama Bob, and all 'em and get the hell out of Detroit. *Shit, I need to rest. I just need to shut my eyes for a few minutes and think.*

Greedy, taking notice that Justice thankfully had calmed down, took the opportunity to soothe her children's cries, putting them back in the bed. She left her young cousin sitting on the couch pouting. Thinking quickly, Justice realized that at this point Greedy was his only ally. But Cuzzo had to get the fuck on, period. He wasn't a fool. He'd seen how Cuzzo's gay ass used to be sizing him up like chick. So for once, tonight, he decided to use that to his advantage.

He took his drenched shirt off so his wife beater would show off his chiseled muscles and his jailhouse tattoos.

"Look, Cuzzo, my bad on all that. A nigga just high as a fuck, you know." He licked his lips. "It's just late, and I wanted to get my dick sucked in peace. You know how it is." Justice tugged on his manhood.

Stupid as the day he was born, drama queen Cuzzo fell right into Justice's trap, welcoming his apology for almost choking him to death. "It's okay I guess." His eyes widened as they focused on Justice's now-rock-hard dick.

"Okay then, we cool?" Justice stuck out his hand, encouraging Cuzzo to give him a play. "We cool?"

With his own dick standing at full attention and his asshole throbbing, Cuzzo eagerly gave him a play, willing to just get a chance to touch the dude he always wished was gay or at least a homo thug.

Just as Greedy reentered the room, she saw her cousin and baby daddy making nicey-nicey. Rubbing her huge stomach, she exhaled with relief. "I'm glad y'all done made up and shit. Y'all gonna make a bitch have this baby months early!"

"Hey, y'all got any pills around here?" Justice abruptly questioned, already knowing the answer before he asked. "I feel like getting my mind right, and you know X gets a brother in the zone." He winked his lazy eye at Cuzzo. "That shit have a brother freaky as a motherfucker!"

Still watching Justice like a hawk, Cuzzo's dick jumped while his mouth watered at the very thought. He'd dealt with all type of dudes, both black and white, who were on the down-low, and if his gaydar senses were correct, Justice was, suddenly after months of bashing, giving him all the signs indicating he wanted to walk on the dark side.

"Naw, baby," Greedy said apologetically like it was her fault. "But Li'l Ro got some down the way. You want me to go cop?"

"Naw." Getting up, stretching his arms back, Justice made sure Cuzzo could get a full view of what he was really working with. "I got a better idea." Standing behind Greedy, rubbing her shoulders, kissing on her neck, Justice never took his eyes off of Cuzzo. "I'ma run down there and grab some, plus a beer from the after hour. Why don't you jump in the shower and I'll be back to handle that!" Justice schemed as Greedy smiled.

"All right, daddy," she quickly agreed, not having had any sex for over two weeks.

"You want me to walk with you?" Cuzzo leaped to his feet, slipping on his flip-flops, praying his hunch was on point. Unknowingly he'd gone right along with Justice's game plan, even volunteering to go with him on his own.

"Whatever." Justice didn't want to seem overly anxious heading out the door. "It don't matter. Just hurry your sissy ass up!"

Right then and there Cuzzo knew the shit was definitely on and popping. Normally ain't no way in sweet hellfire a hood Negro, born and raised in Detroit and cut like Justice, would let a flashy diva like him be seen walking with him whether it was day or night.

Only a few houses down from Greedy's, Justice made his move. "So how long you been taking it in the ass?"

"Why you always so rude?" Cuzzo paused, feeling brave enough to nudge Justice's arm. "Besides, how you know I take it in the ass?"

Looking around the quiet block for signs of nosy witnesses, they continued to walk. Then Justice put his game into full motion. "Well, do you or not? I wanna know!"

"There's a couch in the old, abandoned weed spot around the way," Cuzzo boldly announced, hoping he wouldn't get socked in the grill. "You wanna see? I can show you better than I can tell you!"

Justice didn't mutter a single word as he followed Cuzzo, who was wearing a pair of white shorts that tightly hugged his ass like a glove. Trying not to watch the young man who talked and moved like a female, the half-crazed Justice thought back to one of his former cellmates who used to brag about hitting dudes off in the shower all the time. *Maybe there's something to this bullshit.*

Going around the side of the vacant house, Cuzzo pushed the unlocked door open with ease, prancing over the threshold as if he'd just won the lottery in three different states. "Come on in," he purred, sucking his pearly white teeth. "Don't be scared. I don't bite."

"I ain't never scared! Believe that!" Justice slowly shut the weather-beaten door behind him, going up the small flight of warped stairs leading into what was once the kitchen. With each awkward step he took toward the dining room where Cuzzo was at, Justice's heart-beat increased, knowing he was about to take another life. *This faggot about to die. How the fuck he think I want his gay ass! I ain't no homo!*

Standing face-to-face, Cuzzo leaned over, snatching a cushion off the old couch, stained with God knows what. Tossing it between them on the filthy floor, he took a deep breath in anticipation of the obvious. As the one streetlight on the block fought to shine through the broken windows of the empty house, Cuzzo wasted no time dropping down on his knees. Unzipping Justice's jeans like he was an expert, the diva gazed up into Greedy's man's face. Blinded by being horny, Cuzzo mistook the strange expression of sheer confusion for that of lust. "Tell me to suck ya dick, daddy!"

Part of Justice was enraged by Cuzzo's suggestion as his hands clenched firm, ready to beat him to death, while the other part of him was wondering why some sissy down on his knees had his pipe rock hard in antici-pation of getting some head.

"What you say?" Justice stalled for time, trying to fight the urge and understand his strange desire.

"Never mind." Cuzzo reached his soft but still man-size hands into Justice's boxers, pulling out his stiff hookup.

Before the mad-dog killer could object, Cuzzo's warm breath got closer, and his wet, moist mouth began making the dick feel at home. The loud sounds of slurping seemed to echo throughout the empty house and bounce off the walls. Justice's legs grew increasingly weak. Falling back on the couch, Justice grabbed a tight handful of Cuzzo's weave, ramming his head downward so he had no other option except deep throating him.

This ain't me! This ain't me! This bullshit ain't me! repeatedly ran through Justice's delusional mind as Cuzzo kept sucking away. *But the shit feels so good!*

The untimely tremor of Moe Mack's phone shocked Justice out of his dizzy, sex-induced trance and back into reality. Back to the true reason he was in an old, dilapidated house with this gay motherfucker. Desperately trying to not explode and bust a nut in Cuzzo's mouth was easier said than done as Justice's head dipped backward and he let out a silent scream. Hell yeah! With Cuzzo swallowing every drop of cum like a champ, it was a sin and a shame what happened next. Still down on his knees with a grin of complete and utter satisfaction, Cuzzo's carefree existence quickly took a drastic change.

"Don't you wanna hit it from the back?" he seductively whispered as Justice shoved his now semi-limp dick back in his boxers.

"Why in the fuck would I wanna do that faggot-ass shit?" Arrogantly, Justice stood up, fastening his pants, acting as if what he'd just done, getting his dick sucked by a dude, weren't as equally flame-throwing gay as Cuzzo, who was down on his knees doing the sucking.

"Huh? What you mean?" As Justice stood towering over Cuzzo, his voice cracked as if he was about to cry once again.

Without as much as a second thought, while most of Detroit's god-fearing citizens slept before attending early morning church services, Justice yanked a terrified Cuzzo by the neck with one hand squeezing, while pounding his fist on the side of his temple with the other. Delivering seven or eight swift blows to his forehead, he then let Cuzzo's feminine-shaped body hit the floor. With a pool of blood leaking from the rear of his skull, Cuzzo's bulging eyes shut for good.

Raising his shoe, Justice then judgmentally peered down at the dude who'd just moments ago given him so much pleasure, and proceeded stomping him in the mouth. Pausing his tirade, allowing a few crackheads who were roaming the streets in search of a late-night blast to walk past, Justice noticed a few of Cuzzo's broken teeth lying on the floor. *Smile now!*

Once again, like clockwork, Bama Bob was calling, only this time on Justice's line. *I done had enough of this sucker blowing my shit up like he pay the bill!* "Yeah, lame, speak on it!"

"Yo, dude! What in the fuck is wrong with you, bitch nigga!" Bama Bob was stunned that Moe Mack's killer finally answered, but he didn't miss a beat letting him have it. "We know you did that foul-ass bullshit to ol' boy and 'em!"

"Yeah, and what, nigga? What?"

"That's all you gotta say and shit?"

"What the fuck else your country ass wanna hear?" Justice barked.

Bama Bob was growing more pissed by the second listening to Justice acting like he was some sort of a boss. "Why don't you stop hiding like a punk and bring your coward ass out in the open? Then we can really see what's really up! You can kill females and little kids like it ain't shit! Come kill my grown ass! You already know what it is!" he heatedly vowed. "Ol' boy looked out for you, taking you under his wing when ain't nobody else in the game wanna fuck with ya retarded ass!"

"Whatever." Justice spit a stream of saliva through his teeth, landing it on Cuzzo's toothless face. "Ya homeboy Moe was grown too, wasn't he? But then again, he did cry like a little girl when I was doing his fake ass proper! 'Waa, waa, waa. Please don't kill me, Justice, please! I wanna live. I wanna live,'" he mocked Moe Mack's finally moments, further agitating Bama Bob.

"I swear to God on everything I love!" Bama Bob promised revenge. "Ungrateful motherfucker, just come see me! I got something for your slow, ugly-looking ass waiting at the hip! Come see me! Or better yet, we can knuckle up! It ain't no thang!"

"Why in the hell would I do some dumb shit like that?" Justice nonchalantly taunted. "Right about now I'm busy about to turn over in my bed and get some pussy from your mother. So stop calling and texting me like we fucking! I'll see you when I see you, Country Bama!"

Having had gotten the last word, Justice turned both his and Moe Mack's phones off, not wanting to be disturbed anymore while he tried to figure out his next move. And now with Cuzzo out of the way, he could at least get one good night's sleep at Greedy's.

Bending down, he removed Cuzzo's pink rhinestone cell phone off his hip, sticking it in his back pocket. Getting a hold of both Cuzzo's clean-shaven, smooth legs, Justice dragged his lifeless body behind the couch. Making sure no one could see any part of him, he grabbed his flip-flops off the floor, tossing them also behind the couch. Blank faced, with no remorse, Justice shoved the couch all the way back, wedging

Cuzzo's small frame against the paint-chipped wall. Taking Cuzzo's cell out of his pocket, he then sent Greedy a text pretending to be Cuzzo, informing her that he'd run into a few friends and would holler at her later. *Her pregnant dumb ass so hot for this dick she'll believe any fucking thing.*

Before leaving the abandoned house, Justice smashed Cuzzo's phone against the wall. Content with getting Greedy's cousin out the way, he bent down, picking up three of Cuzzo's broken-off teeth, shaking them in his hand as if they were a pair of dice. *Oh, well, it is what it is. I had to do what I had to do!* he dumbly reasoned for getting his dick sucked by another man.

Still on his original mission, Justice copped two ecstasy pills, then slid past the after-hour spot, grabbing a forty of Old E. Taking it to the head, he put his game face back on, going inside of Greedy's house. Belching no sooner than closing the door and putting both dead bolts on, Justice offered her an explanation about Cuzzo not being with him.

"Hey, girl, your cousin is a straight-up slut bag!" he proclaimed, lying. "We get up the way, and he sees a group of other fuck boys and breaks out with them!"

"I know, he texted me," Greedy giggled, happy Cuzzo left her alone with her sometimes man. "He always doing some crazy mess like that."

Justice laughed inside as she played right into his hands. She just as dumb as he was. *That shit must run in they family.* "Fuck that fag! Damn, trying to be nice to that punk with his sissy ass!"

His crude comments were to be expected. If he'd said anything other than what he was saying about Cuzzo, Greedy would automatically know something was seriously wrong and start with all the questions, not stopping until she got satisfaction.

Chapter Thirty-one

Bama Bob couldn't believe Justice had the balls to talk to him like he had. But then again, he and the rest of the tightknit crew, NFL 4 Life, were still in shock that Justice had even flipped out, murdering their homeboy and connect Moe Mack in cold blood. Each being born in the streets and true to the life of hustling knew death or jail were the only ways out of the game. However, anytime a player died by the hands of his own or was a victim of snitching, trust it wasn't ever a good look, even in Detroit where dudes were hard.

"All right, y'all." Bama Bob paced the floor, ready to stomp a mudhole in Justice's backside. "That closed-eyed bastard gotta fucking go! Ya feel me? Not only did he do Moe Mack, but he did his own homeboy, Cree. Right about now, we don't know if Cree was riding with that fool, but fuck it, he got to go on the strength of both our brothers!"

Rallying the crew to regroup and hunt down the weak link in their organization, Keith stood silently by allowing his right-hand man Bama Bob to do what he did best, which was handle shit. Brokenhearted, Keith had just returned from consoling his best friend's parents. He informed them that at least, thank God, their one and only grandchild, Moe Mack's namesake, was spared the violent death his parents suffered. After reassuring them their son's killer would be brought to justice, whether by the Detroit Police Department or by the hands of extreme vigilante justice, he wouldn't rest until Justice paid in full.

"Listen up, everybody." Keith, visibly shaken, had blood boiling in his eyes. Scanning the room for signs of more possible weak links in the crew who had disloyal thoughts brewing, he continued, "Moe was a fucking solider! Y'all know that! There wasn't a time me or him ain't stand tall for all y'all asses!" Visibly choked up, he shook his head while they all nodded in agreement. "So on the for real, a guy like me got eighteen racks large plus lawyer fare for anyone of y'all who can lay that no-good, slimy-living motherfucker down for good."

As Keith reached deep in his pocket, showing the entire squad the dough and validating that he meant business, their mouths salivated with hunger, each willing to do just about anything to be the one who got that bread. Never mind that there was a full-blown depression in the D and everyone needed extra ends, especially $18,000, but the props the soldier who brought back Justice's head on a stick would earn behind the task was worth its weight in gold. So with Yak, Denard, and Bama Bob each breaking off and politicking with their respective street lieutenants, they each promised Keith a swift outcome and told him to keep those racks ready to pay off.

"Oh, yeah, dig this here! One more thang!" Keith wanted to put them up on the low-key information update he'd received before leaving to get himself another stiff drink only forty-five minutes before the sun came up. "My girl Jazmine called and told me that punk was spotted over on the east side somewhere. He was in a cab or something like that. So if y'all know any bitches he fucks with over there, east, or any family he got, get at it! We wanna catch his sucker ass and deal with him Linwood style before the cops do!"

With the sun finally coming up and signaling a new day for Detroit residents, some hoped that going to church would purge their sins while others slept in after a long night of partying. Jazmine had just gotten off from working a mandatory double shift and was pulling up in the driveway of Keith's suburban home. Still trying to come to grips that Moe was gone, she rang the doorbell and stood silent in the early morning cool air, wondering if there really was a heaven for gangsters, pimps, and hoes.

"Hey, girl. What up doe?" A worn-out Keith pushed open the screen door, letting her inside. "You heard anything else or what?"

"Yeah, I just came from hollering at my boy down at homicide. He slid me these pictures and a confidential copy of the crime report. We probably need to jump on this shit as soon as possible!" She revealed a manila folder with the letters DPD stamped on them.

Keith led her to the dining room table where one of his many female friends he dealt with was just pouring him a hot cup of coffee. "You need a cup?"

"Hell yeah. Ya girl been up for close to twenty-four hours straight and counting." Jazmine reached for the mug as soon as the girl brought it in. "And considering how I feel, I don't wanna sleep 'til that buster is dead or at least locked the fuck up!"

Spreading the horrific murder scene photos out across the huge marble table, Keith gagged. Feeling like he wanted to throw up in his mouth at the sight, just as Jazmine felt the moment she'd first laid eyes on them, his eyes watered. Yeah, the snapshots of the kids slumped over with dried-up green vomit around their mouths was terrible to see, and certainly, the ghastly way Cree was ultimately sent home to God or the devil was definitely no walk in the park. Even looking at NayNay, who neither one of them could stand but tolerated for the sake of the baby, was awful. However, staring at their long-time homeboy Moe Mack, with his face blown half off, was a gruesome memory neither of them would soon forget.

After getting themselves mentally together, Keith and Jazmine carefully examined the police report. There they read the investigative conclusion from detectives. Moe Mack had been alive for quite some time, probably being tortured, before he was actually murdered execution style. Also, Cree was most likely fighting with the suspect before he was killed with the fireplace poker that'd come back with Justice Richards's prints all over it. NayNay's paperwork had yet to come back. Lastly, the duct-taped children, which was a no-brainer for authorities considering the evidence recovered from the kitchen counter, were poisoned, dying almost instantly.

"Here's what we need that might give us some info on Justice's whereabouts!" Jazmine pointed out, setting her coffee down. "They wrote the address from the boy Cree's ID. If we swing by his house, maybe we can get some answers as to where his boy Justice lays his head."

"Yeah, maybe you right." Keith stood up from the table, having seen enough of the heart-wrenching pictures.

"The only thing is we need to jump on the bullshit right about now. Last night they ended up towing Moe's Beemer, and you know ol' boy left some pistols stashed under the driver's seat. So you know nine outta ten, one of them bitches is gonna come back dirty." Jazmine divulged more classified information that only the Detroit police were supposed to be privy to. "Not to mention there were drugs all up in the car, so the damn DEA is fighting with the ATF, and both of they asses bucking it out with the department."

"Shit, the streets gonna be hot!" Keith snatched his car keys off the table, heading toward the front door and out onto the porch. "Hotter than a motherfucker!"

Jazmine, a sworn officer of the law, followed as she tucked her badge, dangling on a chain around her neck, underneath her shirt. "You know how we gotta do during an election year! Heads gotta roll!"

Trailing Jazmine's truck, Keith drove in complete silence. He'd never thought that he and his homeboy would part like this so soon. They had plans of retiring from the game damn near millionaires in three to five years. They often kicked it about taking their girls to the Bahamas and living like true kingpins. But now that fantasy was over. The pipe dream was now no more than a nightmare. Justice had ended that with two bullets, just like that.

As the sun shined brightly, Keith glanced at his diamond-encrusted watch then focused back on the road. It was exactly eight-twenty in the morning when he and Jazmine pulled up in front of the address that was documented as Christopher Weaver's place of residence.

"So this is it, huh?" Keith questioned Jazmine as they headed up the walkway. "Somebody in here better know something!"

Jazmine tugged his arm, stopping him just before his foot hit the first stair. "Listen, I'm used to dealing with victims so chill. Let me handle this."

"Victim?" Keith quickly snarled. "That fool Cree was all up in that bullshit no matter what in the fuck jumped off when they got there! Them two was like Batman and Robin!"

"Babe, just fall back. We don't really know who actually lives here or what they know yet!" Her tone was serious, and since her badge could ultimately be on the line for what they were about to do, Jazmine convinced him that they'd do this wrong-as-hell bullshit as right as possible.

Agreeing to keep his mouth shut, Keith knocked on the gate as Jazmine held on tightly to his arm just in case he couldn't control himself. A few minutes later an elderly woman, more than likely Cree's grandmother, came to the door.

"Yes?" She nervously shook as she spoke. "Can I help you?"

"Yes, we're friends of Christopher." Jazmine gave her a faint yet convincing smile. "And we wanted to both offer our condolences for your loss."

Cree's grandmother had never seen any of Cree's friends except that no-good Justice, who the detectives who were there earlier claimed may have taken her grandson's young life. "Well, baby, y'all come on in." She naively welcomed the devil into her home. "His girlfriend is getting dressed, and I'm getting ready to leave for church as soon as the senior van gets here. See, I haven't missed a service in close to nine years now, and this morning I need to call on Jesus and my church family for strength." She held on to her cane for support as she unlocked the gate. "But any friends of Christopher are always welcome in my house. Y'all come on in and have a seat."

Staring at the assortment of family pictures on the mantle and coffee table, it occurred to Jazmine and Keith that even though Cree was more than likely in on the botched robbery turned murder, he was still someone's relative. Just as the church van blew its horn, Cree's very pregnant girlfriend emerged from the back bedroom to see Granny off.

"So you knew Cree?" With swollen, red eyes she rubbed her stomach. "What's y'all name? I ain't seen y'all before."

"Listen, umm . . ." Jazmine opted not to divulge her name but wasted no time starting the mini interrogation as Keith looked on. "I know this is kinda bold and you're grieving, but we're trying to locate Cree's sidekick, Justice. You know him, don't you?"

"Yeah, of course." Lowering her head, crying, her voice cracked as she shielded her face from the strangers' view. "The police said he was the one who killed Cree and all those other people on Fullerton. That motherfucker ain't shit! Cree was supposed to be his boy! I told Cree that nigga wasn't shit and now look! He gone! He gone!"

By her reaction when Jazmine mentioned Justice's name, it was easy to see there was definitely no love lost for him in that household. Hopefully, she'd be able to provide some information to bring them one step closer to ensuring Justice met his maker: Satan.

"Look, yeah, you right. That dude Justice is the one who did it. Everybody knows!" Keith added fuel to her grief-stricken outburst, using it to his benefit. "Cree was a good guy. He used to kick it about you all the time around the way," Keith coldly lied, not having had more than two, maybe three direct interactions with Cree. "That's why we're here!"

"Yeah, girl, that's why we're here." Jazmine consoled the young pregnant teen as she started to shiver. "We're trying to find out where that idiot lay his head at. Cree was our boy too, and how Justice played him was straight-up foul! So do you know where he might be at?"

"Not really." She wiped her tears with an old piece of tissue. "Like I told the police who was here earlier asking questions, his ugly ass stay wherever one of them stupid females he hang with let him stay."

"Well, do you know any of them? Maybe? See, like I said, we was cool with Cree and the rest of them, and if that nigga did do that grimy mess, we wanna make sure he pay." Keith pulled out a big knot, peeling off a couple of hundred-dollar bills like it wasn't shit, putting it in the trembling hands of the mother-to-be. "We know you got that baby coming, and now thanks to that animal, you gonna straight be out here on your own, struggling! But the family, we got you!" He beat his fist on his heart.

Cree's baby mama was stunned. Her child's father was dead, and NFL was all for anything that would bring the killer to justice. "Hey! He did used to fuck with this tack head on the east side named Greedy." She proudly stood to her feet, wanting to help any way she could. "I hate that bitch!"

"Greedy?" Jazmine confusedly frowned. "That's the female's damn name? Greedy?"

"I guess so. I don't know her like that, but Cree told me a few months ago she was supposed to be pregnant by that monster." She rubbed her stomach while the tears ran down her face. "I was bugging 'cause the tramp already got four or five kids! Dumb bitch!"

Jazmine knew it was only a matter of time before the girl remembered even more. "The east side, huh?"

Keith was anxious, feeling like they might actually catch up with Justice sooner rather than later. "Oh, yeah, do you know where the girl Greedy live at?"

Still holding her belly, the young female squinted her eyes, trying to remember. "Naw, not really. Me, Cree, Justice, and her went out to Red Lobster one night, and by the time we dropped her off at the crib, it was late as hell, and I was buzzing. I do know it's off Mack Avenue, deep, deep east," she announced, wiping all the tears from her face, having a major flashback about the good times. "I ain't never really dealt with the girl again after that night because I found out one of her hoodrat friends was trying to get with Cree behind my back!"

"Oh, yeah." Jazmine reassured her she knew how grimy females could be. "That was fucked up! Well, do you know where that female lives at? The one who tried to get with Cree?"

Keith was losing patience with all the back-and-forth "As the Hood Turns" saga, and he excused himself, leaving the girls to talk. He went out to the car so he could call Bama Bob and see if there were any updates.

Walking over to the hall closet, Cree's girlfriend busted back out in tears as she saw all her man's winter jackets hanging up. "Hey, can you get that old duffle bag down for me?" she asked Jazmine, who quickly obliged. "I forgot about something."

Sitting back down on the plastic-covered couch, she dumped the contents of the bag on the floor. Sorting through the huge pile of old discarded cell phones and what seemed like fifty or sixty black tangled chargers, she summoned Jazmine to help her. "I don't remember which one it was for sure, but it was a Metro PCS I know. That damn Greedy and her girl was playing on my phone so much I had to change my fucking number, and when I did, I upgraded." She kept tossing all the T-Mobile, Sprint, and Verizon cells to the side, while Jazmine separated the Boosts and off brands. "But I know I locked Greedy's number in for sure. I know I did!"

Finding a possible three cellular phones, both females went through the task of matching the chargers since, of course, each battery was dead. Just as Keith walked back in, they were plugging in the last phone, checking through the long list of contacts.

"Here it is, under 'Stank Hoe!'" She forced a smile, waving the phone in the air. "This that bitch number!"

Jazmine informed Keith they'd found Greedy's number, and hopefully, it hadn't been changed. Before attempting to call, the trio plotted what exactly they wanted the young girl to say in the way of finding out if Greedy had seen Justice lately or at least had any knowledge of where he might've been hiding at.

Deciding to place the call from one of Keith's throw-away minute phones, they put it on speaker. As luck would have it, the number worked and started to ring.

"Now let's hope it's still Greedy's number," Jazmine whispered.

As the voicemail kicked in, Cree's girl laughed with disgust. "Yeah, that's her dumb ass! Still with all the music and then saying, 'You know what it is, boo boo, leave it!'" she mocked, shutting Keith's cell and ending the call before leaving a message.

"Maybe the girl ain't up yet!" Jazmine pondered. "It's only just nine."

Keith snatched the cell from Cree's girl once again, pushing talk. "Well, that slut need to wake the fuck up!" Listening to the annoying sound of the voicemail once more, he decided to take matters into his own hands. "Dig this." He motioned to the very pregnant girl. "Grab your shoes and let's head east. Maybe you can remember the street if you see the area."

Not really wanting to go anywhere with complete and total strangers, no matter how much they knew about Cree and wanted to smash Justice, Angie declined Keith's offer. "I don't think I can leave. I wanna help, but I just need to lie down for a while. My head is starting to pound like hell. I need to rest. I been up all night!"

Jazmine knew Keith's temper was about to explode, and she ordered him to go back out to his car and wait for her. Putting her career on the line, she then removed her badge from underneath her shirt, showing the apprehensive, scared teen she was an officer with the Detroit Police Department, but also a friend to Cree. She soon made her realize that without her assistance, Justice, the man who tragically ended her unborn child's father's life, might get out of dodge if she didn't do all she could do to help.

"Do it for Cree and your baby," Jazmine bargained, playing mind games. "Here you is living with him and his granny and y'all wasn't even married. He loved you, girl!

Show him the same kinda love and at least try to help us find Justice!"

Five minutes later, Cree's baby mama was climbing up in the back of Jazmine's truck. They followed Keith to drop off his car over at a friend's house, then all three of them skirted off, heading east.

Chapter Thirty-two

Waking up with a smile plastered on her face, Greedy looked over in the bed next to her. There she saw the fifth man she claimed was her baby daddy. Her other four children each were by different men who all walked out on her the moment they found out she was pregnant. Greedy was known around the Detroit club circuit as a party girl. So it was one thing for a guy to fuck the dog shit out of her in the back seat of their car or even in the men's bathroom, but to spend time with her and actually consider making her wifey was out of the question. If she could get a man to spend the night, she would be in pure heaven. Even though Justice was far from being a prize and oftentimes, if not all, treated her like shit on a stick, she seemed drawn to him. He could do no wrong that Greedy couldn't seem to forgive, even kicking her ass or whipping the skin damn near off her children.

Growing up the black sheep of her family, also being twenty years younger than her three siblings, Greedy was wild from the time she hit kindergarten and would probably remain wild until the day she died. That's why she and Cuzzo were so tight. He was also the black sheep from their fold, and since she was estranged from her mother, they were as thick as thieves. He was the only one, besides her kids, she'd kill over, unless of course Justice was involved.

"Damn, I love your no-good ass! I don't know why but I do." Greedy leaned over, kissing a snoring Justice on his lips then trailing her wet tongue down to his disfigured chest then onto his morning, heavy dick resting on his thigh. Taking it in her mouth, Greedy woke her new baby daddy up with the greeting most men prayed for on a daily basis. "Yeah, baby, cum, cum, cum!" Greedy jerked at Justice's stiffening manhood. "That's it! Yeah! Hell yeah!"

Now feeling the strong encouragement from his hands on each side of her head, Greedy had no idea whatsoever Justice's mind was back in the old, abandoned weed spot with Cuzzo sucking him off. Just seconds before he was about to let loose a hot load in her mouth, Justice harshly flipped a horny Greedy over on her pregnant belly, punishing the pussy from the back like there was no tomorrow in sight. No sooner than he was sexual satisfied, still high as hell off the two ecstasy pills and all the liquor he'd consumed the previous night, he collapsed on the mattress, falling back into a deep, coma-like sleep.

Tiptoeing out the bedroom, Greedy snatched her food stamp card out of her purse and grabbed her house keys. "Y'all be quiet out here. Justice is still asleep, and y'all know how he gets to acting when y'all make all that noise!" she informed her sometimes-boisterous kids who were sitting on the floor, glued to the cartoons on television. "I'm going to the store. I'll be right back. And you," Greedy said, pointing at her oldest daughter, barely eight but smart for her age, "you be especially quiet!"

With the intention of making Justice a huge home-cooked breakfast, Greedy started her walk toward the market. Turning on her cell, she kept on her hip, surprisingly to the unwed mother, at nine-thirty on a Sunday morning it started to ring. *Who in the fuck?* Greedy stared at the strange number before answering. "Yeah, hello!"

"Hey, Greedy." Angie acted like they were homegirls as Jazmine and Keith listened in.

"Who is this?"

"It's Angie, Cree's woman."

"Unh unh, what is you calling my phone for?"

"Well, I was trying to get in touch with Justice. Cree wants me to give him a message, and it's kinda important. So is he with you? I need to talk to him."

"Bitch, please! My phone ain't none of Justice's and I definitely ain't no messenger. So you can get the fuck on with all that bullshit!"

At the urging of Jazmine, Angie continued trying to reason with her. "Listen, Greedy, can you just tell me if you know where he's at?"

"Say what?" Greedy stopped dead in her tracks so she could truly give Cree's once-smack-talking girl the business. "Girl, you can stop this shit right now! The last time I talked to your fake butt you was promising me an ass kicking. So unless you ready to make good on ya promise, don't be calling my phone with no mess low-key trying to find your man. 'Cause, see, a ho like me know where mines is and that's asleep in my bed! Now fuck you!" *Wait 'til I tell Cuzzo about that silly skank calling me! She lucky I don't sic my girl back on Cree again!* Greedy powered off her phone, not in the mood for any more "a bitch who can't find her man" calls, and she went on her merry way to the Arab-owned market on the corner. The fact that there was an abnormal number of police cars patrolling out and about in the streets didn't seem strange to Greedy, as she was on top of the world with Justice back at her house, in her bed.

Hearing Greedy being so coldblooded and callous made not only Jazmine and Keith pissed, wanting to sock her dead in the mouth, but Angie also. Here she was acting as if she was proud to have a piece of trash like

Justice as her man, even after all the crimes she had to have known he committed the day before.

"Maybe you can put one of them GPS tracking things on her phone and find out where she at." Angie felt her baby kicking as she started grasping at straws. "Or a satellite thing."

"Sorry, sweetie." Jazmine sympathized, knowing ol' girl was mourning the loss of her baby daddy but still trying to stand tall with them. "For right now, we just gotta see if you recognize any landmarks that seem familiar."

Barreling down Mack Avenue, doing sixty in a thirty-five mile-per-hour zone was of no concern to Jazmine, who had her police radio on listening to updates of various crimes being reported throughout the city. With Keith laid back on his cell phone, finding out Bama Bob's exact whereabouts, Angie suddenly yelled out, having Jazmine turn right.

"I kinda remember that schoolyard facing that row of old houses. Plus, it just dawned on me, Greedy's house had a lot of poles in the front yard."

"Poles?" Keith quizzed, fed up with her immaturity and ignorance. "What kinda poles?"

Angie stared at every house, on each passing block, explaining what she meant. "They were poles sticking up where a fence is supposed to be, but it looks like somebody stole the fence part."

Momentary having a laugh at Greedy's expense, they were soon interrupted by Jazmine's radio blasting a report of a deceased body discovered in a vacant house less than a quarter of a mile from where they were. Thinking it would be in their best interest to at least swing by the crime scene and check in with her homicide buddy, Jazmine headed in that direction. Keith took that as the perfect opportunity to have Bama Bob meet up with them and take him back to his car. He'd had just about enough of Cree's baby mama's confused, backward ass and her juvenile way of talking.

Greedy's hands were full of plastic bags containing all the groceries she needed to prepare a breakfast fit for a king, not to mention the Sunday paper, which housed all the latest sales fliers. Deciding not to use one of the jitneys that always hung around trying to hustle for a couple of dollars while getting their old-school flirt on, she enjoyed the morning's clear blue sky. Not especially anxious to get back to her four kids, even though Justice was there in her bed, hopefully dreaming about her, Greedy decided to be nosy. Watching a swarm of police cars race by and stop a few blocks over, she headed in that direction. With all the empty lots in Detroit, a person could easily stand on one street and tell a nigga what they were doing damn near six blocks away.

Walking through the beaten-down dirt path the local residents had made, Greedy found herself standing amid a quickly growing crowd of early morning onlookers who weren't too high, drunk, or just plain fucked up from the previous night to be awake.

"Wrap that tape all the way around and secure the perimeter," demanded one officer who seemed to be in charge. He was wearing a suit and a tie, and his eyes were weak in appearance, as if he hadn't slept in days. "And, all you people, please step back. Please."

Whispers from neighbors, speculating about the identity of who was lying dead in the condemned house or who they wanted it to be, filled the air. Some wished it was the boy who broke their windows. Another hoped the local car thief was dead, and others wished it was one of their own drug-addicted family members.

As the gossip traveled from ear to ear, Greedy placed her bags all onto one forearm as she took her cell off her hip, powering it back on. *Damn, let me call Cuzzo and see if he's up yet! I gotta tell him about Cree's bitch before I get home. Damn voicemail!* Greedy slid her phone back on her hip as a dark SUV swerved up with a female jumping out like she was the shit. *Oh, she one of those hoes who wishes they was a man! Them police bitches kill me, wanting to be all tough!* Greedy hunched her shoulders as the female pulled her badge out so the other cops could recognize her as she ducked underneath the bright yellow crime tape.

Just as she'd had enough of standing around, waiting for the answer to the million-dollar question, the officer in charge took out his notepad and started talking to the cop who was driving the truck. Loving to be in the next person's personal business, Greedy eased over near the semi-private conversation and ear hustled.

"Yeah, he was discovered by those guys over there. They say they were looking for bottles, but from the way they're dressed, we know they're scrappers."

"I just swung by to check in. I know you already went beyond the call of duty, but have you heard anything else?" Jazmine batted her eyes at the detective, hoping he'd give her more hush-hush information on his search for Justice Richards, who'd been justifiably labeled the Kid Killer.

"Sorry, babe, it ain't nothing new yet. The ATF and DEA is all on the chief's back, so you know he's on mine!"

"Well, lunch is on me next week when shit calms down in the city. How about that?"

"I'll have to take you up on that." The detective perked up. "But first, now I gotta deal with this young homo who's up in there stuffed behind a couch." He motioned to the abandoned house behind them. "Our victim got blond streaks and painted toenails. Shit, all my men thought he was a she when we first arrived!"

Jazmine laughed at her colleague's animated description of the deceased, as one of the inquisitive neighbors loudly butted in.

Chapter Thirty-three

"Here, take a few more dollars for that baby of yours. I'm about to bounce." Keith handed Angie a small stack of twenties to go with the dough he'd given her earlier, and he resumed his conversation. "Yeah, man, come a few blocks over from where y'all at and you should see Jazmine's truck," Keith instructed Bama Bob. "Just fall back, and when she's through checking some shit out we'll meet you arou—"

Before Keith could end his sentence, Angie leaned over from the back seat, screaming in his ear and tapping him on his shoulder blade. "Oh, my God! Oh, my God! That's that ho! Right there! Right fucking there! That's the bitch! That's her!"

Keith sat up from his gangster lean position so he could get a better look at who Angie was pointing at. "Look, baby doll, ain't no more bread all right?" He stopped what he thought was a con game before it got started. "I'm done with this dry-run nonsense!"

Throwing the money on the front seat and on the floor of the truck, Cree's baby mother took offense. "Don't nobody want your money," she shrieked, holding her stomach. "I'm telling you that's that bitch Greedy standing right over there next to ol' girl!"

Reaching over in the middle console, Keith removed the minute throwaway cell, pushing the last number dialed, which was Greedy's. After two or three rings the female who was now talking to one of the officers took her cell off her hip, shooting the incoming call to voicemail.

"Aw hell naw!" Keith fought not to get out the truck and knock Greedy's head off her body if she didn't take them to Justice, but considering all of Detroit's finest standing around, he opted to call Jazmine and put her up on game.

Overhearing what she thought had to be a big mistake; Greedy interrupted the plainclothes policeman and the female cop he was talking to. "Excuse me." Her breathing intensified, and her stomach turned in knots. "I just heard you say there was a young guy inside of that house, with nail polish on his toes. Is that what you said?"

Embarrassed that the pregnant woman had heard his disrespectful, off-hand comments about the deceased, he tried cleaning it up. "Listen, it's true. There is a young man inside the home. Would you happen to have any information that might help us to identify him?" He knew it was a long shot. She was probably no more than a nosy neighbor trying to have something to gossip about later when she stood in a long line to play her lottery numbers or return a bag of bottles to the store to buy herself a beer. However, he humored her just the same, pulling Greedy over to the side away from the crowd. "The poor young man didn't have any ID on him. So right now he's a John Doe."

Shaking like a heroin addict needing a fix, Greedy informed the detective she thought, from what he'd just said to the other officer, referring to Jazmine, that the body in the old weed spot might've been that of her younger cousin. "Did I hear you tell her the guy inside looked like he was a girl when you first saw him?"

"Yes, we did think that, although there was extreme trauma to the overall facial area." He looked down at his notepad, taking out his pencil. "What did you say your name was?"

Ignoring his question and answering it with a question of her own, Greedy started to panic and hyperventilate.

"Oh, my God! Does the guy have white shorts on?" She thought back to what Cuzzo was wearing. "And blue and white flip-flops with one of them stupid-ass blue flowers on them?"

Jazmine could tell by the expression on her coworkers face, that more than likely, the pregnant girl's general description was fitting that of what he had written down in his notes concerning the deceased. "Listen," Jazmine interjected, trying to ease the tense situation. "You need to calm down, and let's see what else you can remember about the last time you saw your friend."

"You mean my cousin," Greedy corrected her, holding the grocery bags in her arms close. Her hands quivered trying once again to call Cuzzo's cell phone. She prayed that he'd answer.

"Okay, sorry about that." Jazmine reassuringly touched her arm, seeing she was pregnant as well as distraught. "Cousin."

The detective asked her if her cousin had any special birthmarks or maybe tattoos, ear piercings, or permanents scars. "Can you think right now, or do you need to have a seat in the back of one of the squad cars until you catch your breath?"

With the neighbors watching Greedy, who they all knew, start to talk louder, they focused all their attention on her. She was now on display and would be on the top of the gossip list for the evening. "No, I'm good! I'm good!" Greedy rocked from side to side, tapping her foot. "My cousin has a tattoo of a big-ass butterfly on the left side of his neck with the words 'Sexy Bitch' written inside of it. It can't be! It can't be! No, no, no!"

"Okay, sit tight," the detective begged as Greedy's cell rang and she shot the call to voicemail. "I'll be right back okay? And calm down. It might not even be him, all right? Just let me check things out."

Jazmine tried making casual conversation with the pregnant girl as the officer disappeared inside the house to compare the information he'd just been provided with. "When is your baby due?" After finding out the date from the frantic, stricken female, Jazmine stepped a few feet over as her cell rang. "Hey, Keith, I'm almost done here!" With the noise from the crowd growing louder, Jazmine stuck one finger in her ear, not sure what she just heard him announce. "Say what? Where? Right there? The one I was just talking to?" Immediately returning to the crying female's side to verify Keith's claim, Jazmine was unfortunately met with the detective offering the girl the sad, devastating news.

"I'm so sorry, miss, but can you come with me over to the car?" The detective held her arm, trying to offer support. "Are you a blood relative by chance? I need to find out what your cousin's government-issued name is."

"For what?" Greedy screamed out, having watched enough episodes of *Law & Order* to figure out what was going to be said next. "I need to go inside that house! I need to go inside! Cuzzo! Cuzzo!" She ripped away from him, trying relentlessly to break through the yellow tape that was separating her from seeing the dead corpse she now knew was family. "Please! Please!" She struggled as Jazmine cruelly yanked her back, having her own selfish, private agenda with the girl, knowing she was the missing link in finding Justice.

The detectives, along with the neighbors, were stunned the pregnant female had so much strength. Greedy was going berserk, swinging her arms. Not caring, she let the groceries fall to the concrete pavement, surely breaking the newly purchased eggs in one bag.

"Calm down! Wait, wait, please!" the detective coaxed. "We need your help. When was the last time you saw your cousin alive? Can you tell me that?"

Just then the Sunday edition of the *Detroit News* fell out of one of Greedy's other bags. When it landed, opening up, the huge bold headline along with a grayscale mug shot immediately brought Greedy back to her senses and reminded her of the last person who was with Cuzzo: SUSPECT SOUGHT IN KID KILLER FAMILY MASSACRE.

"Oh . . . my . . . fucking . . . God!" Greedy's pain-filled ear-piercing screams could be heard blocks away. "My kids! My kids!" Recognizing the man's picture on the front page as Justice, who was back at her house, alone, unsupervised, with her children, she broke out, hitting the lots.

Signaling for Keith to follow, Jazmine instinctively wasted no time running right behind on Greedy's heels. "Hold up! Hold up!" she repeated, avoiding broken glass, garbage, and old tires. "Slow your roll! I need to ask you something!"

Not listening to anything the plainclothes police officer had to say, Greedy refused to let her protruding belly slow her down from reaching her four children before something happened to them. *It can't be true! It can't! It can't! Not Justice! How could he?*

Around the corner, two gravel-filled lots to the left and lastly one burnt house to the right, three houses from the dead end, like a puzzle or a maze Jazmine now understood how a slew of criminals could dip and disappear in their own neighborhood if they knew all the shortcuts. *Damn this shit is crazy! Detroit is fucked up!*

Nearing her house, Greedy felt like she was close to passing out in the middle of the street, but she kept it moving. Running up the toy-scattered pavement, Greedy got up on the porch, taking two stairs at a time and twisting her ankle in the process. Not feeling any pain, Greedy yanked open the raggedy screen door and tried turning the knob on the main door. *Fuck! It's locked.*

Hearing the unmistakable sounds of cartoons from the television blaring through the door, the panicked mother banged with one hand, searching for her house keys with the other. *Please let my kids be okay! Please!*

Snagging her pants on one of the fenceless poles that Angie described earlier, Jazmine sprinted up the stairs and was posted right behind Greedy as she finally found the key, putting it in the dead bolt cylinder, turning the knob. *Shit! I wish at least I had my vest on!* With her gun out and one already up top, the young task force officer who was trained to kill cautiously waited.

Chapter Thirty-four

Wondering what in the hell was going on and what exactly Jazmine had said to Greedy to make her take off running like that made Keith jump over to the driver's seat as soon as he saw Jazmine's signal. Throwing the truck in reverse and trying to navigate through the narrow streets and all the news trucks and reporters that were just showing up, he and Angie finally bent a few corners. Also confused, Bama Bob, who had just pulled up and parked right behind Keith, was now also in pursuit, playing follow the leader.

"Yeah, y'all. Get ready for some bullshit to pop! It's on!" He placed a call to Bama Bob as he steered Jazmine's overpriced truck.

Recklessly, Keith drove down one-way streets and ran into several dead-end blocks trying to keep up with the two running females. Easily getting turned around, luckily Bama Bob spotted Jazmine cut across an alley, and they were seemingly back on point in the chase.

Following the detective's direct orders to bring the fleeing pregnant female back for questioning and back up his girl, Jazmine, a police squad car was also struggling, doing the same thing Keith and Bama Bob were attempting: trying to figure out where their fellow officer and the pregnant ghetto track star had gone. As the uniformed cops watched the two trucks break traffic law after traffic law, they let it go because their main priority was finding not only the mystery female but protecting one of their own: Jazmine.

Shoving the door with the force of five grown men, Greedy rushed inside the noisy home. Panting, out of breath, she rested her hand on the wall, counting her children, who seemed undisturbed by the door flying open or the female complete stranger who was standing behind their mother with a gun in her hand.

"One, two, three." Her eyes searched the entire room, looking for her oldest. "One, two, three." Greedy did a head count again as Jazmine stood guard with her department-issued weapon drawn.

"How many kids you got?" Jazmine's trigger finger itched, hoping Justice was somewhere in the house hiding so she could put something hot in his ass for murdering Moe Mack.

Praying her baby was just fixing herself or the younger kids a bowl of cereal like she often did when Greedy was passed out drunk, gone partying, or preoccupied in the rear bedroom with a "special friend," she went in the kitchen. Not getting her prayers answered, Greedy wobbled back through the kitchen door with a gigantic butcher knife clenched in her fist. "Four. I got four."

Bending down, taking matters in her own hands, Jazmine whispered to the kids, sensing some real gangster shit was about to jump off. "Hey, y'all, where is your big sister at?"

"Yeah." Greedy demanded answers clenching the wood handle tightly. Her lip curled. "Where's Eboni?"

"We sorry, Mommy! We sorry!" the next two oldest whined as tears started to flow. "We didn't mean to make noise to wake him up, but the TV was so funny, and we was laughing too loud."

"Where the fuck is your sister?" Greedy snatched the child up, shaking her by the arm. "Where is she? Huh? Where is she?"

"He said if Eboni went back there he wouldn't spank us," the innocent, small child cried, pointing toward Greedy's bedroom, "and we could keep watching our shows."

Experiencing sharp cramping in her side after listening to what her child had just revealed, Greedy held her belly, racing down the hallway in spite of her fast-swelling ankle. Wasting no time kicking her bedroom door almost off the hinges, the oftentimes neglectful mother was furious. Oh, hell naw! "Get your motherfucking hands off my daughter! Nigger, is you crazy or what?" Greedy couldn't believe her eyes and what they were seeing. The unfit single parent smoked weed around her kids, cursed around them, and even took them with her to shoplift from time to time, but what see was faced with now made the expectant mother of four shake with immeasurable rage. "Come over here, Eboni! Get over here right now! Hurry up!"

Barely eight years of age, Greedy's oldest little girl was perched down on her knees at the edge of the bed with Justice's rock-hard dick in her mouth, sucking him off like she'd been doing it for years.

With streams of gigantic tears flowing down her face, Eboni froze in fear, trying to explain, as if she were to blame for what was going on. "I'm sorry, Mommy!" She sniffled, still attempting to hold Justice's swollen manhood in her tiny hands. "We didn't mean to make any noise to wake him up! I'm sorry. I'm sorry! Don't be mad! Mommy, he promised he wouldn't leave you! He promised!"

Embarrassed and ashamed of what she was hearing, Greedy took hold of Eboni's flowered pajama shirt, taking her out of harm's way as she swung the huge butcher knife at an unremorseful Justice. Cocky, he didn't flinch or even move a muscle to get out of Greedy's way and what she intended doing. "You grimy-ass nigga! I trusted your punk ass! You ain't shit! Nigga, I'm gonna kill you! That's my baby, you fucking child molester!"

Removing his arms from behind his head, Justice gave her a demonic half-cocked grin before leaping off the bed, with his dick still standing at full attention and his pants down to his knees. He was every bit of Kamal's grandson. This proved it. His actions over the past twenty-four hours, not to mention a lifetime, were better than any blood test. Still spinning off the ecstasy pills, he made no excuses for his despicable actions. "Bitch, I wish the fuck you would try to cut me! You'd be wasting your time! You can't hurt me, slut! Nobody can!"

"What? You got me twisted!" Greedy pushed Eboni behind her, stepping up to do battle.

Delusional in his thoughts, the murderer now turned child molester gripped up on his dick, asking Greedy if she wanted to come finish what her young daughter had started. "Don't worry, baby doll." Justice jerked his hands, stroking the shaft. "There's plenty left for you. Oh, li'l mama good as a motherfucker, don't get me wrong." He motioned toward Eboni. "But you know like I know all this thick nut I got would've been too much for her little throat to handle. Maybe in a year or two from now she'll be ready! What you think?" He winked at the shivering little girl.

"I'ma kill your black ass! And where is Cuzzo? Huh? Huh? How could you, nigga? I hate you!" Raising the knife once again, determined to kill the grown man who'd violated her child and without a doubt murdered her cousin, Greedy suddenly doubled over in pain. Clutching her stomach, reality set back in as she quickly realized that the monster she wanted dead so badly was also the father of her unborn child. Dropping the knife to the carpet, Greedy hugged her frantic daughter. "It's all right, baby, don't cry! Don't cry. I'm sorry I left you. It's okay."

Still standing like he'd done no wrong, the brazen Justice, dick in hand, yelled out, "I knew you couldn't hurt me! I told you nobody can! And fuck that faggot Cuzzo! That was an easy kill!"

Coming out of the shadows, Jazmine emerged with her gun pointed directly at Justice's head. "You's a sick-ass motherfucker, nigga! Straight up!" she argued, easily persuading Greedy to take her child out of the bedroom and make sure she was okay.

"You stanking bitch!" Justice belted out to Greedy after instantly noticing Jazmine's badge. "You called the damn police on me!"

Slamming the door shut almost as hard as Greedy had kicked it open, Jazmine bit down on her lower lip, something she always did when she was about to fire off a few rounds. "Get over near the wall and shut your fucking damn mouth!" she ordered, wanting to hurl getting a good look at his bare scar-mutilated chest. "And if you think a bitch playing, try me, you fucking animal!"

Slightly hesitant, Justice wisely did as he was told. "Can a nigga at least put his dick up, or do you want some of daddy's big lollipop too?"

Jazmine wanted nothing more than to immediately put the muzzle of her pistol to the back of Justice's head and empty the clip, but she wanted him to first know why he was about to die. "Go ahead. Put your little thing away. Damn molester! You lucky I didn't let her cut the son of a bitch off!"

"Then what would you have to suck on?" He deliberately mocked Jazmine, knowing an officer of the law wasn't going to just shoot him in cold blood. "Matter of fact, come on over here. You is kinda cute!"

"On everything I love, my nigga!" Jazmine got ghetto with it. "Your ass is about to feel some hot ones! You think you can just kill a brother and it's all good! Shit don't work like that, homeboy! Not at all. You should know better."

Leaning back against the dresser, shaking off the effects of the pills he'd taken, Justice's lazy eye started to twitch. "What kinda police is you?" He looked her up and down, staring at the barrel. "Why ain't you calling for backup?"

"Come on, Justice." Jazmine called him out by name, flashing a hand gesture that made him quickly change his facial expression. "Why I need to do that? You know how the game go, don't you, fam? Cree knew, and my big homie Moe Mack knew."

"What you say?"

"Boy, you heard me!" Jazmine ridiculed with contempt, sucking her teeth. "You should've known better than to bite the hand that feeds you! That's the first rule of the game! And you violated it!"

"Wait a minute, I know you." Justice kinda recognized Jazmine from a crew cookout at Rouge Park one summer. Realizing that his psychotic reign of terror was coming to an end, he tried to take a cop anyhow, zipping up his pants. "Listen, let me explain!"

With a strong grip on her nine aimed at Justice, who was no more than a savage dog needing to be put down, Jazmine raised the sleeve of her T-shirt, revealing a tattoo that read the unmistakable words NFL 4 LIFE. "Negro, please, you already know!" Once again she bit down on her bottom lip, firing a shot off directly toward his repulsive face.

Chapter Thirty-five

Bringing the SUV's tires to a screeching halt, Keith stopped right on the money, coming close to causing Angie, who was not wearing her seat belt, to fly in the front and almost go crashing through the truck's windshield. "There she go! Right over there!" Spotting Greedy on her front porch coming in and out the house angrily tossing clothes and other items into the front yard, Keith knew for certain he was in the right place. Swinging the door open, before he could place his Kenneth Cole loafer on the running board and search for Jazmine himself, the police squad car sped up, blocking his exit.

Knowing he was also following the two females, with guns drawn, the cops dashed over to Keith, demanding to know if he had any knowledge of which direction their fellow officer had gone.

"Damn, lower y'all guns!" Being a black man in Detroit, or America for that matter, Keith instinctively threw up his hands, proving to the police that he was unarmed. "Jazmine Coleman is with us. This is her truck!" he quickly announced, with Bama Bob inconspicuously watching from down the block.

Satisfied the driver and his pregnant companion Angie meant them no immediate harm, the uniformed patrolmen called for additional backup to their location. Cautiously they ran up the walkway scattered with toys and clothes, approaching an overly distraught Greedy and four bawling kids. "Where is Officer Coleman?" the burly white cop insisted to know as his rookie partner kept his gun pointed at the open door. "Which way did she go?"

Surrounded by her petrified children, Greedy stopped throwing Justice's belongings and shut her eyes, shaking her head for bringing that monster into their lives. "She's in the back room, down the hall, second door to the left."

Knowing time was ticking and her safety was on the line, the two patrolmen made the split-second decision to not wait for backup and search for Officer Coleman themselves. Upon entering Greedy's house and turning off the loud television, they secured their immediate perimeter. Step by step, kicking a few items out of their path, the duo headed down the long, dark hallway.

The closer the white cop got to the closed bedroom door, he heard voices. Not being able to make out what the people behind the door were saying, he knew for sure one voice was that of a female and one was that of a man. Not wanting to waste any more time or risk the life of Officer Coleman, the veteran cop shoved the door off the loosened frame just as a shot was being fired.

"Argg, son of a bitch!" At the very second the booming blast of the gunshot rang out that was fired at Justice, Jazmine was pushed on the right side of her body and knocked into the low-sitting TV stand. Trying to regain her balance as soon as possible, the tactical field-trained officer broke her fall, grabbing a hold of a bookshelf. Never once dropping her nine, ready to fire once again, Jazmine defensively aimed at the person coming through the door until the white policeman loudly announced himself.

"Freeze! Detroit Police!" He scrambled to make sure the guy across the room, whose picture was posted on every newspaper and television set in Detroit, wasn't armed and his comrade was all right.

With Jazmine back on her feet, she and the white cop both approached a moaning Justice.

Crying like a true bitch, the once-boisterous self-proclaimed "Hood Warrior" had broken glass from the window he'd fallen into, covering his bloody face. "I'm hit, I'm hit!" he groaned, holding his head.

Not giving two shits about what the murder suspect was saying, the oversized policeman flung him over on his stomach, snapping the cuffs on as tight as he could possibly get them. "Shut the fuck up!" Grinding his knee into Justice's spine, the father of six thought about his own kids, two of whom were the same age as the boys Justice was accused of poisoning. "Nigger, you lucky I don't kill you myself!"

Normally Jazmine would be offended if the white man said the N word or manhandled a black suspect a little bit too roughly for her taste, but no amount of brutal over-the-top behavior was uncalled for under these circumstances. In the case of dealing with Justice Richards, it was one of those anything goes moments.

Dragging him out in the hallway, then turning on the lights, all three officers flipped the Kid Killer over, discovering that, unfortunately for the good taxpaying citizens of Wayne County who'd have to foot the bill for a trial, Justice wasn't dying from a gunshot wound to the head, but had only been grazed. The majority of blood on his face had to have come from the cuts he suffered from the broken window.

Shit! Jazmine thought as a disoriented Justice mumbled about her trying to kill him. *I never miss. If it weren't for the door hitting my arm, this buster would have been dead for sure!*

After hearing shots fired, a huge number of police cars swarmed the block. They were joined by a slew of reporters who were just covering Cuzzo's murder, followed by a lynch mob of hostile neighbors calling for Justice Richards's head delivered on a silver platter. Keeping Greedy and her children segregated from the judgmental crowds, who blamed her for harboring the fugitive, was a task in itself. With the family of five all huddled together in an unmarked sedan with dark tinted windows, one part of Greedy hoped Justice was now dead while the other prayed he could change for the sake of their unborn seed. However, after being given a Sunday paper and reading the long, detailed article of the crimes the soon-to-be father of her child had been accused of, she knew that wasn't possible.

Jazmine, knowing she'd missed the only chance she would get to avenge Moe Mack's death, walked out to her truck, breaking the bad news to Keith, Bama Bob, and Angie, that regretfully Justice was still very much alive. "That jackass got nine lives. Another inch over and he'd be coming out in a body bag instead of handcuffs!" she hissed, staring back at Greedy's house.

Rubbing his hands together, Keith smiled. "It's all good, fam. We got dudes on the payroll in every county jail, detention center, and fucking penitentiary from here to Ohio to Indiana and back. Trust he gonna get got! That's a given!"

With the cameras rolling, the chief of police was planted front and center on Greedy's front grass, talking to reporters as if he himself singlehandedly captured Justice. The irate crowd erupted in insults, death threats, and boos as the infamous Kid Killer was dragged out shirtless in handcuffs with a bloodstained bandage wrapped around his head.

Uncharacteristically, not muttering a word as numerous microphones were shoved in his face, the newly apprehended Justice Richards was roughly paraded through the street then tossed in the back seat of a squad car headfirst before being whisked off. There was no "Fuck you!" No "Nigga, do you know who I am?" No "Suck my dick," or mean mugging. No "I'll kill ya ass!" And not even a "Bitch, get that shit out my face!" Detroit's public enemy number one remained silent, leaving all of the city's residents standing there in person and watching on channels two, four, and seven breaking news to only speculate what could be going on in that sinister mind of his.

Chapter Thirty-six

"Good Tuesday morning, Detroit. I'm downtown standing in front of the Thirty-sixth District Courthouse. And with this past weekend being one of the deadliest forty-eight hours recorded in Michigan history, the court clerks have been working overtime crossing the t's and dotting the i's, trying to ensure no clerical mishaps in the over nine high-profile arraignments that have already taken place over a twenty-four-hour span. Now depending on who you ask, today might be the worst. It's been a rollercoaster ride in gathering evidence, witness statements, and deciding what specific charges will be filed today against Justice Richards, who has been nicknamed by the media, residents, and authorities as the Kid Killer.

"The prosecutor's office reportedly has been overrun with citizens willing to step up and help bring a much-needed end to the one-man murderous wide-scale rampage that claimed the lives of eight people, including those of two small boys. Sources say Mr. Richards, apprehended Sunday on the far east side, is apparently lodging a hunger strike, refusing to eat, and is also refraining from making any statements thus far. So we can only wait today and see what unfolds. We'll also have reactions from the families of the victims on our broadcast at noon, as many of them are just arriving to the proceedings. This is Jayden James live reporting for Channel 7 Action News."

***

As Judge Curtis sat back in the leather chair in her private chambers, the same social worker who'd been present in the courtroom the day Justice was taken away for good from his belligerent, defiant mother entered, taking a seat.

"It's been a long time, Judge," the now-retired woman spoke. "I never thought I would be back inside of another courthouse after I left the job."

"Yeah, almost twenty years to be exact," Judge Curtis reminisced, looking at her various degrees, certificates, and framed newspaper articles nailed to the wall. "It was the first week I started out over in family court."

Showing a faint smile, considering the reason for their reunion, the elderly woman took a deep breath. "I never thought in a million years this sort of thing could happen, but it has. God help me for being selfish and not completely honest from the beginning."

Judge Curtis removed her eyeglasses, setting them on the desk. The once-innocent baby that she and the woman in front of her had saved from his mother's ungodly influences was now the talk of the town and the perpetrator of violent acts that were deemed unspeakable even in the most awful of households. "I've read this file over and over and wanted to try some way to avoid doing what we have to do, but I can't. When I got your call, I was in total shock."

"I know," the retired social worker agreed. "I can't help but wonder if somehow this was my fault and I could've stopped it. For the past forty-eight hours my conscience has been killing me. I've been trying to find a way to deal with it, but I can't." She openly wept. "After today, everything in my life will change for good. I only pray God will forgive me for holding back on the truth. It's been far too long."

"Listen, you can't blame yourself. You did what you thought was best all these years. The only thing we can do now is make it right." Judge Curtis reached for the phone, lifting the receiver to her ear. "Now I just got off the phone with the psychologist before you came in, and we need to consult with the prosecutor and the defense attorney and bring them up to speed with the urgent business we need to take care of after Mr. Richards's arraignment."

Entering the courtroom, inquisitive spectators along with distraught, infuriated family members were seated, packed like sardines shoulder to shoulder, waiting to get their first glimpse at the calculating creature who'd robbed them of their beloved father, mother, daughter, sister, cousin, son, and friend. Taking into consideration that emotions would be running at an all-time high, extra security precautions were taken. Not only were Wayne County sheriffs standing on post throughout the courtroom and building, but also heavily armed Detroit police officers stood guard on the streets.

With news cameras ready to capture every moment of the proceedings, not only were residents of the Motor City anticipating Justice's defense of his heartless actions, but also the world that'd stood up taking notice of how the crime-ridden town would deal with a savage individual such as the notorious Mr. Richards.

Chapter Thirty-seven

"All rise. The Thirty-sixth District Court of the State of Michigan is now in session." With an expression of seriousness, the court bailiff made his normal speech as the chamber doors cracked open. "The Honorable Judge G. Curtis residing."

"Thank you." She sternly nodded, knowing all eyes were on her. "You can all please take your seats."

Shuffling through what seemed like tons of paperwork, the judge shared a few private words with her clerk, then summoned her to begin with the most anticipated arraignment of the morning. "Case number 217-66883-A72: the State of Michigan versus Justice Richards."

The specially assembled team of prosecuting attorneys waited behind their wooden table, ready to wage battle as Justice's lone court-appointed defense council fixed his tie, optimistic that this case and its infamous client would gain him worldwide recognition and possibly a shot at making partner in his law firm. Finally, dressed in an old, mildewed jailhouse-issued jumpsuit, Justice, who had several minor bruises he magically somehow obtained while being fingerprinted and booked courtesy of Detroit Police, was led out in shackles. Instantly he was met by jeers, threats, and insults, causing Judge Curtis to bang her gavel repeatedly, demanding that order be restored in her packed courtroom.

"I hope to God you die in your damn sleep, mother-fucker!" NayNay's sister and mother to the two small boys he'd poisoned shouted out to him. "You ain't about shit! What about NFL 4 LIFE, nigga?" she screamed in tears, having lost three family members in Justice's crime spree.

"You're an animal! How could you take our son from us?" Moe Mack's parents sat astonished that their only child was dead, leaving them to raise his baby.

Barely able to stand, the cab driver's mournful wife shouted out in her native tongue what was no doubt a curse of torture and a slow death toward the young man who'd made her an early widow.

"Order in the court! Order in the court!" The judge helplessly watched rage erupt from one side of the room to the other as armed guards surrounded a hard-faced Justice, who seemed not to care as he defiantly made eye contact with each person.

"She was my baby!" The mother of the teenage girl he'd randomly smashed into the liquor store building held on to a picture of the adolescent as she wailed.

Cree's elderly grandmother rocked back and forth in prayer with her Bible clutched tightly, as a pregnant Angie tried consoling her while needing consoling herself.

Cuzzo's weeping mother refused to sit next to her sister or bad-seed niece Greedy, who she ultimately blamed for her son's heinous death. A subdued Greedy hyperventilated, struggling mentally, trying to cope with carrying the offspring of a murderer and child molester. It was growing inside of her, kicking every morning and fighting to be born. Greedy now seethed at its very existence. The fact that her aged mother, whom she hadn't spoken to in over a year and a half, was there trying to offer comfort and make amends meant nothing to Greedy, as did the heartless look Justice had just given her from across the venue with standing room only.

After a group of loud-talking, neck-rolling, finger-snapping, gum-smacking, flame-throwing male friends of Cuzzo's tried to jump over the handrail, promising to scratch Justice's demented eyes out, the woman in charge had enough. Shrewdly observing that the volatile atmosphere was going to get worse before getting better, Judge Curtis made the wise decision to clear the out-of-control courtroom of all spectators and possibly ban the news agencies from broadcasting live.

"Order in the court!" she bellowed again, trying to regain some normalcy to the proceedings. "Can the officers please escort everyone out except for council, the defendant, and those five people over there? The scheduled arraignment will take place this afternoon, and it will be closed to the general public."

Following instructions, the various Wayne County sheriffs strategically placed around the explosive, emotionally charged courtroom assisted each individual to make their way out into the hallway. They were ordered to exit from the building as soon as possible with as little controversy. When all the occupants, with the exception of those Judge Curtis requested to remain seated, had been vacated, she started an unorthodox speech directed toward Justice, who had yet to say a word.

"Okay, Mr. Richards, I know you weren't expecting to hear what I'm about to say," Judge Curtis said, gazing into his hardened eyes, "but after consulting with the psychologist who evaluated your mental state, Dr. Thomas, whom I sure you remember, sitting to your right, and both sets of attorneys, we feel it's in your, as well as the State's, best interest to deal with a prior moral situation."

Justice leaned back in his seat, as nothing the judge was saying mattered to him one bit. From time to time he glanced over at Greedy, who was one of the people allowed to stay. Arrogantly he blew kisses.

"Are you listening, Mr. Richards?" Judge Curtis inquired, trying to regain his attention. "We feel the system has somehow failed you. Even though you are here in my courtroom under some of the most atrocious and appalling acts that I have seen in my twenty years on the bench and thirty years of practicing law, I still feel it would be an injustice not to try to right this wrong." Somewhat piquing Justice's interest, judging by the expression on his face, she continued. "As I studied your past criminal conduct, I can only shake my head in disgust. Your history started with petty shoplifting at nine years of age, followed by several assaults, multiple breaking-and-entering charges, fraud, and quite a few car jackings. And of course you know why we are here today: homicide, vehicular manslaughter, home invasion, breaking and entering, child molestation, and weapons charges. Being placed in foster care, instead of the courts trying all we could to locate possible other family members willing to take you in, was definitely not beneficial to your upbringing."

Greedy couldn't believe her ears or the cold, hard facts of whom she'd been sleeping with and had the awful misfortune to be impregnated by. *Why did I even hook up with you in the first place?* she contemplated spitefully, peering at Justice. *I should've listen to Cuzzo and stopped fucking with you a long time ago when you got caught kissing my homegirl at the club. Damn!*

"Look here, Judge!" Justice finally broke his silence, standing. "I don't know really what in the fuck this bullshit back down memory lane got to do with what's happening now, but real talk you can miss me with all that!" With two sheriffs shoving him back in his seat, Justice wasted no time continuing his rant. "I ain't about to be all up in here trying to take no cop to nothing or go out like I'm a punk, cause I ain't! I'm a hundred percent Linwood all motherfucking day and all damn night!"

"Shut your mouth talking to the judge like that! You understand?" one officer hissed with his teeth clenched. "Or I'll shut it for you!"

Somewhat restoring order, Judge Curtis went on. "Listen, Mr. Richards, I realize you don't know exactly who I am, but if your attorney will give you the documents to look over, I'll explain. See, when you were a baby, I was the one who signed the final paperwork dissolving all of your biological mother's parental rights."

"Okay, and so what? You did me a favor, because if the bitch didn't want me, I sure in the fuck don't want her ass! If it's fuck me, then you know it's fuck her!" Justice remained insubordinate as the cop gave him another dirty look, promising him a beat down when they got back behind closed doors.

"I swear it wasn't like that," one of the women handpicked to stay in the courtroom shouted out. "I was out of my mind back then. I'm sorry!"

With the attention of everyone now focused on the small woman with thick black and gray cornrows braided toward the back, Justice's lazy eye opened. "What you say?" he quizzed. "Who in the fuck is you? What kinda bullshit is y'all trying to pull?" He turned, facing the judge for answers.

"I'm your mother, Justice, that's who I am. My name is Joi Richards." She apologetically rose to her feet as the female deputy sent to guard her watched the unfolding drama along with the other courthouse occupants. "I'm so sorry that I wasn't there for you when you needed me the most, but those drugs had me messed up bad. I was emotionally damaged, and I know you are too. I didn't know what I was doing or saying half the time!"

Justice looked at the woman claiming to be his mother as if she were an alien. Then he looked at the judge, and then back at the woman who was in tears fighting the maternal urge to run across the room and embrace her only son she hadn't seen since the day he was taken away.

"Is this shit supposed to be for real or what?" He cynically laughed. "Listen, you old bitch! You ain't nobody to me but another ho with a slit wanting to get fucked, you understand? So get on with the 'I'm your mother' act. It ain't playing with me. I walk these Detroit streets alone and always have! Bitch threw me away like garbage!" He for once, since killing his homeboy Cree, secretly regretted not having a friend on his side. "I don't give a shit about taking a life 'cause y'all motherfuckers took mine a long time ago!" He lifted his restrained hands, ripping down the material on his jumpsuit, revealing all the wounds he'd suffered at the mercy of various foster care providers and group homes over the years. "And being scared ain't never been a motherfucking option to a real street warrior!"

Judge Curtis was stunned at the vulgarity she was hearing, but she allowed the obviously overwhelmed Justice to continue his outburst, getting it out of his system as Dr. Thomas suggested be done. "Mr. Richards, the court indeed feels your pain and does sympathize, but you can trust when I tell you that, without a doubt, this is your birth mother."

"Okay, dig, so what if it is?" He toughened up, frowning at Joi. "What you want me to do about it, run over there and kiss the old bitch's ass? Come on now. Be for real. And why after all this time is y'all telling me now? Why now?"

Judge Curtis hesitantly responded to Justice's question, knowing full well all hell was going to break loose. "The honest reason it's so vitally important to reunite you with your family is that ironically enough you've been charged with molesting your niece."

"My niece? Man, what in the fuck is you talking about?" Justice defensively raised his voice for being accused of a crime he knew he hadn't committed. "I ain't got no family!" He mean mugged Joi once more. "I been out here alone from day one! Ain't that right, bitch?"

A confused Greedy leaped to her feet, full of questions herself. "What other little girl have you done this to, you fucking freak?"

"Tramp, shut the fuck up," Justice yelled at her with no remorse, adding insult to injury. "Don't worry, only you and your baby getting this big dick!"

Having to be physically restrained by officers as well as her mother, Greedy was ready to kill him on the spot. "Let me go! Let me go! He got me fucked up!"

"Wait a minute, baby. Calm down, please." Greedy's mother tugged at her crazed pregnant daughter's arm while taking an old yellow envelope out of her purse that contained a few documents with gold raised seals on them. "I never wanted it to come out like this, but when I saw the news reports, I knew I didn't have a choice."

"What in the hell is you talking about, Mom? Huh?" Greedy snatched away from the now-retired social worker. "What did you do? Tell me! Tell me!"

Handing her the paperwork disclosing the twenty-year hidden family truth, the once-proud mother lowered her head in shame. Tracy "Greedy" Rodgers was legally adopted at birth. Conceived out of rape at the hands of a prison guard, Tracy was biologically Joi Richards's daughter. That cold, hard fact was incredible, rendering all speechless. She was Justice's younger sister.

"I'm so sorry, Tracy." Mrs. Rodgers lowered her head once more, knowing how hurt, devastated, and confused her adopted child was.

"My mother? I'm adopted? What? What you talking about?" In denial, Greedy stared over her shoulder at Joi, her alleged birth mom. Holding her stomach, the puzzled mother-to-be darted her eyes at her baby's daddy, her newly discovered brother, Justice Richards, the same man who had molested Eboni, her firstborn. "What you trying to say? I'm confused! You lying! Why y'all lying to me?"

Justice was as blackhearted as he ever was, never letting the next man see him sweat or show emotion. Here he was meeting his mother for the first time and couldn't care less. It'd just been confirmed he had indeed violated his niece's innocence and didn't bat an eye in the way of remorse. Lastly, unknowingly impregnating his long-lost sister Tracy, who he knew as Greedy, Justice sat back in the chair almost enjoying the torment he'd caused in everyone's lives.

"Well, ain't this about some dumb shit." Justice jumped to his feet once more as the courtroom officers, attorneys, the woman guarding Joi, the doctor, and the judge shook their heads, not knowing what other hidden secrets would come to light. "You motherfuckers acting like I'm the bad guy! I ain't do jack shit but play the cards you once-a-month-bleeding bitches gave a nigga to play! So now all you broads sitting in this three-ring circus, kangaroo court wanting to blame me! Hell naw! I ain't taking the weight! Y'all need to be on trial, not my black ass! Say what y'all want, but I made the best outta some fucked-up shit. I came from nothing. I made it out of the system! I'm gonna be all right!" he proclaimed before demanding to be taken back in the bullpen.

Consumed with guilt, knowing her former drug addiction and long, ongoing prison sentences had caused all this chaos in her children's and grandchildren's lives, Joi reached for her birth daughter's hand to apologize. Immediately pulling away, about to faint fearing what physical and mental abnormities her unborn baby would probably suffer from the incestuous affair she was unknowingly having, Greedy broke down.

Watching both her children in agonizing pain, Joi Richards had to make a choice to help one of them at least live a halfway normal life. Knowing everyone was caught up in the moment, the mother of Tracy and Justice took the split-second opportunity to unexpectedly leap over the wooden banister. Once over she grabbed one of the sheriff's firearms. With love in her heart, she let off one round, striking Justice, her son, in the rear of the head right before he made it out of the courtroom doors.

"I can't let you live like an animal anymore! Neither one of your grandmothers was about shit either! We was all fucked up back then. You just like your father, grandfather, and great-grandfather were: savages! I know it's my fault, but I know you'll be all right now. The shit gotta stop! God help me!" Dropping the gun, Joi Richards fell to her knees, begging forgiveness for what she felt she had to do. Instantly she was tackled then handcuffed as her other child starting hemorrhaging, causing the expecting Greedy to go into premature labor.

Considering the immeasurable crimes the arrogant youth had committed and the many innocent lives he'd altered, no one rushed to call for medical attention as Justice lay bleeding out on the courtroom floor. With a pool of blood flowing from a huge, gaping hole in his cranium, he knew he couldn't cheat death.

Fuck all y'all! Go ahead, let me die! I'd rather be free in hellfire than live locked up on earth! They always got love for a nigga from Tha D! Justice's mind grew dark as the devil welcomed him home to finally meet his kin.

Minutes later, Greedy and Justice's tiny son was born on the marble courtroom floor. The fifth generation of the terror-tainted bloodline had been released upon the world. The system had truly failed yet another family.

The End